CORPORATE GUNSLINGER

CORP⊙RATE
GUNSLINGER

A NOVEL

DOUG ENGSTROM

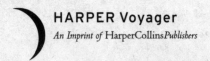

HARPER Voyager
An Imprint of HarperCollinsPublishers

CORPORATE GUNSLINGER. Copyright © 2020 by Doug Engstrom. All rights reserved. Printed in the United States of America. No part of this book may be used or reproduced in any manner whatsoever without written permission except in the case of brief quotations embodied in critical articles and reviews. For information, address HarperCollins Publishers, 195 Broadway, New York, NY 10007.

HarperCollins books may be purchased for educational, business, or sales promotional use. For information, please email the Special Markets Department at SPsales@harpercollins.com.

Harper Voyager and design are trademarks of HarperCollins Publishers LLC.

FIRST EDITION

Designed by Renata De Oliveira

Library of Congress Cataloging-in-Publication Data has been applied for.

ISBN 978-0-06-289768-8

20 21 22 23 24   LSC   10 9 8 7 6 5 4 3 2 1

This is for my mother and father,
my first teachers of perseverance

CONTENT WARNING

Corporate Gunslinger is a story about the training and career of a professional gunfighter. As such, it is permeated with depictions of gun violence, including graphic descriptions of gunshot wounds and character death. It also portrays abduction and suicidal ideation.

CHAPTER 1

In front of her, a door that leads to the dueling field. Behind her, an exit. Between them, Kira Clark weighs the prospect of killing and the possibility of dying against the certainty of a life in servitude. The changing room clock gives her eleven minutes and forty-two seconds to make her decision.

She could take the exit and forfeit the match. Walking away before a duel starts is a highly informal way for a professional gun-fighter to resign, but she wouldn't be the first. It would feel pretty good for about a month, maybe two, but then her money would run out, her creditors would foreclose, and she would become their property—theirs to do with as they pleased, for the rest of her life.

The only real way out is forward, through the scanner and onto the dueling field to face Niles LeBlanc. Make that Niles fucking LeBlanc: professional gunfighter, high-caliber asshole, and poor, dead Chloe's contemptible ex-boyfriend. Kira brings her cold focus to bear on all the reasons he deserves to end the match with a bullet in his heart.

Right on schedule, fear breaks her chilly concentration, ar-riving as an awareness of her body's vulnerability so acute that it sparks a deep ache in her chest. She wraps her torso in a self-hug and breathes, timing her inhalation by count and forcing the exhale to last twice as long. True to the promise of her first acting instructor, her muscles relax, her heart rate slows, and her mind goes blank. The terror flows through her, past her, around her . . . and then it is gone.

The anxiety used to spook her, feeding a fear that she was too weak for the job. Twenty-nine gunfights after her first match, it's simply part of her changing room routine, like pulling on the dueling tunic with the TKC Insurance logo stitched on each shoulder, slipping her feet into the glove-soft boots, or attaching her ID chip to the box holding her personal effects.

She unwinds her arms and focuses on how Niles will see her, closing her eyes to shut out the changing room's office-bland decor and bought-by-the-pound corporate artwork. She will enter the field as a deadly apparition, wearing the company colors of forest green and slate gray, her blonde hair clipped into the helmet-like shape of the gunfighter's cut, and her eyes like two chips of stamped steel. She drives every hint of softness or compassion from her face, tightens her abdominal muscles, and straightens her spine.

Then the words, spoken only for herself: "I am death. I am terror. I am blood."

She gives herself over to Death's Angel, her role for the duration of the duel. Playing her longest-running and most popular character, she will step onto her greatest stage to give her largest audience a life or death performance.

She speaks the final words of her personal incantation: "Show time."

CHAPTER 2

Although it was only 9:00 a.m., Kira's first day as a gunfighter trainee already featured a payment glitch that nearly made the hotel manager call the cops and a hassle getting onto TKC property when somebody hung a Society for the Prevention of Dueling flag from the main gate and chained themselves to the entrance. Now, on top of all that, she faced a broken elevator in her new home. Was this the shape of things to come, or was it getting all the bad luck out of the way at once?

Standing in the stairwell, Kira sighed. The company tried to dress up the Logan P. Jameson Building by referring to it as "educational accommodations," but it was clearly a dorm. No denying going back to a dorm was a step down, though the steps up posed the most immediate problem—dragging her baggage up the three flights of concrete stairs flanked by thick-painted steel railings. She adjusted her backpack, took a new grip on her suitcase handle, and resumed her slog to the fourth floor.

Though having the elevator fail on moving day was a bad sign, the building probably wasn't that much worse than some places she'd lived while trying to balance food, rent, and loan payments against a small and uncertain stream of income. Once they got the elevator working again, it would probably be better than either the third-floor walkup she'd lived in during her first months in New York or the basement place with the iffy plumbing. Best of all, she'd have a year . . . as long as she didn't quit or flunk out. A year meant twenty-six loan payments. More financial stability than she'd had since leaving college. But first, climb the stairs with suitcase in tow.

Like all dorms on moving-in day, good-natured insults and bursts of profanity filled the air, accompanied by the underlying smell of mustiness, industrial-strength cleaners, and sweat. On the landing just before her door, the voices from her target floor became clearer—loud, boisterous, and uniformly male.

Shit.

The floor map from the trainee information packet on her handset showed her room at the opposite end of the hallway. To get to it, she'd have to pass through a mass of just-moved-in guys somewhere between the ages of nineteen and thirty. Walking in alone, a twenty-six-year-old blonde would get the kind of attention dogs would give a steak if it tried to stroll through a kennel.

Should she make it a confrontation? Establish herself as a person who wasn't going to be messed with, even for something as random as a catcall? Risky until she got the lay of the land. But appearing vulnerable might be risky, too. Better to make the first encounter neutral.

She pulled a set of bright-orange over-the-ear headphones from her backpack and set the noise cancellation to maximum. With the phones in place, she brought up some dance music on the handset. Unless somebody delivered his taunt with an air horn, she wouldn't hear it.

Time to run the gauntlet. She hardened her face, squared her shoulders, and opened the fire door.

A loose scattering of young men, furniture awaiting placement, and bags of trash lined the hallway. A couple shirtless guys lounging against the right wall watched her pass, as did a guy in an Iowa Cubs T-shirt wrestling an armchair through a doorway, but if they said anything, the pounding rhythm drowned it out.

Noise cancellation really might be the best invention of the twenty-first century.

She squeezed past a dresser left sitting sideways and maneuvered her luggage through the same narrow passage. A few more feet across the industrial-gray loop carpeting, and she'd be home free. She tapped her handset, and a green light flashed on the door. Her key token worked. A quick turn of the handle, a pull on her suitcase, and she was inside.

She pivoted and found herself facing a black-haired teenage guy in a powder-blue T-shirt, staring at her with big brown eyes. What the hell was this? She pulled the headphones off, and although she kept one hand on the door handle, her voice conceded nothing. "Who are you?"

He startled. Was he surprised at her tone or surprised she'd spoken at all?

"I-I'm, ah—"

He looked like a kid and she'd taken him by surprise. The T-shirt and jeans were both badly worn and out of fashion, as were the shoes. Nothing suggested he was used to getting his way. She could probably do a good enough teacher-voice to send him packing, and then slam the door shut behind him.

A voice sounded from the bathroom. "That's my baby brother, Lorenzo."

Lorenzo looked at his feet.

The voice's owner emerged. A few years younger than Kira, she was built like a rugby player, with a body so short and squat she seemed almost square. "I'm Chloe Rossi."

"I'm Kira Clark. I guess we're roommates."

Chloe dressed much like Lorenzo—clothes either purchased at a thrift store or about to go there.

She nodded toward her brother. "Lorenzo came along to help carry, and with . . ." She waved to indicate the hallway Kira had just passed through. ". . . you know."

Kira took her hand off the door handle and stepped farther into the room. "Pleased to meet you both."

A few awkward seconds ensued, in which Lorenzo managed to say "Hi," but mostly stared at Kira as if she'd just emerged from the ocean naked on a half shell. Chloe eyed him with a mixture of amusement and annoyance.

If this was going to move forward, it was apparently on Kira to do something. "Look, Chloe and I have an early start tomorrow. Mind if I unpack?"

Chloe turned to her brother. "Thanks for the help, but she's right. We've got an early day coming."

Lorenzo accepted his dismissal, but he stopped at the door to address Chloe. "You'll be at the house Sunday? After Mass?"

Chloe frowned. "If I can. It's my only day off."

"Mom and Dad expect you. Especially now."

After a few seconds of nonverbal standoff with his sister, Lorenzo turned to Kira. "You can come, too. Mom makes great spaghetti."

A vision washed across Kira's mind: a big table full of good food, surrounded by people talking and laughing, with the smell of cooked meat and spices in the air—basil, thyme, and oregano. In the middle of it all, a place for her. Like Professor Fowler's parties for students who couldn't go home for Christmas, or when the Carlyle family had the whole cast over for dinner at the end of a play's run. She shook it off. Lorenzo was just a smitten teenager looking for an excuse to stare at her some more. All she needed was a polite deflection. *But still . . .*

"Thanks. I'm still figuring out my schedule."

Lorenzo responded with a small bob of his head before leaving.

Chloe looked after him for a moment, scratched a russet curl that had somehow survived her hairdo's transition into the gunfighter's cut, and turned her attention to Kira. "Sorry about that. He's a good kid, but he's a kid."

Kira responded with a noncommittal shrug. "No problem."

"I took the left side, but I'm not unpacked yet." Chloe pointed to a suitcase and a couple of boxes on the far side of the room. "Do you care?"

Kira dropped her backpack. "Right's fine. I can't see much difference."

The room's mirror-perfect split represented another step back to college-like living, along with the desk, chair, dresser, and single bed on either end of their quarters, all made from the same cheap, heavy wood. The durable gray carpet, extended from the hallway, confirmed the impression of space that had seen a lot of hard use and expected to see a lot more.

Kira unzipped her backpack and unloaded her portable terminal, Empire State Building paperweight, data pad, and a stylus onto the desk. The rest of the unpacking went easily enough; there were some advantages to selling almost everything for moving money.

The big gray bag sitting on the bed turned out to be full of uniforms in shrink-wrap. Kira tugged at it.

Elbow-deep in a moving box, Chloe announced, "They said to try them all on, to make sure they fit. Do the boots, too."

Kira dragged the bag into the bathroom. It opened with a pop and released the smell of freshly extruded synthetic fibers and an illustrated guide explaining how everything should fit and what to check.

She unpacked the first tunic, shook out the wrinkles, and did the same for a pair of pants. They used the same design and materials as professional gunfighter's uniforms, but the two-tone beige color scheme marked the wearer as a trainee. The reflection in the full-length mirror made it obvious the uniform's color didn't do her hair or her complexion any favors, but it fit. With the drawstring pulled, the pants hugged her hips just tightly enough to feel secure but didn't restrict motion. The tunic sleeves ended where her wrist joined her hand, exactly as the directions said they should. Her name, in block letters over her left breast, was spelled correctly. The company logo was indeed printed on both shoulders, though there was no escaping the fact it looked like a midair collision between the letters TKC and a Cubist rendering of a seagull. It didn't express "security, stability, and competence" to her, but she wasn't the target audience. She didn't have any assets to insure.

The soft leather boots fit like socks and smelled like hunting and work. Their tan color complemented the uniform, and when she stood, the pants ended just above the foot and fell high enough in back that her heel couldn't get caught in them.

The bathroom lighting and gray wall made her image in the mirror look like a publicity still. Which is what it was, really. For the next year, she would play Kira Clark, gunfighter trainee. Like her three months as Juliet, nearly six months as Ophelia, or her five glorious, well-paid weeks as the Higgins Sky-Yacht Services Girl—before Higgins and most of the corporate treasury departed for a non-extradition country.

Kira worked through all seven uniforms and two pairs of boots, focusing on the look and feel of the clothes while trying to ignore their purpose.

A lot could happen in the next year. Legislation restricting debt slavery could pass. Lawsuits overturning punitive charges in her contract could move forward. A decent job could turn up. And, if none of that happened, she had twelve months to think about what to do next. Ideally, an option that didn't involve shooting at anybody, getting shot herself, or adding repayment of her signing bonus to her already monstrous pile of debts. Potentially, those were some hard choices. But for now, all she had to do was play the part.

God knows she'd spent enough time and money learning to do *that*.

She pulled the seventh tunic over her head, shook it into place, struck a pose, and checked the mirror. How should a gunfighter look? Or more to the point, how should *she* look, as a gunfighter? Not angry. An angry young blonde wouldn't be taken seriously, especially because she was only 5'4". Something else, then. Efficient. Competent. Cold. Like Beatrice the Assassin in *Bellamy Beach*. She straightened her back, squared her shoulders, and adjusted her expression. A relaxed, alert, and utterly unsympathetic face stared back from the mirror—a lioness sizing up a herd of gazelles.

A paid killer.

That's what Rob had called her that last night in New York, right before he put a gob of spit between her feet and stalked off down the street. He'd been drunk, not to mention mad because she'd abandoned his play just three weeks into the run, but he wasn't wrong. On the other hand, it was pretty damn easy to be critical when nobody was trying to foreclose on *your* life.

Time to try the look out on an audience. Kira returned to the main room. "What do you think?" She took the same pose she'd taken in front of the mirror and spoke in her character's voice: low, cool, and flat, with an undertone suggesting she didn't really need the opinion she was soliciting, but chose to be polite.

Chloe, seated at her desk, looked up and blanched. "Holy shi— Pardon my French. You look good."

Kira laughed. No need to stay in character now that she'd seen the effect. "Thanks." She patted the pants. "These things are ridiculously comfortable."

"Yeah, they're taking good care of us. I mean . . ." Chloe spread her arms wide, taking in the space around her. "Take a look at this room! I heard the food's good, too."

Kira forced a smile. Where had Chloe lived that made a glorified dorm room seem upscale?

Kira changed back into her street clothes and hung the uniforms on the front rod of the closet.

Chloe talked while unpacking another box. "So, the class list says you're from New York?"

"No, I grew up in Iowa. Ames. My parents worked for Iowa State." Kira rolled her suitcase under the uniforms and shoved it to the back. "I went to New York to be an actress."

"Well, that sounds cool."

Kira let her shoulders fall along with her face. "It didn't turn out the way it does on vid."

Chloe placed a statuette of Mary into what looked like a small shrine on an open shelf. The space already held a cross with a rosary draped on it and what looked like an icon of a saint Kira didn't recognize. Did gunfighters have a patron? They certainly needed one.

Her unpacking done, Kira pulled her chair from the desk and sat. "What about you? Where are you from?"

"Des Moines. South side. Born and raised." Chloe folded a box flat and stacked it on top of the others. "They say sometimes they have to send gunfighters out of town, and the Guild makes them get fancy places for us. You know, those hotels where it's more than one room."

"Suites?" *That was a sudden move from the topic of where Chloe was from.*

"Yeah." Chloe's face brightened. "Suites. You think it's true? You think they really put us up in suites?"

"I don't know. I haven't thought that much about being a

gunfighter. I'm more worried about getting through training."
With the big cut after the sixth week looming ahead, staying
focused on graduation was a plausible reason not to talk about
what they were training to do.

Chloe didn't respond. Instead, she opened another box, set
a picture frame on top of her dresser and turned it on. A gray-
haired man and woman stood together, beaming. Two younger
men stood to their left, with Chloe standing in front of them.
Standing next to Chloe, Lorenzo looked even younger than he
had a few minutes ago.

Kira smiled at the image. "So that's your family."

Chloe brushed the edge of the frame wistfully. "Yeah, that's
us all right. Mom and Dad, Michael and Desi, and me and Lorenzo." The picture shifted. An older man hefted a red wooden
ball a little smaller than his hand, his gaze focused outside the
frame. "That's my uncle Luca, about to whip Desi's butt in bocce
ball." The picture shifted again, this time to a baby on a blanket.
The camera had caught the infant with a smile breaking out on its
face and its pudgy hands in midwave. "That's my nephew, Alex."

"What do your parents think about you being a gunfighter?"

Chloe shrugged. "They're worried about me. But they can't
take care of me forever." Chloe slumped into her desk chair.
"Ever since I dropped out of school, it's been the same thing.
I get a job, or I get two jobs, or I get three. I get a little money
together, get a place and maybe I get a roommate, and things go
pretty good for a while. Then I get laid off, or my hours get cut,
or I get sick and miss a couple shifts or something and *boom*! I'm
back in Mom and Dad's basement, or somebody's couch, and
I crawl out again, and then . . ." She waved her hand, as if to

push her own words away. "Mom and Dad can't work that much longer, and if they quit, they can't have me showing up to put a hole in their groceries. Michael and Anna have the baby now, so crashing there is out. I've gotta figure out how to take care of myself." Chloe's face brightened a little. "I'm doing it, too. I used my signing bonus to put a down payment on one of those duplex places. It's a dump, but Lorenzo and Desi are fixing it up. I'm paying for some of their school, so it helps all of us." She went to the frame and brought up a picture of a nondescript brick building with two entrances and a battered exterior. "I want to rent out one side and live in the other. So, when I'm done here, it's all paid for and I've always got a place to be, and I've always got some money coming in." Chloe worked her fingers, as if they were stiff.

"But they're OK with you shooting people?" There. It was out.

Chloe sat up straight. "The way I figure it, we'll be kind of like cops, you know? We'll deal with the people who won't follow the rules and keep insisting they're right after everybody's told them they're wrong. It's better if they duel with one of us instead of showing up at an office someplace and gunning a bunch of people down, isn't it?" She looked to Kira for agreement.

Kira maintained a neutral expression.

Undeterred by the lack of an answer, Chloe kept her attention on Kira. "What about you? Why are you here?"

Kira squirmed. Might as well go with the truth, as ugly as it was. "I got behind on a lifetime services contract loan and the property recovery teams were coming for me." She shuddered at the notion of becoming *property* that had to be *recovered* by enforcers working for her contract holders. "The signing bonus was enough to stop it." She pulled into herself. What would Chloe think of her now?

Her roommate's eyes went wide. "A lifetime services contract? For what?"

"Student loans. I went to Paget for undergrad, then I got an MFA . . ."

Chloe's brow wrinkled. "Couldn't your parents, like, help you out a little bit?"

Kira took a deep breath. "My parents are dead. Staph infection. Dad got it after surgery, Mom got it from him. I've been on my own since I was nineteen, and I guess I made some bad decisions." People were usually less judgmental if you took some responsibility.

Chloe looked stricken. "I'm sorry, I didn't . . ."

"It's OK. That's just how it is for me."

Chloe's tone shifted toward incredulity. "Don't you have any people at all? I mean . . ."

"Some cousins in Portland, but we don't see each other much."

The shock didn't fade from Chloe's face. "How much debt do you have, anyway?"

Kira looked at the floor. "That's kind of personal."

"Sorry." Chloe sounded genuinely pained. "I forgot. Rich people don't like to talk about that stuff."

Kira frowned. "Rich? I just told you; I'm broke on my ass."

Chloe waved the objection away. "That's not what I mean. You get out of this, you get the right job, or find the right guy, and you'll fit right in." Chloe rolled her shoulders. "Me? I could have more money than the president of TKC, and the minute I open my mouth, people would know right where I come from and wonder why I don't go back there. And that's if they can't tell just by looking."

Kira squirmed again. "I don't know about that."

"Well, I do. But it's OK." Chloe stood. "Do you really want to come to Sunday dinner?"

Kira nodded. "Yeah, if you're going. I guess I'm afraid that on Sunday this place will clear out and I'll be here by myself while everyone else is away, and . . . I don't know, I don't want that right now."

"I get that." Chloe grinned a little. "Though if you tell Mom your whole story, she may decide you're a project and try to fix you up with somebody." She gave Kira an appraising look. "Not that it would be hard. You're pretty enough for three people. Who do you date?"

"Guys." Kira laughed a little. "Just guys."

"Yeah, me, too." Chloe made it sound like yet another limitation on her prospects.

Heavy, running footsteps pounded down the hall. Something big hit their door with a hard, meaty sound, followed by a slap, laughter, and a shouted response with "asshole" as the only intelligible word. A gasp, more laughter, and the footsteps thundered on.

Chloe pointed to the door. "You know we're the only two girls in the class, right?"

"No." Kira folded her arms across her chest. "There was an Adrian and a Rory on the class list. I thought maybe . . ."

"They're a couple big, beefy guys from someplace in Kansas. Lorenzo and I checked."

The room suddenly felt like a small and rather fragile life-boat in a large and rather hostile sea.

Chloe continued. "I think our chances are better if we stick together."

"I think you're right about that."

Chloe's voice became even more earnest. "So let's say we do everything we can to help each other graduate. Deal?"

Kira grinned. "Deal."

CHAPTER 3

Kira enters the scanner, closes the door behind her, and confirms her identity with her thumbprint. It's the third time today she's verified who she is, as if anyone would trade places with a gunfighter about to face another top-line professional.

Hanging at her side, her left hand trembles. Apparently, her body doesn't like the fifty-fifty odds she'll face on the field. No question this will be more dangerous than a duel against an untrained citizen with a complaint over corporate policy and a loss in arbitration. With those, her chance of dying is less than one in twenty-five. But the rewards for the encounter ahead are also far greater . . . beginning with the freedom to never do this again.

She steps into the circle inscribed on the floor of the cylindrical space and faces the AI readout. The scan begins.

The AI searches for hidden body armor, velocity-blunting fibers, implanted aiming aids, or even a button or snap that might alter a bullet's course through her body. Her pullover tunic and drawstring pants are as comfy as a pair of nice pajamas, and they offer about as much protection.

The AI continues its work, and Kira steadies herself by using scene analysis to break down the part she's about to play.

The one-act drama "Death's Angel on the Dueling Field," starring Kira Clark, is about to unfold for a vid audience that might run into the tens of millions. No matter. The tools she used when playing in a basement theater for a few dozen people will still serve.

The questions:

What is Death's Angel literally trying to do?

Win a duel.

What action is she going to perform?

Escape the life. Hundreds of millions in corporate unidollars will flow in response to the outcome of this match, cascading into billions in share price changes, options, and related derivatives. Only a tiny slice will be hers, but that slice will be enough to buy her freedom, with plenty left over to purchase any life she wants. She's been conned by the system, she's been an enforcer for the system, and this will be her final payday. Whether it comes in the form of a huge bank deposit or a cheap plastic body bag is yet to be determined.

It's as if—

This is always the hardest part. The "as if" is the touchstone of the scene, the emotional prompt to guide her words and actions. It should be an event from her life, emotionally similar to the scene, but not close enough for direct comparison.

It's as if I'm auditioning for the Forrest University MFA program.

She'd succeeded on pure craft, using training and technique to show the admission panel the grief of Andromache from The Trojan Women. "But to die is better far than to live wretched." It helped *that Euripides got that right, and it went well enough she beat out 304 applicants for one of twelve slots.*

Today, she'll show the cold, calculating indifference of Death's Angel. Every word, every gesture, will demonstrate she's come to claim what's hers and stepping over Niles's body to do it is all in a day's work.

She puts her once-trembling left hand through the signs she will use to communicate with her second when the door opens. I'm OK and opponent ready *spill from her fingers. Perfect.*

Diana's fondness for her homemade hand signals probably comes more from her days as a Marine directing troops in close combat than the needs of the dueling field, but Kira has always gone along with them. Today, they provide a comforting click of routine.

With a crescendo of nearly inaudible hums, the AI completes its work and reports that Kira is free from any prohibited material or equipment. It opens the door to reveal a white dome covering a field of green pseudograss a little larger than a basketball court with very generous sidelines.

The space is both chilly and acoustically dead—as cool and still as the place in her chest where Kira Clark kept a wide variety of feelings, but Death's Angel maintains only an iron determination to win.

CHAPTER 4

"All right. Listen up!" Alan Peterson held up his data pad to get everyone's attention, like a football coach calling on his team. The tight little knot of ten gunfighter trainees, the portion of Kira's class assigned to Simulator Four, turned to face him. After two weeks in the program, their skill set consisted largely of showing up on time, speaking when spoken to, and maintaining an attentive silence while directions were given. That, and what Senior Instructor Briggs described as "loading and holstering a weapon without endangering yourself or those around you and achieving intentional discharge in the general direction of the target in somewhat less time than it takes my grandmother to locate her handset and remove it from her purse."

Kira maneuvered to the outer edge of the group, where she could see and hear without the taller bodies of her classmates in the way. At last, she had a clear view of the instructor in his green-and-gray uniform; right down to the black bar across his chest signifying Guild-certified status and the one red slash on his right arm indicating his junior rank.

Someone moved in front of her. Kira shifted again, trading

a more oblique angle on the instructor and a little more distance for an unobstructed line of sight. With luck, Peterson would have enough audience awareness to speak up and turn enough to make sure everyone got a good look at anything he had to show them. If this session stuck to the pattern of earlier classes, verbal instructions and demonstrations would be the only reliable sources of information. Handouts and other written materials seemed to be produced and maintained with the idea no one would ever read them, and hardly anyone did. Like Chloe, most of the class struggled with any text more complex than the cafeteria menu, but most of them could repeat a series of physical steps after seeing it just two or three times.

Satisfied he had the group's attention, Peterson continued. "This is the dueling simulator. Some of you may remember it from the tour. The combat area behind me is exactly like a dueling field. It has pseudograss, and it has a centerline, start point, strikeline, and kill boxes all laid out."

He waved toward the space behind him. Unlike the real dueling field, this one was open-topped, allowing an instructor to see the entire space from a control cab well above the combat area. High walls surrounded the field on three sides, topped by walkways where a smattering of advanced trainees, instructors, and staff watched the proceedings.

"Follow me." The group, a loose gaggle of beige ducklings, fell in behind Peterson. He reached a table below the control cab, counted his charges, and continued his presentation. "Today, you'll be armed with a pseudogun." He pointed to a device sitting in the safety stand, its action open. Except for its bright-blue color, it looked exactly like a dueling pistol. Beside it, a rack of thirty bullets sat in a carrier. They were also bright blue. "The pseudogun can't fire a round. However, you are expected to treat it *exactly* as if it were a real gun." The instructor lifted the device, loaded it, and placed it in his holster, taking care to keep the barrel pointed down throughout the operation. "Just like we practiced, OK?" He surveyed the class, checking for their attention. "The pseudogun makes a flash, but it's just a thing called a diode. There's a speaker that simulates sounds, too." The instructor drew the device, aimed it at the wall, and squeezed the trigger. The muzzle emitted a white flash and the sharp report of a 9mm pistol.

"As long as you're inside the simulator, the system can tell where the bullet would have gone if this had been a real gun. That's how we keep score during a practice duel."

Peterson scanned his audience before proceeding to his next point. "When you've finished with your match, go back to the judge's table, remove the bullet, and put it in the case bin." He carried out the action he'd just described, tossing the bullet into the blue plastic receptacle on the table. "These rounds don't have any powder. They just tell the pseudogun it's loaded." Peterson placed the device in the waiting cradle, where it emitted a small chirp. "If you don't hear that chirp, that means the capacitor didn't recharge. Press this." He touched a recessed button just above the grip. "That way, it's ready for the next person. When you're done, go sit with the group." He waved his data pad toward the area where they'd been standing earlier. "Proper handling of the pistol at the judge's table is the only part of today's exercise that will be graded."

In response to that revelation, a ripple ran through the trainees. Upperclassmen had been hectoring them with stories of their first simulator combat since training started, and they'd all assumed their performance in the upcoming duel would have a big impact on their scores.

Peterson stepped closer to the group. "Today is your introduction to the simulator. This is where we provide the most realistic training we can offer. Normally, you'd face off against a mech running a program selected by your trainer, and you'd fire at it with a real gun." He pointed to the three walls of the enclosure. "If you don't hit the mech, one of those walls would stop your bullet." He used his clipboard to indicate the open fourth side. "Since the mech only fires a pseudogun, we don't need a wall on that side."

It was hard to tell for sure at this distance, but the walls appeared to be coated with the same spongy, bullet-absorbing material as their range targets. When tickled with an electrical current, it gave up all the bullets embedded in it. Scooping them up from the ground was a job for trainees whose attention wandered in class or who mouthed off to the instructors.

Two men wearing gray-and-green professional dueling uniforms descended the stairs from the control cab. Peterson introduced them. "Today, you'll be dueling against either Mr. Abrams or Mr. Sanchez."

The men nodded in acknowledgment and took up positions across the centerline at the other end of the judge's table while the trainees watched in rapt silence.

Peterson reclaimed the group's attention. "You may recognize them as professionals in the TKC stable. Because we aren't ready to lose you quite yet, they've only got pseudoguns."

Collectively, Kira's group emitted a nervous chuckle.

"When they squeeze the trigger, the simulator figures out if the bullet would've hit you. If it would've grazed you someplace, you get a tingle. If they score a substantial hit, you get a shock. If they hit your head or heart, you get a big shock."

A hand went up.

"Yes, Mr. Lopez."

"Are they wearing shock suits, too?"

The instructor paused, as if he might offer a comment, but instead he pointed to the gunfighters, and Mr. Sanchez held his arm out and pulled the sleeve back, revealing the wire-laden skin suit beneath. It was the same gesture the trainees used when they arrived this morning, to show the instructors they'd dressed as ordered.

Petersen addressed Lopez. "In the unlikely event you or one of your classmates manages a hit, these gentlemen will feel it."

Peterson's tone left little doubt that Lopez had stepped in it, and put himself about one impertinent question away from spending some of his precious off hours scooping bullets or scrubbing toilets. Another ripple passed through the group, this one created by trainees reflexively putting some distance between themselves and Lopez.

"Are there any further questions?"

There weren't.

"All right, when it's your turn, come to me. I'll be standing here like your second. Load and holster your weapon, and then it's the standard dueling rules we've all seen on vid. Mr. Abrams, Mr. Sanchez: Would you please demonstrate?"

The two gunfighters came to the table, loaded their pseudo-guns, and assumed their positions on either side of the centerline that split the field in half.

"You and your opponent get into position, and the Wall goes up." The instructor made a sweeping gesture, and a featureless gray hologram the same height as the barrier walls covered the centerline, rendering the other side of the simulator field invisible from where Kira and the trainees stood.

"Walk to the start point when you're ordered to do so." The instructor pointed to the center of the combat area, where half of a large red circle protruded on the side of the barrier the trainees could see. From a speaker just below the cab and just above the score displays, a recorded voice spoke. "Combatants, please advance to the start point."

Sanchez walked along the Wall. Presumably, Abrams was doing the same thing on the other side, although no one on Kira's side of the hologram could see. Sanchez reached the start point and turned, facing away from the barrier.

"See how he's standing inside the circle with his back to his opponent?" Sanchez stood with his toes on the edge of the red area, placing him as close to the kill box—about ten paces away—as he could get. The class nodded.

"Good. Now, he'll be told to march, and he'll walk to the kill box." The instructor pointed to the two-meter-deep area marked off on their end of the field. The trainees turned, like sunflowers finding the light.

"When you get to the kill box, pivot and fire as soon as you're ready. Remember, your opponent is doing the same thing."

The recorded voice sounded again. "Proceed on my count. 1 . . . 2 . . . 3 . . ."

Sanchez timed his strides with the voice's cadence, but he departed from the strikeline that showed the shortest distance to the kill box. He reached the box and became a blur as he turned. He stopped with his gun drawn and at eye level. It flashed, two pistol reports sounded, and Sanchez jumped slightly, as if he'd been goosed. On the other side of the field, Abrams frantically rolled his shoulder and patted his chest, as if he was trying to get a bee out of his shirt. Eventually, both men stood upright and still.

The recorded voice spoke again. "Please return to the table area, if you are able."

The two gunfighters holstered their weapons and jogged back to their starting positions.

The screen displayed their scores: SANCHEZ, 58; ABRAMS, 44.

Sanchez grinned and punched Abrams in the shoulder. In an actual gunfight, the match would have been a "bleed-off," the winner determined by who could remain standing the longest with the injuries they'd received. The simulator handbook said the score was the system's best estimate of how badly they'd damaged each other, based on the location of the hit. The scale awarded 100 points for an outright kill, and anything over 90 indicated a severed spine or shattered bone that would guarantee a fall and an immediate loss.

The instructor signaled for attention. "All right, for today, you'll be on the gunfighter's side of the field." He pointed his clipboard to the open side of the combat area. "Mr. Sanchez and Mr. Abrams will trade off on the mech's side. You'll each get one match to start, and you can repeat as many times as you like. Any questions?"

There were none. TKC's allocation of only two professionals

to duel against ten trainees was a clear indication of what their chances were.

The instructor waited a few seconds, and then pointed to the patch of pseudograss on the left of the control cab where they'd first assembled. "Wait there until I call you."

Kira went over and sat, cross-legged, to watch the drama unfold. Soft popping noises sounded from other simulators nearby. Were those demonstrations, or were the other groups from their class that much faster?

"Chas Evans."

The first up was a tall, wiry guy built like a basketball player. He tried to outdo Sanchez by barreling straight down the strikeline, using his long legs to get to the kill box first. He lost time on the pivot, and Sanchez's shot left the trainee doubled over and clutching his belly, the pseudogun still in his holster.

"Timothy Ramirez."

Despite a fast walk down the strikeline and a rapid pivot, Tim wasted his shot, firing straight back the way he'd come, only to discover Abrams standing a few feet to the right.

"Thabo Young."

Thabo looked like he might have outdrawn Sanchez, but his shot went wide and Sanchez administered a sting on his leg that forced him down on one knee, triggering the fall indicator and a loss.

"Curtis Johnson."

He fouled out by drawing his pseudogun before he got both feet in the kill box.

"Kira Clark." She scrambled to her feet and jogged to the table.

"Give me your left wrist." Kira held out her arm, and Peterson held his data pad near it until the device chirped. He spoke gently. "Ready for the suit test?"

Kira nodded, and jumped slightly at the tickle on her bicep.

"OK, your suit's synchronized. Go up and load your weapon." He pointed to the judge's table.

Kira went through the load and holster routine, and Peterson nodded. Good. That probably meant she had full credit on this part of the exercise. She assumed her position, Sanchez assumed his, and the Wall went up. What should she do? With her relatively short legs, there was no way she'd get to the kill box first. What if she took a diagonal route? It would take longer to get there, but the rules said the Wall didn't come down until both combatants were in their kill boxes. She turned pretty fast and might have a chance if Sanchez had to spend time looking for her.

The recorded voice sent them to the start point. There, she stood in the circle, pointed forty-five degrees off to the left. The voice called cadence, and she began her march to the far corner of her kill box. She turned and drew. Sanchez turned toward her as her gun came up. A flash from his muzzle. She pulled her trigger and a burn started over her heart. The burn became agony and she dropped the gun as she brought her arms to her chest, desperate to make the pain stop.

When it was over, she found herself folded over her own knees in the kill box. Peterson knelt down next to her. "You OK?"

Kira sat up and drew a ragged breath. "Yeah. I mean, I think so. What?"

"You took one through the heart. You died."

"Oh. That's why I feel so bad."

"Yeah." Peterson smiled a little and patted her on the shoulder.

Would getting hit in the heart for real be more or less painful than what she just experienced? She pushed the thought away; she didn't need to deal with that right now.

She started to stand and stopped. A faint whiff of ammonia, and her crotch was damp. *Damn.* On top of everything else, she'd pissed herself.

She looked down as heat rose in her cheeks. "I'm sorry . . ."

Peterson pulled her to her feet. "It's OK. It happens. You took a jolt at 80 percent of max. That's enough to mess up anybody. Go back to your room, clean up, and get some lunch. I'll take care of the pseudogun and mark you complete. I know you've got that part down."

"But I want to go again. You said we could."

Peterson shook his head. "There's no point. It takes twelve to fourteen hours to recover after a hit like that. What's your afternoon class?"

"Self-care first aid."

"That's good. I'll sign you out until then." He clapped her on the shoulder. "Food, rest, and a shower. You'll be fine."

Her voice came out small and ragged. "OK, thanks."

Fuck it all. Pity. Only two weeks in, and she was getting *pity*. She faced the expanse of open space between her position and the double doors leading out of the simulator area. The audience on the catwalks turned their attention to other simulators, and her group of trainees shifted their attention to Peterson, anticipating his next call. Best to make a run for it now.

Once through the doors, she found her locker and retrieved her purse. In the empty hallway, sounds and thoughts echoed. *What would this be like when the bullets were real?* She'd be someplace else by then. And if she wasn't, this was still better than foreclosure. Wasn't it?

She shut the locker and sagged against it, squeezing her purse close. Inside, her handset buzzed for attention. After a couple of deep breaths, she fished it out and checked the message. It confirmed she hadn't been selected for an arts education liaison position she'd interviewed for just before leaving New York. "*. . . a large pool of well-qualified candidates, and at this time we have decided to move forward with a candidate whose skills are a better match . . .*"

Another door closing. How long did she really have? She'd been telling herself gunfighter training would last a year, but after today, what were her chances during the big cut next month? When they winnowed her class down to its final size, would she even be in it? And if not, then what?

Nothing to do about it now except what Peterson said: clean up, food, rest, and keep at it. For right now, get clear of the hallway before classes let out and everyone saw her with wet pants. She shambled toward the dorms. Her handset buzzed again.

This time, it was a rejection from a Des Moines recruiter. They didn't represent people enrolled in training programs.

Fuck it all.

CHAPTER 5

Kira adjusted her grip on the cardboard box containing two sets of ear protectors, a misappropriated dueling pistol, and sixty rounds of stolen ammunition. Chloe studied the darkened break area between their position and the entry doors of the Advanced Firing Range as if it were a linoleum-clad no-man's-land. Two hours before the range's official opening time, shadows filled the place, and Chloe jumped at all of them.

Under the circumstances, Kira couldn't blame her roommate for hesitating, but they needed to get moving. Kira pitched her voice to an urgent whisper. "Remember, if anybody asks, a tech told us to carry this stuff over and put it in Firing Point Two. We don't know anything else about it."

It was a plausible story if you didn't think about it too hard. Trainees who hadn't even cleared their six-week test were fair game for a menial assignment from just about anyone. The door guard hadn't even bothered to ask when he checked the access tokens on their handsets.

Chloe wavered now, though, peering into the farthest and darkest corner over by the restrooms to see if anyone lurked in the shadows. When she finally nodded, Kira led the way through the neat checkerboard of steel-legged tables surrounded by spindly plastic chairs. Were professionals that much neater than trainees, or was the cleaning service more diligent with them? For the benefit of anyone watching via camera, Kira maintained the slow meander of a person sent on a pointless errand and resisted the urge to look back to see if Chloe followed. At last, they reached the puddle of light near the firing point doors. Chloe fumbled with her handset for the key token.

"Hey! What are you doing there?" The harsh voice belonged to a short, compact man in a green range manager uniform.

Why the hell was he at work so early?

Kira responded with wide eyes, a warm smile, and a soft voice. "Oh, we were just—"

"It's OK, they're with me." All three of them turned to face the voice. A tall, muscular woman emerged from the darkness of the break area, a set of ear protectors hanging around her neck. The three red slashes on her tunic's right sleeve identified her as a senior instructor. The name stitched on the uniform identified her as *Reynolds*.

The range manager faced the instructor, fists on his hips. "You're supposed to escort trainees in the professional area at all times."

"I'm sorry. I was in the restroom." Nothing in the instructor's tone or body language conveyed the smallest suggestion of regret.

The manager looked toward Kira and Chloe as if they were escaping prey and pushed his sleeves up to his elbows. "Can we talk about this?"

The instructor keyed her handset, and a green light flashed on the firing point door. She nodded toward Chloe and Kira. "Go on in and set up. I'll be along in a minute."

Kira and Chloe entered the firing point vestibule, and the outer door clicked shut behind them. Chloe hissed. "We are in for it. That was *Diana Reynolds*."

Kira dredged her memory for the name. Nothing. Chloe stared back at her, wide-eyed. "You've never heard of her? She *killed somebody*."

"The instructors are former gunfighters. They all killed somebody."

"I don't mean like an opponent, I mean like an *actual person*. They say when she was a Marine in Iran she—" Stirring at the outer door cut Chloe off, and they moved from the vestibule to the firing point, closing the second door behind them and leaving the mystery of why Chloe was so flummoxed by the idea of a Marine who killed people for another time.

Unlike the open range where trainees practiced, each station of the professional facility was fully enclosed by solid, slightly curved walls running all the way from the firing point down to the target area, like a vast hallway coated with sound deadening, bullet-absorbing material, open at the top to give the noise someplace to go. The firing point had enough room for two people to stand comfortably among the controls, a storage shelf, the pistol safety stand, and the hanging gun belts that shared the space. It would be tight with three. Overhead, a ventilation fan pulled so hard it stirred Chloe's hair. The space felt like a generating station Kira had visited as a kid—immense, clean, and quiet. Ms. Reynolds entered, and the generating-station illusion became complete. The unmistakable thrum of power now vibrated through every particle of air.

Kira and Chloe pressed together to make room. In the confined space, the senior instructor seemed even taller and more imposing than she had outside. She had to be at least six feet tall, maybe a little more. Kira searched for an opening in the older woman's expression or bearing. Nothing but calm gray eyes, a widow's peak of dark hair setting off a stern expression, a strong jaw, and a relaxed, all-business posture. Whatever Ms. Reynolds had planned for them, Kira wasn't going to flirt their way out of it.

She pointed to the box in Kira's hands. "Go ahead."

Chloe confirmed her view of their change in fortune as a trip from the frying pan straight into the fire by crossing herself and looking down. Kira opened the box.

The instructor leaned forward to inspect the contents and leaned back against the storage shelf. "So, how much did Pete charge?"

Chloe shot a panic-stricken look at Kira.

There was no way out of this but the truth. Kira responded with her best matter-of-fact tone. "Twenty unidollars for the pistol, twenty-five cents each for the bullets. An extra ten if we don't clean it and return all the brass."

"The access tokens?"

Kira swallowed hard. "He threw those in for free."

"He must like you. He usually charges five." The instructor turned her attention to Chloe. "Or maybe it's because he's friends with Niles LeBlanc. Niles sent you to Pete, right?"

Chloe seemed to be making a serious attempt to disappear into the floor.

Ms. Reynolds prompted. "Upperclassman doing his girl-friend a good turn?"

Chloe's voice came out in a whisper. "I'm not exactly his girlfriend."

"Ah." The instructor folded her arms. "So those 2:00 a.m. check-ins from his apartment are friendly visits?"

Chloe remained silent.

"It's your life, and I'm not telling you what to do, but this job attracts psychopaths." Real warmth flowed into Ms. Reynolds's voice as she tried to make eye contact with Chloe. "Be careful, OK?"

Chloe responded with a single nod of her head.

"All right. Explain to me why a couple new fish are sneaking into the advanced training area at oh-dark-thirty with stolen gear."

Kira squared her shoulders and plunged in. "We're afraid of getting cut in the six-week trial. We heard we're below the cutoff, but we think we can make up for it if we do some extra work."

"Hmmmm . . . And who told you about your position?"

"We . . ." Kira hesitated. Was she saying anything that might get someone in trouble? "We heard some guys talking at break. One of them saw a class rank, and they said we were down in the bottom fifth."

"I see."

"They said we were old and slow." Chloe seemed almost surprised she'd spoken.

Ms. Reynolds shifted her attention to Chloe. "'Old and slow'?"

Chloe withered under the instructor's gaze.

Kira responded. "Look, Ms. Reynolds, we're six to eight years older than most of those guys, and, you know, reflexes . . ."

A smile played across the older woman's face. "Let me show you something."

She put on the gun belt, tapped a command into the control panel, and held her hand out. Kira placed the pistol in it—the weapon's eleven-inch barrel pointing at the floor and its single-shot break action open. Kira waited while the instructor inspected the pistol, then handed her a carrier with ten bullets. Ms. Reynolds placed the carrier within easy reach of the firing line, put on her ear protectors and signaled for Kira and Chloe to do the same. Once assured everyone had protection in place, Ms. Reynolds stepped up to the firing line with her pistol loaded and holstered.

The drill signal sounded, pitched to the same range as normal speech so the noise-canceling ear protectors would allow it to pass. The instructor's arms became a blur, fully visible only when she reached final firing position. The gun barked. With a smooth, unhurried, almost mechanical motion she removed the casing, reloaded the pistol, and returned to the ready position. She repeated the exercise until she used the carrier's last bullet. The ceiling vent sucked away final wisps of gun smoke and a hologram displayed her results—an average of 1.97 seconds from draw to hit, the hits all within the solid black circle around the target's heart.

Ms. Reynolds placed the pistol on the safety stand and removed her hearing protection. "I've got seventeen years on either one of you."

She unbuckled the gun belt and handed it to Chloe. "Your turn."

Chloe adjusted the belt for her larger waist, loaded the weapon, and put her ear protection back in place. She stepped up to the firing line with the gun in her holster and her hands at the ready position.

Diana's voice was curiously soothing. "This is baseline. Show me where you are so we know what to work on, OK?"

Chloe nodded.

A chime announced the start of the exercise and a random interval later, the fire signal sounded. Chloe responded with a smooth draw and a shot at the target.

Chloe dropped the gun to waist level, broke the action open, yanked the casing out, and tossed it toward the case bin. She missed. While she scrambled to retrieve the errant bit of metal, Diana made a clucking noise and shook her head. "Relax, relax, relax. The timer stops when you hit the target. It doesn't start again until you draw. On reload, just be fast enough not to irritate people waiting their turn."

Chloe huffed, mumbled something . . . but did relax a bit and reloaded smoothly.

Chloe ran through the ten rounds in her rack, and Diana ended the exercise. The display awarded her an average time of 2.53 seconds, the hits in a random pattern all over the target's chest area and two clean misses.

Diana studied the pattern in silence for a few seconds before addressing Chloe. "Not bad, but when do you put your finger inside the trigger guard?"

Chloe paused before she replied. "When I bring the gun up, I guess. I'm trying—"

"You're missing." Diana held her hand out, index finger extended. "Your finger stays outside the guard until the sights have stabilized on what you want to hit." Diana folded the extended finger into her hand.

Chloe bit her lip. "But the speed . . ."

"You only get one shot. The worst thing you can do is waste it. 'Don't point the gun at anything you don't want to destroy; don't touch the trigger until you know what you'll hit.'"

At Diana's recitation of the training maxims, Chloe bowed her head and let her shoulders droop. "Yes, ma'am."

Diana's voice softened. "Don't worry about speed. Worry about form. Get the movements right and speed will come."

Chloe set the gun on the stand, released the gun belt, and handed it to Kira.

Diana tapped something into the command console and offered no further comment.

Kira stepped up to the line, ear protectors in place and the gun heavy on her thigh. She drew a deep breath and focused, shutting out both her fear and the weight of Diana's gaze.

"Try a wider stance."

Kira obeyed. By the time the chime announced the exercise's start, Kira's world included nothing except the gun and the target. At the draw signal, her right hand found the weapon and extracted it from the holster, meeting her left at waist level. Her thumb flicked off the safety as she raised her arms, and when she had a clear view of the sights and the target, she squeezed the trigger. She reloaded and continued the exercise, repeating the actions while holding everything else behind a haze of inattention. It would all be there when she was done. When the casing from the last bullet hit the bin, Diana called a halt.

The hologram scoreboard gave Kira an average time of 2.39 seconds, but her hits fell in a tight pattern, most of them in the darkest three circles near the target's heart.

"Nice job. You're pulling a little left; allow for that next time."

Kira turned away from the display and faced Diana. "OK. Thanks."

The instructor's attention remained on the control panel. "You two have class at eight?"

Kira and Chloe nodded.

Diana looked up. "That's a yes?"

Kira and Chloe stumbled over each other's affirmative responses.

"OK, that's it. Clean the pistol and put the brass in the box."

Kira ran a cleaning rag through the pistol barrel while Chloe fetched the case bin.

"It's two weeks until the evaluation. Can you two meet me in the lobby of this building at six every morning from now until then?"

Kira's chest became light. "Sure!" She picked up the box. "Do we need to bring—"

"No, I'll take care of it." Diana held out her hands. "You two get to class. I'll take this back to Pete."

The lightness disappeared. "Is Pete going to get in trouble?"

Diana looked as if Kira had told a joke only Diana understood. "No. Shaking down trainees for beer money is minor. But he needs to know somebody's paying attention."

Slowly, Kira surrendered the box.

With the container in her custody, Diana added. "Pete won't deal with you in an 'unofficial' capacity again, and neither will anyone he knows. But that won't be a problem for you."

"Why not?" Chloe blurted.

Once more, Diana produced the joke-that-only-she-got smile. "Because now, you know me."

CHAPTER 6

Kira emerges from the scanner onto the dueling field. She stops, absorbing the vastness, her isolation, and the silence. As always, it feels like an empty theater that will never fill.

Diana arrives, a pillar of calm. Her uniform is nearly identical to Kira's, except for the large TKC logo on the front, rather than the shoulders. Since no one is shooting at Diana, there's no danger of it becoming a target. Kira flashes her hand signs, indicating her readiness and her estimate of Niles's preparedness. Diana flashes hers in return. Field OK. Expected second.

Kira nods in acknowledgment. Tom Dryden, Niles's third and longest-lasting second, will guide him through the match. Good news for Kira and Diana's strategy.

Diana turns and leads the way to the judge's table in silence. Kira follows, seeing more of the broad, muscular expanse of Diana's back than the administrative area they're approaching. Her second's hair is grayer than when they first met, and that's at least partly Kira's fault. Delivering a win today will all but guarantee Diana's place in the Guild's Hall of Champions, and Diana's share of the purse will underwrite her retirement from the dueling field. Surely that will make up for the times Kira straggled into work late and tried to phone it in, only to have Diana snap her back to the reality that she was preparing to face real bullets.

Maybe it's even enough to repay her for the times Kira terrified Diana in a way the older woman could only express as anger.

They arrive at their destination. Kira stops short of the centerline and turns to face the judge's table. Everything is in place: Diana on her left, the centerline on her right, and the combat area at her back.

Behind the table, the two wards in brick-colored body armor cradle their stun rifles with easy precision. Beside them, the EMTs look small and out of place, preservers of life in a temple dedicated to death. The judge stands over them all, aloof on his elevated bench, protected by a transparent plastic shield and the dignity of his red satin robes.

Gun belts, holsters, and dueling pistols are laid out on the table in sets, along with the bullets—one each, standing at attention, light bouncing off the polished casing. All part of the show. In her mind's eye, Kira sees one of the steel-jacketed 9mm rounds penetrate her tunic and rip through her body, leaving shattered bones and ruined organs in its wake.

She turns to Diana for . . . what? Comfort? Reassurance? Guidance?

Her trainer responds with a small nod and another hand signal: you are ready.

CHAPTER 7

Kira fidgeted outside the briefing room door. The firing range portion of her evaluation had gone well. At least it looked that way. But had it gone well enough to impress Diana? The only way to know for sure was to open the briefing room door and hear what she had to say, and Kira didn't dare—she just had to wait. She fidgeted some more. Her handset buzzed. Appointment time. She pressed the entry chime button.

A calm alto voice responded. "Come in."

Kira entered. Diana looked up, pointed to the open seat across from the room's tiny worktable, and tapped something into her data pad. "Sit."

Kira perched on the edge of the chair, her back ramrod-straight and her shoulders in a knot.

At last, Diana smiled. "Congratulations, you're no longer a new fish."

"Thank you." Kira's shoulders unwound a little. Good news so far.

Diana turned her data pad's display toward Kira. "You threw a tighter pattern than anyone in your class—a little off center, but not enough to hurt at this point." The display changed. "Your speed just missed the top third. There's room to improve, but that's good enough for now. If you keep at it, you'll have no problem with the November evaluation."

Kira squirmed a little. "Do you think I have a shot at the Regional Cup?"

Diana looked thoughtful. "Hard to say. That's competition with people from thirty companies in four different cities, and we don't know anything about most of them. Besides, it's not until graduation."

Kira licked her lips. "Is that why they keep being vague about the cash prize?"

Diana smiled a little. "No. That's because the Guild locals bargain for the companies' contribution. A couple thousand one way or the other sets the tone for contract negotiations. But, it's usually around forty thousand unis for first place, half that for second, and about ten for third."

The calculator in Kira's head spun. Even after taxes, that first prize could repay her signing bonus with some left over. She'd still need a job with a high enough salary to make her payments, but it wouldn't have to be gunfighting.

Diana slapped the table, pulling Kira back to the here and now. "You've got other things to do in the next ten months. Don't worry about the Cup until the quarter before graduation." Diana's face became more serious. "They made a deep cut this time. A fourth of your classmates won't be here tomorrow."

Kira's shoulders knotted again. "Chloe?"

"I can't tell you another trainee's score, but you won't have to break in a new roommate."

"That's good." Kira eased back into her chair once more.

"Here's your overall standing." Diana adjusted the display and pointed to a line just below Kira's rank. "Here's the lower edge of the top fifth." She set the pad aside. "Do you have any questions?"

Kira chewed on her cheek. She had a question, but was asking it a good idea? She'd been lucky, she'd survived the cut, and she should let it go. Thank Diana for her help, hope she'd be willing to help again, and say no more.

But if she could get Diana to exercise her prerogative as a senior instructor and become a mentor for her and Chloe . . .

Calm gray eyes watched Kira from the far side of the worktable, as if they could see the struggle going on inside Kira's head.

Kira pulled up close to the table, put her elbows on it, and forced herself to meet Diana's gaze. Nobody did favors for people who didn't stick up for themselves. She tried to keep her voice casual. "Are you going to keep working with Chloe and me as your mentees?"

Diana looked as if she'd tasted something unexpected, but not unpleasant. "Why do you think that would be a good idea?"

Kira swallowed to clear the dryness in her throat. "We improved when you worked with us. I got faster and tighter. Chloe is more accurate and more consistent." She swallowed again. "We might make good clients when you rotate off instructor duty. If we work together, maybe the AI will match us." It sounded weak, even as she said it. Asking Diana to take them as mentees was begging for a favor, no two ways about it.

Diana sat back and contemplated Kira. "Your aim is excellent, your reflexes are good, and you focus better than anyone

I've ever worked with. Your first day in the simulator was interesting, too."

Kira frowned. "I died."

Diana almost laughed. "That's nearly inevitable." Kira looked puzzled, and Diana leaned closer and spoke in a confidential tone. "It's a setup. The point of the exercise is to show the people who think they know everything that they don't know anything. So we toss you into a new environment and pit you against people at the top of their game. The ones who know firearms suffer the worst. They think growing up around weapons or owning a bunch of fancy pistols makes them better gunfighters. They don't realize how different and artificial the dueling field is."

Kira rolled that over in her mind. "OK, but I still died."

Diana chuckled. "Because you scared the crap out of Sanchez."

"What? You just said we had no chance."

Diana took on the same calm, matter-of-fact tone she might have used to explain the basics of a good grip. "New fish are even more predictable than citizens. They fixate on the strike-line, march right down it, and then draw and turn as fast as they can. It's never fast enough, but they think it's all about speed, so they keep trying. The only reason everyone doesn't die in the first round is the professionals play with it. With a real opponent and live rounds, you always go for the kill, but in this exercise, they can afford to hit people in the leg, wing them on the bicep, or put off-center shots through the abdomen just to drag it out. You can mess around when your opponent is slow, you know where they'll be standing, and nobody is in danger." She pointed to Kira. "But you decided to march for the far corner of the kill box. What were you thinking?"

Kira sighed. "I knew I couldn't outdraw Sanchez, but I knew I could turn pretty fast. So I thought if I showed up in an unexpected spot, I might have a chance."

"So you were thinking about tactics."

"I guess. But it didn't work."

"You didn't have the speed or the skills to carry it off. But when you weren't where Sanchez expected, he panicked and killed you outright." Again, Diana grinned a little. "All his other opponents in your group, too. It was a short session."

So that hadn't been as big a disaster as she thought. What else was she wrong about?

"Were we . . ." Kira shifted uncomfortably, searching for both words and an emotional position. She forced herself to look at Diana again as she delivered her question. "Were Chloe and I ever as far down as we thought we were?"

A smile stole across the instructor's face. "No. You were both always in the top third."

"Then what about—?"

"The class rank people were talking about?"

"Yeah."

"That was a hearing test. It's measured in the percent of your original hearing you've lost. You and Chloe have good ears, which put you near the bottom."

Heat rose in Kira's chest. "You knew that."

Diana remained calm and silent.

"But you let us think . . ." Kira trailed off, not trusting herself to say more. Did she even want Diana as a mentor now?

Diana folded her arms and leaned on the table. "I don't know who left the results out, or why, but I knew what was happening. I let it play out because it told me something I needed to know."

"Which was what?" Kira couldn't keep the suspicion out of her voice.

Diana leaned back and swung one leg over the other. "There are three things to do when you're down: quit, keep doing what you're doing, or do what it takes to get back up. Any one of those can be right, but most people are too quick to quit. Especially if they're identified as talented and gifted."

Kira's jaw twitched. That tag had followed her all the way to graduate school, and it had done at least as much harm as good.

Diana continued. "You have potential, but that's nothing if you can't recover after a setback." She smiled again. "You recover well."

"So you want to mentor me and Chloe."

"I want to mentor *you*."

Kira frowned. "Look, if you think I'm scrappy and recover well, Chloe is like twice that. She got the tip that got us into the training center."

Diana took a breath. "Chloe's a scrapper, I'll give her that. Life dealt her a shitty hand, and she's busted her ass for everything she has. But she doesn't have your raw ability. I'm looking for people to take as clients when I rotate off instructor duty. You're right about the AI. If we work together and request each other, we'll probably be matched. I can only take five, and I need to be selective."

Kira stared at the tabletop. If she took Diana's offer, was it really betraying Chloe? She'd done what she could do. It was Diana's decision, not hers. Besides, Chloe didn't even like Diana.

She was still afraid of her, even after the prep sessions. Anyway, there were nearly ten months until graduation. She could broach the subject with Diana again later, after she had the chance to feel things out a little more . . .

Diana folded her arms and leaned on the table again, continuing in her matter-of-fact tone. "It's your decision, but you should know some things that aren't public record. First, I've never worked with a trainee who failed to graduate. Second, my clients live. In a typical class, only about a third stay alive to complete the twenty-six matches they owe TKC after graduation. For my clients, it's half. That's the best record in the Guild."

Kira's throat tightened, and she struggled to get the words out. "A third? They keep telling us we have a 96 percent chance of walking off the field alive if we're good enough to get through training."

Diana got that amused look again. "Six and a half years of college, and you never took a stat class." It wasn't a question.

"No, but how . . . ?"

"If you lose 4 percent of the class on every match, by the time you complete twenty-six matches, only a third are left. Cumulative odds are like compound interest. It's a little worse at the beginning and a bit better at the end, but that's how it works."

Kira folded in on herself. To stay in the program, she needed to pass three quarterly evaluations, and Diana could help with that. With any luck at all, something would turn up on the outside before survival rates became important to Kira. For Chloe, though . . .

Kira read the scene. Her teachers had always said acting

was as much about what your partners were giving you as what you did. Across the table, Diana's face remained calm, but tight shoulder muscles showed through the uniform. Though her arms lay in a relaxed-looking fold, two fingers tapped her forearm. All of which meant . . . Diana had something at stake here, too. Kira would never have more leverage than she had right now.

She stood. "Thank you, Ms. Reynolds. You've been a great help, and I appreciate the offer, but Chloe and I are a team. It's both of us or neither of us."

Diana rose in turn, the faintest flicker of surprise crossing her features. "You don't have to decide right now. Talk it over with Chloe, but understand I'm doing what I need to do."

"I know, and I understand. But Chloe and I promised each other. I'm doing what I have to do, too."

Kira turned and walked to the door.

Wait for it . . .

She put her hand on the door handle, pressed down—

A voice from behind her: "All right."

Kira stopped, but didn't turn. Diana shouldn't see her face right now.

"Both of you."

Kira let out a breath, composed her expression, and walked back to the worktable. "Thank you. You won't regret it."

Diana pointed to the chair. "Sit down. If we're doing this, we need to talk."

She then moved back toward the table but didn't seat herself. "Here's what I'm offering: Work with me a couple mornings a week, maybe some evenings. We'll drill, assess your performance, and see if I can help. If we like working together, we request each other at graduation. If the AI matches us, you become my client, and I become your second."

Diana paced in the tiny open area on the far side of the table as she continued. "You've got natural talent, but that's nothing without work. My job is to make you the best gunfighter you can be. To do that, I need you to follow my orders. Ask questions if you don't understand, but I expect you to follow through even if you don't. Can you do that?"

Kira nodded. "Yes."

Diana stopped pacing. "I'm going to ask Chloe the same question, and she needs to agree, too."

"I'm sure she will. I'll talk to her."

"All right—good. Let's start by meeting Wednesdays and Fridays at 6:00 a.m. Wednesdays at Simulator Four, Fridays at Firing Point Three."

Kira keyed the dates into her handset.

"Also, you don't have a concealed carry permit."

"I don't own a gun."

Diana resumed pacing. "It's time to fix that. Understand not everyone buys the idea you're an instrument of society. Some people want personal revenge. Being a woman makes it worse." Diana stopped and keyed something into her handset. "Carry any time you're outside the training facility or the arena complex. As a trainee, you aren't in much danger, but I want you to form the habit."

Kira hesitated. "OK."

Diana ignored Kira's reaction and continued. "My husband owns a security company. Come down on Sunday at three thirty for your concealed carry training. Once you get your permit, we'll work on making you a street fighter. That's very different from winning a duel."

Kira flinched. That was a chunk out of her day off. Not to mention another reason to avoid becoming a gunfighter. But she keyed the appointment into her handset. "OK."

"We'll loan you a pistol until you get a sponsor. Then you'll carry theirs; that's part of the deal."

Kira frowned. "They keep saying not many of us will get sponsors."

A smile pulled at one corner of Diana's mouth. "You'll be one who does."

"Because people think I'm pretty." Kira's frown curled into a grimace.

"That helps." Diana sat down again. "And if that's the case, so what? Use it. But you'll get sponsors because you've got presence. Combine that with a good dueling record and you'll get a good contract. Especially if you negotiate for yourself as hard as you just did for Chloe."

Kira tried to keep the smile off her face. "I think I can do that."

Diana settled in, with her too-relaxed-to-really-be-relaxed face. "So, if we're going to be partners, we shouldn't have secrets."

"OK . . ."

"How did you know I'd fold?"

Loyalty test? Genuine curiosity? Probably best to be truthful. Kira licked her lips. "Well, I knew at the Battle of Baravat, Major Diana Jensen . . ."

No facial reaction from Diana, but her fingers started tapping the desktop at the mention of her Marine rank and maiden name.

". . . lead a counterattack to keep an Army battalion from being captured, even though her commander was dead and she was outnumbered and outgunned. She pulled it off, but got her right leg all shot to hell. They gave her the Navy Cross for it. I guessed the person who did all that might respect someone who wouldn't cut a friend loose."

Diana sat back in her chair, openly studying Kira. "They said you were a smart one. Where did you get all this?"

"I asked around." That was a reasonable characterization of two weeks spent badgering anyone on staff who seemed to know anything about Diana, tracking down every available piece of public information, and obsessively posting questions on every forum for veterans of Iran that didn't immediately kick her out.

"So, you know about my manslaughter conviction."

"I know you did seven years in Leavenworth and came out with a dishonorable discharge." Kira waited for a reaction, but got nothing at all this time. "All the details are behind the National Security seal." Kira folded her hands. Maybe her new mentor would fill in the blanks.

Instead, Diana pulled her chair up to the table. "There's good reason for that."

Kira still said nothing.

When Diana finally spoke, she used a brisk, no-nonsense tone. "It doesn't give anything away to say I'm guilty as charged. I wasn't railroaded, I wasn't framed, and I didn't take the fall for anyone else. I screwed up, an innocent person died, and I probably got off easier than I deserved." She fixed her eyes on Kira. "Does that change anything?"

It seemed like it should matter, but there was no denying that it didn't. Kira shook her head. "No. It's not like you're teaching me to dance."

CHAPTER 8

Kira swept through the apartment door, pushed it shut behind her, and held her grocery bag aloft like a prize won in battle. "Butter brickle." Though they'd been out of the trainee housing for nearly three months and graduation was just around the corner, bringing home food to share with Chloe retained its novelty.

Stretched out on the couch in the living area, Chloe laughed. "How did you know?"

"I always know my roomie's breakup food. It's a gift." In truth, it was memory. Nearly a year of living together and talking with the seemingly endless array of family members who passed through the Rossi household on Sunday afternoons had packed Kira's head with facts about her roommate.

Kira loaded the ice cream into the freezer and set her purse in its place on the serving bar. "How's it going?"

Chloe swatted the data pad with the back of her hand. "I don't see why they make us learn anatomy. It all just means 'shoot for the middle of the chest,' right? That's where all the important stuff is."

"Well, there is knowing how to take care of yourself if you get hit."

"I suppose."

"And do damage assessment if you're in a bleed-off."

Chloe made a face.

Kira could mention part of the reason was to emphasize the trainee's fragility, to reinforce the "kill or be killed" ethos of dueling that their instructors pushed at every opportunity, but she didn't bring it up. Instead, she propped herself against one of the sofa's arms and eyed her roommate sprawled across the seat. "Look, it's not like they're going to fail you based on the written portion. All the points are on the simulator eval, and you're doing great at that."

Chloe flipped over the data pad. "How's yours going?"

"Well, Ms. Reynolds let me quit early tonight, so either I'm in good shape or she's given up."

"You're in good shape. She never gives up." Chloe sat up and tipped her head toward the freezer. "Why don't you help me eat that? I need a break."

Kira hung her jacket on a serving barstool, exposing the holster on her shoulder. Wearing a weapon in the apartment still troubled Kira, but Chloe seemed to take it in stride. It would probably bother Chloe more to have Kira disappear into the bedroom to remove the holster just as the ice cream came out.

Chloe pulled the ice cream from the freezer and a scoop from their utility drawer. Kira extracted bowls from the cupboard and found two suitable spoons among the mismatched sets in their silverware drawer. Chloe filled the bowls, and they took their places at the serving bar.

Chloe took in her first spoonful and closed her eyes as a beatific expression crossed her face.

Kira grinned. "You really know how to get a lot out of that."

Chloe smiled an embarrassed smile. "It's good. I miss Niles less already."

Kira laughed. "Good. That's the point." She fiddled with the ice cream in her bowl. "Do you really miss him all that much?"

"No, not really." Some heat entered Chloe's words. "He could be a real jerk. Like when we first got together, it was this huge deal whether he was going to call me his girlfriend or not. It was like it was this prize I had to win or something." She scowled. "I should've seen it. But, you know, sometimes you want somebody, and if it seems like somebody's interested . . ." Chloe dug at her ice cream.

"You'll find somebody better." Chloe's venting was good. Part of the process.

"Not that it would take much. He was a dick about my family, too. He wouldn't come meet Mom and Dad because 'oh, that's just too big of a thing right now.'" She rolled her eyes. "And then he kept insisting I come see him instead of being with them and getting all pouty and mad whenever I'd go to Sunday dinner or church or something." Chloe's ice cream bore the brunt of her remembered anger as she stabbed at it with her spoon. "But the thing that tore it was when he took a swing at me."

Kira froze. "Really? You never told me that."

Chloe looked down. "I guess I'm embarrassed I let it get that far. But yeah, I was over at his place and I got this handset message about a class getting rescheduled or something. All Niles sees is that it's from a guy and he just flipped out and started screaming at me. Pretty soon we're standing in the middle of his apartment and we're both yelling, then all of a sudden he hauls off and swings for my face."

Kira's stomach became hollow. "He *hit* you?"

"He tried." Chloe smirked a little. "He's not the only one with gunfighter reflexes. I blocked it." She took a spoonful of her battered ice cream and continued. "But I told him we were done." Chloe looked to the far corner of the room, as if a scene only she could see played out there. "Before she was married, Mom lived with a guy who hit her. More than once. She always told me, 'If a man lays hands on you, that's the end. I don't care if you're married with three kids. Pack 'em up, call a driver, and get the hell out. No turning back.'" Chloe looked to Kira again. "All I had to do was get my stuff out of his dresser."

"He let you do that?"

"Oh yeah. The moment I blocked his arm, he knew he'd messed up. He got all weepy and everything and started saying it's only just because he loves me *so much*." She snorted and stabbed at her ice cream again. "Asshole. Mom warned me about *that*, too."

Kira nodded, though the hollow feeling had spread to her whole abdomen. "You did the right thing, no question."

"Yeah. I just need to graduate and get through this." Chloe scraped together the remains of her ice cream and scooped it into her mouth. "Save money and stay alive. I don't need any guy shit to worry about."

"Yeah, it's just too hard right now." Kira took another bite of ice cream. "Just focus on what we need to stay alive and get out."

Chloe pushed her bowl aside. "You know, I keep meaning to ask you this. All that time you were in New York—"

"About two years." Where was Chloe going with that question?

"OK, two years. In that time, couldn't you get . . ." Chloe paused, her face and body shifting. "Couldn't you find a guy who would, you know, take care of you?"

Kira laughed, but couldn't keep the tinge of bitterness out of her voice. "I'm in for way more than anybody is willing to spend on a friend." She cocked her head a little for effect. "Even a really, really, *special* friend."

Chloe lowered her eyes and Kira continued. "And for anything more permanent . . . if a guy is rich enough not to be scared by my debts, he's also rich enough he doesn't have to settle for somebody like me. I've got no family and no accomplishments except some parts in theaters nobody has ever heard of and a couple of commercials."

Chloe nodded. "So, I guess we've both got to take care of ourselves. And each other."

"Exactly."

They cleaned up together, and Kira went to her room. Having her own room was the best part of leaving trainee housing. TKC wanted to get the upperclassmen established off campus before they faced live bullets, and the company's concern seemed warranted. Some of the younger guys were showing up late, in dirty uniforms, or hungry as they worked out the mysteries of living with no one to cover the domestic details. If they couldn't survive doing their own laundry, how were they going to survive a gunfight?

For Kira and Chloe, though, it felt like a step up and a return to normalcy after living in the dorms, and their rankings rose accordingly.

Kira had almost unbuckled the first strap of her shoulder holster when her handset warbled for attention. Voice call.

She popped the device loose from its belt clip and checked the display. "Hey, Marla. What's up?"

Her friend's northern Minnesota lilt was as strong as ever. "Kira! I've got good news."

"Really?"

"You bet. Remember that assistant manager thing we talked about?"

"I thought that fell through a year ago." When Marla had delivered that news, Kira dialed the TKC recruiter without putting the handset down.

"It did, but it's a new fiscal year, and I found a different funder. Same responsibilities—assist me with everything from donor relations to PR to filling in for ushers."

Kira's breath caught. "Are you still paying $55,000?"

"Only fifty."

Kira sucked on her teeth. "After my payments, that doesn't leave much."

"Well, I've been talking to the board, they really like you, and we can furnish on-site housing."

"On-site?"

"They built this place with a space for interns. We're using one of the old bedrooms for storage, but we could clear it out. There's a microwave and hot plate, and a shower down the hall. It's not ideal, but I think it would work."

CORPORATE GUNSLINGER   63

"Yeah. Maybe." Would it be that much worse than sharing a bathroom with Chloe? "How long is the grant?"

"It's three years to start. After that it renews annually for a total of five."

Kira pulled her arms across her chest. This was a shaft of daylight, but no more than that. "Look, here's the thing. To get out of this gig, I have to make enough to pay back my signing bonus."

"There isn't any money for that—"

"I know. But there's this contest at the end of training. All the training schools in the region compete, and the person with the best final evaluation gets a cash prize. It's enough."

"Sounds as though you're going out on a little bit of a limb there."

"I've been doing that since day one. Can you wait until next Friday?"

"OK, but I can't hold this door open forever, you know."

"I know, and I appreciate what you've done, but I don't have much room to maneuver. I really need this. Please?"

"I'll do what I can."

"OK, thanks. I'll let you know by next Friday."

The connection clicked off.

Kira flopped onto the bed. Was this even really a way? She'd have to calculate the after-tax on that salary, and it was going to be a tight fit, even without rent. And what about the length of that grant—three years? Maybe five? What would happen then? There wouldn't be enough cushion to build a cash reserve. She'd have to have something lined up before the grant ran out. How likely was that? Still, five years was a long time. Hell, three was a long time. Something would turn up, just like it was turning up now. But her current payment plan ran for seventeen years. Could she really keep this up until she was the same age as Diana? *One step at a time . . .*

Out in the main living area, the door chimed. Chloe answered. A male voice, the clunk of the door opening to the limit of the chain. Kira stood. Indistinct words filtered in.

". . . want to talk!"

Niles. Yeah, it had to be Niles. Too bad when TKC sold his contract to United Re, his new employer hadn't shipped him off to a different state.

"Yeah . . . only when you want something . . ."

Chloe was holding her own. Kira put her jacket in the closet but kept her shoes on and left her gun and holster in place.

". . . tell me to . . ."

". . . pull THAT shit on me!"

". . . done!"

A loud thud, overlapping bursts of profanity, and the sound of something hitting the floor.

Kira entered the hall. Niles stood in the doorway, the door's chain hanging loose. Chloe lay on the floor, rubbing her face. Niles leg was cocked, as if he were about to kick. On his right side, a quick-draw holster with a pistol in it.

"Hey!" Kira made her voice firm and loud, but not a scream. She held her gun in a two-handed grip, legs apart, slightly bent. Too far away to be rushed, too close to miss. Chloe on the floor and out of the line of fire. The hallway beyond Niles: empty. She could shoot him without endangering anyone else.

Kira kept her sights on the center of his chest. Niles held his right arm tense and ready, but he didn't move. He wasn't that reckless.

He looked Kira up and down, and then produced a derisive snort. "Don't act like you've got the balls to use that thing. Everybody knows you don't."

Kira shifted to a low, flat, cold tone. Almost as cold as the space inside her chest. "Niles, you're armed, you've assaulted my roommate, and you've broken into my apartment. I find you threatening." Kira brought her finger inside the guard and let the pad rest on the trigger. The hallway behind Niles remained clear, and Chloe made no move to get off the floor.

For a split second, something flashed across Niles's face. Anger? Contempt? Maybe the realization of how bad his situation was. "OK. Misunderstanding." Very slowly, and with exaggerated caution, Niles raised his hands. "That's all this is. Just a big misunderstanding."

Kira said nothing, and her gun remained steady.

Slowly and carefully, Niles backed out the door, his eyes fixed on Kira. When he was halfway down the hall, he turned and ran.

Chloe pushed herself upright and rubbed her jaw. "Jesus, Kira. You could have killed him."

Kira lowered her weapon, reset the safety, and holstered it. She wasn't even breathing hard. "Yeah, I could have." She stared down the hallway. "He knew it, too."

CHAPTER 9

Tension pinches at the back of Kira's neck. What the hell is taking Niles so long? Has he taken the door? Or is he just delaying to ensure he makes the final entrance? Kira relieves the stiffness by rolling her head.

On the ceiling and walls, cameras scuttle like bugs. Their motion is a dance negotiated between the AI seeking information to assist the judge and a human producer trying to wring as much drama from the proceedings as possible. To the producer, that little moment between her and Diana must have been a godsend, an emotional oasis in the desert of prematch proceedings. The commentator's booth and match's media feed are probably abuzz with speculation on the hand signal's meaning and Kira's emotional state.

The door to the opposite-side changing room bursts open, and Niles bounds onto the field wearing the royal blue and silver of United Reinsurance. He jogs to his place beside Kira like a star basketball player trotting onto the court for introductions, his second trailing behind like a towel carrier. After giving the judge a cursory nod, Niles puts on his what-a-good-boy-am-I smile and tilts his head to face the cameras.

Jackass. If the rules allowed his ridiculous porkpie hat on the dueling field, he'd probably be waving it.

He turns to Kira and flashes a hand sign. I'm OK.

Kira's breath catches. The bastard broke Diana's code, and now he's sticking his vulgar, leering, bro-douche self into the space between her and her second. Niles sees the look on her face, and he smirks.

The judge sounds a chime and recites the rules of engagement. Niles resumes his preening for the cameras.

Kira reviews her plan to kill him.

CHAPTER 10

Chloe exited Simulator Thirty-Seven, her face stoic. For the hundredth and final match of her qualification series, her mech managed a 62-point shot to her lower chest, while she'd administered only a 27-point shoulder graze in return. The loss hurt in the battle for class rank, but Chloe's sixtieth Qualification Week victory on Thursday had already ensured her future as a TKC gunfighter.

Kira greeted her at the edge of the simulator field. "Hey, you're done!"

Chloe rubbed a spot on her lower ribcage. For the qualification, the shock suits administered little more than a hard tickle, but the irritation could persist. "I thought I had it until it turned." She looked back to the field, where the mech had already assumed the start position, and the next trainee verified his holster settings with an instructor. "Damn, those things are fast. The turn block is loose, though. It overshot when it brought the gun around and couldn't zero in fast enough. That's what saved my butt."

"Thanks, that's good to know."

For the final two days of the seven-day event, operators jacked the mechs' parameters, enhancing speed and accuracy to such an extent that when the trainees fought their last five matches, they faced the equivalent of another professional gunfighter.

Kira's early victories had earned her a late slot in the final round, giving her a chance to see the mech settings in action before she faced them herself. To ensure fairness, the Guild required all mechs used in the evaluation to be the same model and software version, as well as being brought to the same physical specifications. Though a mech's response contained a unique element in every run, the rule gave competitors who studied other matches an advantage.

Kira had watched other trainees compete until the events blurred together in her memory.

She returned the gear bag she'd been holding for Chloe. "Check your handset and see where you're at."

Chloe frowned. "I'm not sure I want to know." But she fished the device out of the bag.

The Guild site displayed her personal results. It showed the 35-point deduction for her last match, then displayed her standing in the Regional Cup competition: currently twenty-seventh overall, with the possibility of going as high as twenty-second or as low as thirty-fourth, depending on how other trainees performed. Kira clapped her on the shoulder. "Hey, that's top fifty for sure, maybe top twenty-five. You're getting a bonus!"

Chloe brightened a little. "That'll be nice." The bump in starting pay wasn't much, but it would let her put a little more toward either her duplex or her brothers' education fund, and Chloe treated every uni as if she were still working uncertain hours for even more uncertain tips.

The screen updated with the results from other matches around the region. Chloe's position changed to twenty-sixth, with a max of twenty-third and a minimum of twenty-eighth. Chloe clicked the device off and put it back in her gear bag. "I can't watch. I'll go nuts." She pointed to the snack kiosk backed up against a simulator wall. "Let's get something to eat."

To lend a festive air to the event, TKC not only provided free food, but splurged by populating the broad walkways between simulator clusters with kiosks whose staff made sandwiches fresh, rather than vending machines that dispensed pre-wrapped food of uncertain age and provenance. Kira drank in the luxury of watching the attendant spread mustard by hand and apply the turkey slices to the roll with a small flourish.

In the walkway, trainees stood in little groups of three to five, juggling snacks, drinks, and handsets. The vendors hadn't brought quite enough small, stand-up tables for everyone.

A giant banner declaring TKC Insurance's "Guiding Principles" hung from the ceiling. Probably because of its height and size, this one had escaped being defaced by the marker-wielding artist who had routinely adorned "Customer Focus" with a stick figure viewed through gunsights and "Passion for Performance" with a graveyard. The doodle rumored to provoke the most ire from company management was a bouquet of flowers with a tag reading "TKC" propped against a tombstone. That one went next to the words "Respect for People." The vandal had been so successful that for the last three months, building maintenance had almost given up displaying "Guiding Principles" posters in the gunfighter training areas.

At the kiosk, Chloe ordered a pastrami and Muenster on rye, with a side of spice chips and a bottle of milk. Kira ordered a protein shake.

Chloe cocked her head toward Kira and provided an explanation the attendant hadn't asked for. "She's still in the running."

The attendant broke into a wide grin. "Well, congratulations, Ms."—there was the briefest pause as he checked the name on Kira's uniform—"Clark." He studied Kira with a bit more than casual interest, as if he were trying to place her. His face brightened. "Good luck!" He handed her the protein shake and moved on to the next customer.

Kira glared at Chloe.

Chloe grinned back. "I couldn't figure out how to tell him about you being one of the Cup contenders, but he probably knew already."

An instructor finished his meal and left one of the standing tables open. Chloe gathered her food and moved toward it.

Kira trailed along. "How could he possibly know? He probably doesn't even understand how it all works."

Chloe snorted. "He probably knows the standings better than you do. When I worked for General Catering, the gunfighter fanboys would give you just about anything to swap places if you got a Qualification Week shift."

"Really?"

"Oh yeah. When you win, tomorrow he'll be on some fan

site, and be all, 'Yes, I served Kira Clark before the match. She had a Nature's Rage Extra Mocha Double-Protein shake, and she shook it three times before she opened it.' It'll be his biggest thing all year."

Kira rolled her eyes, twisted the top off the bottle, and took a deep swig of the contents. Chloe was probably exaggerating, but even if the caterer didn't know all the details, he might guess she was doing pretty well. If she won the Cup, paid off her signing bonus, and walked away, would that make his story better or worse?

On a nearby video display, a bald-headed guy in a blue blazer talked his way through the current set of matches. With every company trying to push its trainees through limited simulator space as quickly as possible, the results came thick and fast all week, but now, as one trainee after another completed their hundredth match, he had time to do more than rattle off stats. ". . . becoming clearer all the time exactly who those last three will be."

In deference to fan sensibilities and the Guild's desire for vid revenue, the final matches for the top three contenders would play out sequentially, rather than simultaneously, with the first starting at 7:00 p.m. to hit prime time in the Midwest.

Kira's handset warbled with a tone normally reserved for emergency evacuation messages and Amber Alerts. Heads turned in her direction before she could silence the device. The bright red block on the screen announced: "YOU ARE A TOP THREE CONTENDER. REPORT TO YOUR MATCH IN TKC SIMULATOR THREE NO LATER THAN 6:40 P.M."

Chloe washed down the final bite of her sandwich by

gulping the last of her milk. "We gotta get going. That's clear across campus."

On the vid screen, a red band announcement came up. The announcer touched his earpiece, said he had important news, and the screen displayed a head shot of a young man with brown hair and a square, muscular face—Fred Grahl from the Minneapolis training center of North Star Mercantile Finance. Ranked third going into the final round with 7,203 points, he would shoot first.

Kira pushed toward the display. This was the most she'd ever know about her competition. The announcer said something about his style or stats, but Kira couldn't make it out over the bustle of other people trying to position themselves for a good view.

A brown-skinned, black-haired young man with dark, soulful eyes appeared below Fred's face on the screen. Julian Gomez hailed from Midwest AgriSystems' Des Moines training center, right next to the TKC campus. His 7,256 points placed him comfortably ahead of Fred, and only two points behind Kira. However, those two points were enough to make him shoot before she did, so she would know exactly what she needed to do when she stepped on the field.

Finally, Kira's trainee ID photo displayed, and scattered applause and cheers ran through the crowd around the monitor. The group quieted down just in time for the announcer to note that during the ninety-nine qualification matches so far, Kira had killed her first sixty mechs outright, added five non-sequential kills in later matches, won an additional twenty-six with nonfatal hits, and lost just eight times. Along the way, she'd only died twice.

Hands extended in congratulations, and Kira shook them. Kess Johnson, a former college linebacker, squeezed her shoulder with so much good-hearted enthusiasm that Chloe intervened. "We need to go."

The two friends made their way through the maze of walkways between the simulator clusters, Kira fielding waves and wishes for good luck from trainees and staff as they went.

When they reached a break in traffic, Kira bumped Chloe with her elbow. "Hey, check your standings again. If they've got the top three, you're probably set."

They stopped and Chloe made a grumpy noise, but she again fished her handset from her bag. The screen flashed "Twenty-Fifth Place" over the word "FINAL." Chloe stared at the terminal in disbelief.

"Hey!" Kira patted her friend on the shoulder. "You made it!"

They hugged and laughed.

Chloe wiped her eyes. "I really didn't think I'd get it. I always just miss." She stared wistfully at the display. "Maybe gunfighting is going to work out for me." She grabbed Kira's upper arm. "Now *you* need to go win this thing."

Kira laughed again. "But no pressure, right?"

"Right. No pressure at all."

When Chloe turned to resume their journey, the smile disappeared from Kira's face. Would Chloe really be OK if Kira won and bought her way out? She'd always told herself her friend would be happy for her. And maybe she would be. *But still . . .*

"Hey, come on. What are you waiting for?" Chloe stood in the walkway, looking exasperated.

Kira jogged a little to catch up. "Coming."

At last, they reached Simulator Three. A trainee from the class right behind them checked Kira in, taking her thumbprint on his data pad.

"You can watch the matches with the others." He pointed to a mass of trainees and staff standing around video displays hung along the walkway. "Or you can wait here in the ready box." He indicated a painted rectangle that marked off an area beside the simulator wall. It contained a chair and a small table with two bottles of water. "Either way, be sure you're right here and set to go ten minutes before start."

Kira's handset warbled. Message from Diana. "Congratulations. Coming soon." Like the other instructors, Diana was working as support staff for the qualification matches.

A slight knot formed below Kira's sternum as she keyed a response. "At Sim 3."

If Kira won and left, what would Diana say? Another part of Kira's mind asked why she should care. She was on her own, pure, plain, and simple. It's not as if she had anybody to look out for her. Sure, Diana had been helpful, but she had her reasons. Walking away might hurt some feelings, but if she stayed, she'd be killing people. Assuming they didn't kill her first.

Kira and Chloe watched from the edge of the crowd as Fred marched to the start point with the mech, where they stood back-to-back. On the ward's signal, Fred traveled almost straight down the strikeline, beating the mech to the kill box. A snappy, precise turn left him facing the gray expanse of the Wall. A cutout screen in the lower left corner showed a close-up of Fred with his gun drawn and his eyes darting back and forth, waiting for the hologram to vanish. On the other side of the Wall, the mech planted its pivot foot on the kill box's marker line. When its back leg landed inside the kill box, the Wall came down. The mech pulled the toe of its pivot foot inside the line, drew, and fired. The mech's diode and Fred's muzzle flashed almost simultaneously, and a new cutout screen on the upper left showed where the hits landed. The mech's simulated projectile caught Fred's upper leg, but high and on the outside. The mech wouldn't get many points for that. The inner thigh was a legitimate target, where shattering the bone or inducing a spasm in the femoral nerve could cause an immediate fall, or severing the femoral artery could cause death from catastrophic blood loss in minutes. A hit in the quadriceps was merely painful, and a gunfighter trained with a shock suit could stand through the resulting bleed-off. Fred's shot struck the mech's upper abdomen. On a human, it would have ripped through the liver but missed the spine. The system computer awarded Fred 82 points and the mech 47. The net gain of 35 held Fred's position at third, but unless Kira or Julian suffered a serious loss, it wouldn't be enough to improve his standing.

A strong hand grasped Kira's shoulder, followed immediately by a warm greeting. "Hey."

She turned to face Diana. "Ms. Reynolds. Hi."

"I came to wish you luck."

"Thanks." Kira couldn't look Diana in the eye, but she could at least turn toward her. "Ms. Reynolds, no matter how this turns out, you've been good to me, and I won't forget that."

Diana's smile became genuinely warm. "I appreciate that. I

really do." She clapped Kira's upper arm. "Remember: you deserve to win."

Despite a small twinge in her chest, Kira responded. "Thanks. I'll do my best."

"I know." One of Diana's secret smiles followed the affirmation.

Chloe worked her way to them through the growing throng around the vid monitor. "Hey, Kira, don't you need to go do that thing?"

Kira grinned at her. "Get into character?"

"Yeah, that."

Diana looked over their heads, sizing up the mob gathered on the open side of Simulator Three and the catwalks above it. "We can't get close enough to see. Chloe, why don't you walk Kira to the ready box? I'll find a spot close to a monitor."

Diana and Chloe synched the "Mutual Locate" function on their handsets, and Diana set off on her quest for a place to view the match. Though Kira appreciated the support, it would be good to be alone while she prepared.

She and Chloe pushed through the crowd toward the simulator.

Chloe broke the silence. "You know, maybe this is a bad time to say this, but I really don't like her."

"My dueling persona?"

"Yeah. She's so . . ."

Kira adopted her flat, cold, above-it-all tone. "You're not supposed to like her. You're supposed to fear her."

Chloe shot her a vicious side-eye, and Kira laughed a real laugh.

They reached the ready box.

"Hey." Chloe squared herself up and showed Kira a hard, serious face. "Cut 'em down . . ." She made a blade-like slicing gesture with her right hand. ". . . and walk away." Her hand became a fist with an upright thumb.

Kira grinned. "Thanks."

She handed her gear bag to Chloe, who took it, consulted her handset, and set off in the same general direction as Diana. Kira waited in the ready box, letting her mind go blank until the results alarm she'd set on her handset sounded. She thumbed the unit. The net total it displayed couldn't be real. She called up the match results and stared at the details as they appeared on her handset. A 38–94 outcome had put Julian Gomez 54 points ahead of her. He'd dropped his mech by either severing its simulated spine or shattering one of its simulated leg bones while receiving only a minor injury.

She would have to both kill the mech for the full 100 points and escape without a serious hit herself if she wanted to avoid killing real people in just a few weeks. Only first prize was enough.

Kira put her hands on her head, closed her eyes, and breathed. Concerns about the outcome passed through her. A series of slow, steady breaths relaxed her body and whisked her consciousness clean. She summoned the reservoir of cold and calm within herself. *I am a heart of ice in a body of fire. I am the unmoving center of the storm. I am serene, I am invincible. I am—*

"Ms. Clark?"

She opened her eyes to find an instructor standing in front of her.

"Ms. Clark, it's time."

She gave him an ice-cold smile. "I'm sure it is."

The instructor synchronized Kira's shock suit with the simulator and helped her load the weapon and test the holster. On the other side of the centerline, the mech waited to morph into a new shape for the match. Its face, the same as all the other mechs used in training, offered only a hint of a nose and some eyebrow ridges near the big, flat optical sensors that served as its eyes. The standard wig, brown hair in a unisex cut, did little to humanize it. Combined with the drawn-on tunic and pants, the suggestion of a face gave the device a menacing but somewhat cartoonish appearance, like the evil sidekick in an animated adventure. It embodied the way the company wanted gunfighters to think of their opponents—threatening, but not precisely human.

The morph began, and its pseudo-flesh exterior drew taut as the underlying frame extended. It was going to be tall and lanky. Long legs would make it fast to the kill box but slow to turn, and long arms meant it would be slow to bring the gun to bear and stabilize its aim.

Kira took another cleansing breath and thought her way through the problem. The mech's pseudogun couldn't inflict any serious damage, just a mild shock she could recover from pretty easily. Her mind picked at that fact like a tongue returning to a ragged tooth. Why did that seem so important all of a sudden?

The Wall went up.

"Combatants, please advance to the start point."

She marched to the red half circle poking out from under the Wall and turned, facing away from the mech and toward her kill box.

The mech would expect her to travel straight down the

strikeline and try to recover from her slower walk by turning and aiming faster. Any delay would tell it she'd deviated from that route and would be off to one side or the other when the barrier disappeared. The longer the delay, the farther off center it would expect her to be, and the larger the movement it would prepare to make. It would hedge its bets by keeping its gun aimed toward the middle of the field and sweep back and forth with its eyes to locate her. Once it spotted her, it would try to align its sights and fire faster than she could draw and aim. If it thought she might fire first, it would fire with whatever alignment it happened to have. The hits to Fred's leg and Chloe's lower chest suggested that even at this setting, the program would settle for a quick, decent shot rather than holding out for a great one.

The recorded ward's voice called out again. "Proceed on my count. 1 . . . 2 . . . 3 . . ."

No rule said the participants had to follow the ward's cadence, but everyone did. If someone tried to sprint for the kill box, that would draw a foul and a penalty, but getting out of step, weaving around the combat area, or stopping were all permissible.

"...4...5...6..."

Kira picked a spot five feet to the left of the strikeline, enough to force the long-armed mech to make an adjustment from center.

"...7...8...9...10..."

Kira placed both feet on the boundary of the kill box and stopped. Habits beaten into her brain and body over the last year screamed to enter the box, to turn, to fire . . .

"...11...12...13..."

By now, the mech would be wound up to snap to either edge of the kill box as soon as it could seek a target. She put her hand on the pistol, careful not to pull it from the holster, and executed a half pivot. The maneuver placed her traveling foot deep in the kill box and left her facing sideways, presenting a narrow profile and looking over her right shoulder.

When her foot touched the pseudograss of the kill box, the Wall came down.

Kira pulled her pivot toe inside the boundary line and drew one-handed. Although she extended her firing arm, she kept the safety on and her finger outside the trigger guard. At twenty paces, the mech couldn't see those details, but it would sense her muzzle facing its direction.

The mech's weapon swung toward her.

Her reflexes begged to fire. Her sights weren't stable.

The mech's pseudogun flashed.

Moment of truth . . .

The suit administered a light shock across her midriff, and Kira's body twitched in response. Enough to send her shot wide if she'd been squeezing the trigger.

A recovery breath, a flick of her thumb to turn off the safety, and she was in alignment. The sting probably represented no more than an abdominal graze. Not the clean miss she'd hoped for, but not many points, either. She focused on the front sight. The mech began to turn so it could present a narrower profile. Kira's sights traced a gentle figure eight on its chest. It wasn't turning fast enough to matter.

Finger to the trigger, a soft squeeze, a sharp report, and the kick of recoil.

The mech shuddered and then staggered, tripping over its own feet and falling to the pseudograss, inert.

A thin puff of gun smoke hung in the air. Kira's nose wrinkled at the acrid smell.

She reholstered her weapon and rested with her hands on her knees. She'd eventually pay for her in-match calm with a cumulative attack of the willies, but she needed to keep it together just a little bit longer.

"Please return to the table area."

Kira stood upright. The scoreboard read: CLARK, 100; MECH, 32.

She walked back toward the table. No need to jog, this was the last match of the day. From somewhere behind her, up on the catwalks, a clap began. Someone else picked it up, and by the time she reached the table the applause spread all the way around the simulator. She kept her head down, as if she were still wrapped in her cocoon of total focus.

The instructor took her gun and belt, and the clapping persisted. She needed to do something, but what? The dueling etiquette classes hadn't covered this situation.

She raised her head and turned, her arms behind her back. The clapping died down. She used a sweeping motion to indicate the instructor at the table, the trainee at check-in, and the anonymous operators up in the booth. The clapping intensified. She bowed to the people crammed on the catwalk on the mech side of the field, and then repeated the gesture with the larger group on the long wall opposite the control cab. Finally, she bowed to the mob gathered in the walkway beyond the open end of the simulator. The applause grew to a crescendo, accompanied by whistles and indistinct shouts. Training discipline held, and no one crossed from the walkway into the combat area.

When it had gone on long enough, Kira turned her face up to the control cab and nodded, hoping the operator would understand. The field lights went down, leaving her in post-show stage darkness. She sagged against the table, letting it all soak in as her audience dispersed.

It was a more dramatic close than she could have hoped for, and a good way to end her gunfighting career.

CHAPTER 11

Kira, Chloe, and Diana stood in a little knot near the punch-bowl, each holding a cup of nondescript pink liquid and a tiny plate adorned with a few mints and a miniscule square of the New Gunfighter Reception cake. Diana had already introduced her new clients to most of the important people in the room—TKC managers, Guild officials, and some staff members such as the scheduling clerk and the second-shift facilities manager. The roster largely confirmed Chloe's stated belief that while Diana might not know everyone, she did know everyone who might be useful.

As the excitement drained out of the reception, instructors and new graduates made for the door, exhausted by the ordeal of Qualification Week. The newly minted gunfighters would have two days of paid leave, during which they were supposed to re-view their contracts and consider their new career. The snatches of conversation Kira overheard suggested most of her class would dash off the contracts tonight, either with or without a cursory read-through, and devote the balance of their time off to drink-ing, sleeping, nursing hangovers, and trying to get laid. Kira would spend hers packing, waiting for the deposit for the Regional Cup prize to appear, and getting ready for her move to Minneapolis.

Like the reception, the ceremony that preceded it hadn't amounted to much. The eighty-one qualifying members of the TKC class had filed into the facility's largest classroom, minor functionaries from TKC and the Guild local said a few words, and Kira was called to the front to receive the Regional Cup. They all got their Guild cards and gunfighter's jackets—both mostly ceremonial—while the important action happened on their handsets. The new graduates each received a digital key proving their membership in the Gunfighter's Guild to any system that cared to check for it, along with employment contracts requiring thumbprint certification, committing them to twenty-six gunfights of TKC's choosing.

Diana surveyed the thinning crowd and apparently found nothing worth her attention. "Join me in the Lounge? You can make sure your Guild keys work, and I'll buy you a drink."

Chloe brightened. "That'd be great, Ms. Reynolds."

"My clients call me 'Diana.'"

A look of momentary confusion crossed Chloe's face, and then she smiled as if she'd just been given the key tokens to an exclusive private club. "That'd be great, Diana."

Kira offered her assent to the plan and then unfolded her jacket and tried it on. It fit perfectly, with sleeves ending just below her wrists, lower hem covering her belt, and comfortable accommodation for her shoulders.

It wasn't a bad-looking jacket, though the Guild's predilection for two-tone styles and company colors was on full display.

TKC's slate gray covered the front, back, yoke, and sleeves, while forest green provided contrast via the sides, collar, and cuffs. A subdued version of the TKC logo dominated the left front panel. A quick tug pulled out some of the wrinkles from the unpacking, but it seemed shinier than the jackets worn by the experienced gunfighters, and still carried the chemical scent of new fabric. She might as well wear it now; there wouldn't be many other opportunities.

Diana called Chloe and Kira in close for a conference. "You're Guild members now, but remember you're still unbloodied."

Kira nodded but looked to Chloe to see if she understood what Diana was talking about.

Diana touched an enamel pin on her collar. "You'll get one of these when you complete your first match." She held out the pin so Kira and Chloe could see the inch-wide red circle contained the outline of a dueling pistol.

Well, that's something I'll never have. The faintest tickle of regret played at the edge of Kira's mind.

Diana continued. ". . . the veterans will expect some deference. If you want to talk to someone who isn't a new grad, let them start the conversation, or let someone introduce you. Listen more than you talk. OK?"

"So it's like we're new fish again?" Chloe's voice carried a little disappointment.

"It doesn't last long." Diana gave them a reassuring smile. "Any questions?"

Kira couldn't think of one, and Chloe shook her head.

By this point, the reception had entered full shutdown mode. Only a few small conversation groups remained, scattered around the edges of the room, and the staff clearly intended to usher them out soon. In the center, the servers and room attendants began their cleanup routine, sweeping trash into bins, taking down tables, and folding chairs.

To avoid the early September chill, Diana, Chloe, and Kira crossed to the arena complex using the skywalk. The crowd thickened as they approached the Gunslinger's Lounge. TKC jackets seemed to be the most abundant, although the red and gold of Lucky Pig Financial and the royal blue and silver of United Reinsurance were well represented. Consolidated Trust seemed to be out in force tonight as well, although their obnoxiously bright orange-and-neon-blue jackets might have made them seem more numerous than they were. The line outside the Lounge also contained a small smattering of black-and-gray jackets that identified the wearer as a Guild official or one of the instructors, evaluators, and shop stewards charged with maintaining standards across companies.

Ahead of them in line, a handset alarm warbled. The owner, a short but muscular man who looked about thirty, froze as a towering Samoan bouncer confronted him. The bouncer established the guy was a new ward and gave him directions to Libra's, the watering hole for the neutral staff, on the other side of the arena complex. The trainee handbook said that, by mutual agreement, the combatants of the Gunfighter's Guild and the staff employed by the Association for Dueling kept to their separate facilities, with only a tiny group of Association fraud investigators given access to both. A few of the new graduates openly snickered at the ward's mistake, provoking rebukes from the seconds and trainers. There was no good reason to earn the enmity of an official who served as the judge's eyes, ears, and muscle on the field.

With that obstacle cleared, traffic flow resumed, and they passed through the wooden double doors and into the Guild members' exclusive preserve. The Gunslinger's Lounge looked like a place that had trouble deciding what it wanted to be. Wood tables, thick carpet, candlelit booths, and a long, sumptuous mahogany bar with brass fittings suggested it was a watering hole for the financial elite. Which, given the income of its clientele, it certainly was. On the other hand, the video screens encircling the room suggested a sports bar. It was certainly that, too.

Currently, it served as the main venue for the Qualification Week after-party. People in small, inward-facing groups filled the floor, while others piled in around booths and tables. Most wore gunfighter's jackets in various stages of removal.

Diana navigated the room with Chloe and Kira in tow. As patrons recognized Kira, she received the occasional hand wave or nod, and caught bits and pieces of the discussion going on around her.

". . . see her try that shit with a real bullet . . ."

". . . she froze . . . but brilliant, is what I'm saying . . ."

". . . balls the size of fucking watermelons."

A tall, athletic man in his early twenties made his way toward the group. Diana flashed a joyful smile as he approached. They shook hands, and Diana became more sober. "I'd say I'm happy you're back, but you should have finished three months ago."

The young man shrugged and looked at the floor. "I just have to set myself up a little better, that's all."

"Get that done, OK?" Diana swatted him on the shoulder.

She reached out to include Kira and Chloe. "This is Gary Thomas. He was my client in the last quarter before I rotated to instructor, and now that I'm a second again, he's back."

Kira and Chloe smiled as if meeting a new stepsibling. Gary did the same. He nodded toward a cluster of tables on the far edge of the Lounge, near the big windows looking out over the deck. "Claire has some spaces saved. I'll go help her hold them down." He addressed Diana again. "If you want your drinks sometime tonight, put in a direct order. Floor service is ungodly slow."

Diana acknowledged his advice with a nod, he departed, and their little column resumed its march toward the bar. Diana got the bartender's attention and pointed toward Chloe and Kira. "These are my clients from the new class, Kira Clark and Chloe Rossi."

The bartender became focused.

"This is Steve Olsen, the assistant manager."

In near-perfect unison, Kira and Chloe piped, "Pleased to meet you." Steve awarded them a small smile.

"Steve, I'm buying the first round tonight." She turned to her charges. "What are you having?"

Kira hadn't thought about what she'd be drinking. Now, people waited to hear her choice. Her second, a combat veteran. Steve, who routinely served gunfighters after a match. Beyond them, all the other Guild members who spent their days either engaging in life-or-death encounters, or preparing for them.

This wasn't the moment to order a Pink Squirrel.

Kira put on her best imitation of nonchalance. "Well, what do winning gunfighters drink?"

Diana smiled and addressed the bartender. "That'll be

Angel's Envy for Kira and me." She pointed to Chloe, who responded with, "Same."

"Neat for me." Having clarified her order, Diana gestured toward Kira and Chloe. "You two?"

"On the rocks." Whatever Angel's Envy was, it was probably strong, and Kira wasn't ready to drink it without at least a little dilution. Beside her, Chloe nodded.

Steve bestowed the drinks, and Diana hoisted hers toward her clients. "May you live to learn."

For a split second, Kira drew a blank. Then the response came. "And learn to live." They clinked glasses.

Angel's Envy turned out to be a smooth and potent whiskey. Kira let the burn roll over her tongue and limited her intake to a sip. She'd nurse this one for a while, letting her body absorb it slowly while giving the ice a chance to melt. Despite the celebration, she needed to keep her wits about her, at least until she'd accepted the theater job and told Diana and Chloe about her decision. Though a little bit of alcohol would probably make the last part easier.

Diana led the way toward the windows. A white-haired man in a black-and-gray jacket intercepted her. His jacket's silver piping and epaulets indicated he was a high-ranking official and Diana introduced him to Kira and Chloe as Malcolm Reese, but his title vanished into the background noise and general confusion. Diana listened, her ear cocked toward him, but between his low voice and the dull roar from the surrounding crowd, Kira heard nothing. Chloe sipped her drink and started to fidget. Diana brokered a pause in the conversation and pointed toward the windows.

"Keep going until you see Gary. I'll be along."

Kira and Chloe resumed their journey, but without Diana's size and presence to part the crowd, it was slower going. They wove their way through immovable clusters of people talking and drinking until they finally hit a clear area. Gary waved them over to a table where he sat next to a woman wearing a gold-and-purple jacket with a second's epaulets. Her jet-black hair hung down her back in a French braid.

Gary stepped up to host duties. "Kira, Chloe, this is Claire Bostwick. Former member of Team Diana, now a second over at First Trust."

Claire shook her head. "There are no 'former' members of Team Diana. Some of us just serve under different colors."

Gary acknowledged the correction and made an exaggerated search of the surrounding area. "You lost our fearless leader."

Kira shrugged. "She sent us on. She had to talk to someone."

Claire looked puzzled. "Who was it?"

"Malcolm something." Kira tried to call the person's image back to mind. "Reese, maybe? Older guy. Somebody big with the Guild."

Claire nodded. "He's probably trying to get her to run for office again."

Concern washed across Chloe's face. "Could she still be a second if she did that?"

Claire and Gary exchanged a look that amounted to a short, silent conference. Claire answered. "No, and that's why she won't do it. But she can get some leverage by talking about it, so she's talking."

Chloe frowned into her drink. "Is Diana *always* working an angle?"

The question provoked another wordless conference between Claire and Gary. This time, Gary responded. "Pretty much, yeah. That's how she is who she is."

Chloe looked puzzled. "So, who is she?"

Gary grinned and took a sip of his drink. "One of those people you just don't fuck with."

Claire broke in. "I always thought Diana's vibe was more 'We both know you're not going to fuck with me, because you're so much smarter than that.'"

"Whatever." Gary directed his attention back to Chloe and Kira. "The point being, if you can't be one of those people, the next best thing is to have one of them looking out for you. Diana will do that." He pointed around the room. "Notice how few seconds are here?"

Although most people in the room wore gunfighter's jackets, the braided epaulets that distinguished the seconds from their clients were few and far between.

"All the instructors and seconds have been busting their butts on Qualification Week, they went to their receptions, and now they've gone home. Diana's here. Has she been introducing you around?"

"Yeah." Chloe fingered her glass. "Kind of showing us off." She turned to Kira. "Showing you off, anyway."

Kira tried to frame a response, but Claire spoke first. "Hey, number twenty-five in the region and number seven in a class of eighty-one is nothing to sneeze at." The young second almost glared at Chloe. "Stop selling yourself short."

Gary picked up the thread again. "Diana wants people to know she's got good clients, but she's also marking you, making sure people know if they mess with you, they'll answer to her."

Kira swirled her glass, melting the ice faster and diluting the drink. "So, she took good care of you when you were her client?"

"She takes good care of all her clients. I think she believes that's the purpose of her existence."

A hand came down on Gary's shoulder. "What's the purpose of my existence?"

He grinned up at Diana. "Seeing to the interests of wayward gunfighters incapable of looking after themselves."

Diana responded with mock surprise. "Is there a nobler cause?"

Gary's grin widened. "I can't think of one at the moment."

"I can." Claire tapped impatiently at the table readout. "Faster nacho delivery. I've had this order in since I got here, and it still says '10 minutes.'" She frowned at the readout. "Wait. Dammit—they moved the SUBMIT button and changed the color." She stabbed the display with her finger. "I hate it when they do that."

Gary leaned over to study the order screen. "So you *didn't* order nachos?"

Claire glared at him but said nothing.

Diana maneuvered into an empty chair between Gary and Chloe, and the conversation morphed into some gossip about the local Guild treasurer getting the boot for suspected embezzlement, which in turn kicked off a long chain of topics that started with TKC's donation of some parkland to the city, ran through the political ambitions of a vice president at EMR Trust, and somehow became a discussion about a proposed ordinance to extend the ban on human-controlled vehicles from the core downtown area to the adjacent business districts and neighborhoods. Some hobbyist groups objected, and the council seemed inclined to hear them out. That was surprising, given the group was tiny compared to the number of people who used grid-managed, AI-controlled drivers.

Kira pitched in occasionally while nursing her drink down to a warm buzz and a dry glass. Gary and Chloe fell into a spirited argument about the relative merits of various southside Italian eateries, while Diana and Claire were engaged in a detailed assessment of the prospects for women's basketball in the coming season. The latter conversation was informed by Diana's history as a starting center all the way through college, and Claire's high school play for Des Moines East, leaving Kira in a conversational eddy.

She excused herself and headed for the restrooms. On the karaoke stage near the back, two guys played to the crowd as the long instrumental opening of Queen's "Keep Yourself Alive" ran in the background. Doing the song as a duet was an interesting choice.

As Kira approached the restrooms, she passed men in varying states of discomfort lined up against the wall leading to their door. The women's room was not only lineless, but empty. There was at least one upside to the small number of women in dueling. As she washed up, Kira's handset signaled for attention. Her bank. Kira's stomach churned. With some trepidation, she pressed her thumb to the device's security reader and accessed her account. At least she was out of public view.

It showed a deposit of 35,750.53 unidollars from the Midwest Regional Chapter of the Gunfighter's Guild. Her prize for winning the Cup, minus withholding. The Guild was a stickler for prompt payments, and they weren't going to make a member wait on them. Kira let out a small sigh.

After she repaid her signing bonus, made her next loan payment, and squared up with Chloe on the rent, she'd have a little over a thousand unis to get to Minneapolis, set up housekeeping in the theater's back room, and hang on until her first paycheck hit her account. If it didn't arrive before another loan payment consumed the last of her cash, she'd be down to shoplifting ramen noodles or begging coworkers to have her over for dinner.

She emerged from the restroom, and the dull buzz of party conversation pressed in. Pressure from nearby bodies. From looks. From expectations. Kira tried the door leading to the deck. It opened.

Once outside, her skin tingled in the cool September air. Cleansing, clarifying. Exactly as she'd hoped. With the exterior lights off, no one inside was likely to notice her through the big floor-to-ceiling windows. She could be alone. In the pond beyond the deck, the recirculating fountain churned away, illuminated by bounce-back from spotlights trained on the words "Midwest AgriSystems" on a windowless wall of prefabricated concrete panels. The building housed the company's gunfighter training campus. By all accounts, the facility was similar to the sprawling TKC installation out of sight behind the arena, although a bit smaller.

Inside the bar, a video screen flickered. Kira's face appeared on the monitor, a snippet from a hallway interview conducted right after the match. The display flipped from that to one of her stills, overlaid with her stats. A title dropped into the slide. "'Death's Angel' Takes Midwest Regional Cup."

Death's Angel?

Somebody had given the cold, deadly character she played on the dueling field a name. Did she really want to be called "Death's Angel"?

It was flattering, in a weird sort of way. It might even make a good throwaway line at a donor event—one of those "interesting life" tidbits artists were expected to provide. *"Why yes, it's true, I did go through gunfighter training. They called me 'Death's Angel.'"* Follow the declaration with an anecdote someone who grew up in a gated community would find both horrifying and titillating.

Kira shook her head, turned away, and looked out over the pond.

Chill ate through the thin jacket, and she zipped it up for warmth. She ought to message Marla now, let her know she had the money to pay back her signing bonus and take the job. She leaned on the rail and stared into the dark. Her handset remained in its holder.

The door opened and another guest entered the deck. No mistaking that profile, even in this light: Diana. Her second leaned on the rail next to her, a half-full glass of wine in her hand. "Hey."

Was there any significance to Diana switching to a less potent drink? Kira didn't turn to face her. "You need some fresh air, too?"

"Maybe." Diana turned around, letting the railing support her weight as she faced the window.

Kira mimicked her mentor's position.

"You can see all the types from here." Diana seemed to be addressing the night at least as much as she was addressing Kira.

"Types of what?"

"The types of people who get into gunfighting." She used her wineglass as a pointer. "There's people like Chloe or Asim." She indicated a man whose age, dark skin, and long, thin limbs marked him as a descendant of Sudanese refugees. "They're born into such crappy circumstances, this looks like the ladder out. And for some of them, it will be."

Diana squinted, then pointed out a man with neatly combed salt-and-pepper hair and the black-and-gray jacket of a Guild official. "I picked up Roger Davis during my first rotation as an instructor." She took a drink. "He's got severe ADHD. Parents didn't know how to help him. His school couldn't deal with him, so he dropped out. He got fired dozens of times, but he hit a TKC open tryout on a good day. Once he was on the Guild medical plan, I found a therapist who helped him work out the right mix of meds and coping strategies, and he made it through a year as a gunfighter. He moved into the Guild's training evaluation section, and now he's the Midwest Region's coordinator." Diana settled back against the rail. "As a society, we knew how to help him, but until he took this job, nobody did the work."

Diana aimed her wineglass at a table where a man with a shock of white hair and striking blue eyes held court with a group of young men. "Paul Harris. Longest-serving gunfighter in the Guild—just over three years with Consolidated Trust."

"Three years? How can anybody do that?"

"He's been hit five times, so he spent some time on the disabled list. But he's honestly fearless. He can envision his death intellectually, but he doesn't feel it emotionally. Not like you and I do."

Kira studied the scene. "He's a psychopath."

"I haven't seen a full psych workup, but I'd bet a year's pay he's off-the-charts on the Kirkland Screen." Diana folded her arms across her chest. "No fear for himself, no remorse for his opponents. He's perfect for this job. Maybe he's perfect for this world."

Diana pointed out a short, balding man in a TKC jacket. "Then there's Marty. Discharged from the Army, got divorced, and wound up homeless. He has a tough time in the civilian world, but he can shoot. I'll pick him up for the last three months of his contract when his second goes on instructor duty."

Kira studied the crowd on the other side of the window. "What about me?" She turned to face Diana. "Where do I fit in all this?"

Diana laughed a little. "You and me? We're the fuckups. We had a chance at a different life, and we blew it. Maybe we get it back, maybe we die trying, or maybe we're just stuck here. But we can never quite believe what we've gotten ourselves into."

Shit. Diana was reading right through her.

At their table, Chloe and Claire talked and laughed, oblivious to the outside.

This might be Kira's last chance to get a question answered. "Do you have any regrets about taking Chloe?"

"No. I always wanted Chloe."

Kira scowled. "No you didn't. You said she wasn't good enough to waste one of your picks on. I had to threaten to walk out before you said you'd work with her."

"It's true I said that."

"But . . ." Kira prompted.

"How did Chloe feel about me?"

"She was afraid of you. You intimidated her."

"Even after getting ready for the six-week evaluation?"

"She was better, but . . . Yeah."

"I make a bigger difference for Chloe than anyone else in the class. Her odds of living are almost one-third higher with me than they are with the next-best choice. But she'd never pick me on her own."

"So you used me—"

Diana's voice rose a little. "I *let you* succeed at something you wanted to do. Going to the mat for Chloe also made you pull her in the right direction. You and I both got what we wanted. Chloe got what she needed."

"Does it—" Kira bit back the words, then started again. "Does it ever occur to you that you take an awful lot on yourself?"

Diana's voice became cool and controlled. Dangerous. "Does it occur to you that an awful lot gets *pushed* on me? I'm surrounded by people making life-and-death decisions. If I know the right answer and I don't steer them to it, I'm betraying them."

"Couldn't you just lay it all out? You could have explained everything to Chloe and then let her choose instead of hustling her into it."

Diana laughed a cold, bitter laugh. "Rational consideration of alternatives? That's weak tea, especially for people under pressure. They stick to what feels familiar, they choose whatever gets it over with quickly, they obsess about minor points, and they huddle with their friends. That doesn't always lead to the best option."

"So, did you want me at all?" If the answer was no, it made walking away a lot easier.

"Oh yes. I make a difference with you, too. Not as much as with Chloe, but I'm your best bet for finishing match twenty-six and walking away in one piece."

"How can you be so sure?"

"I'm not. But I know the odds, I understand what it takes, and see a path to survival for both of you."

"And it doesn't hurt that this 'path' happens to give you two of the class's top ten gunfighters."

"There's a strong correlation between surviving and winning. That's part of the reason I can do what I do."

"Which is what?"

"Like I said: find clients who survive if they're paired with me."

"How can you *know* that, though? How can anybody know that?"

"You can learn a lot with enough data and the right analyst." Diana downed some wine, but watched Kira out of the corner of her eye. A challenge.

Kira rubbed her face. Somehow, all the pieces Diana tossed at her made a picture. But what was it? "OK, I can believe you can get at a bunch of gunfight data, but the AI does all the analysis, and it chooses the pairs . . ." Kira stopped, the picture suddenly clear in her mind. "Holy shit, you figured out how to bribe the AI."

"It's not quite that simple." Diana looked amused again. "I play with it."

"Play with it? You mean . . . what? You give it a digital belly rub and it just purrs out the data?"

Diana laughed. "That's pretty close to the truth."

"So, what is the truth?"

"The AI makes digital art. It shows it to me, traces my eye movements, and monitors my pulse while I watch."

"That's it?"

"That's it."

"So it . . . cares that you like its work?"

Diana shrugged. "I don't think my aesthetic judgment matters. Maybe it likes the ebb and flow of data. Maybe it enjoys getting a human to do something for it instead of the other way around. It's an AI. Nobody knows why it wants what it wants." Diana sipped her drink. "But it wants that interaction. A couple years ago, TKC hired a new AI wrangler. He discovered the AI would do its job if he watched the art or not, so he quit doing it. Then the AI found me."

"So, you get it to calculate survival odds and then get it to assign the trainees you want."

"I can't make it do anything. But it will tell me how it decides, and I make sure it sees what it needs to see."

Realization dawned on Kira again. "*That's* why you had us sandbag on the third-quarter quick-draw evaluation!"

Diana awarded Kira the smile reserved for prize pupils performing well. "The AI thinks people in the middle range on that exercise are more successful with me than those at either extreme. So, I wanted you two in the middle."

"Same deal on the variable-sighting exam."

Diana nodded and took another drink.

Kira shifted in place and not just from the cold. Was it weirder that a disinterested entity with inscrutable motives controlled her fate, or that Diana had figured out how to hustle it?

Kira put her elbows on the rail, turning her back to the window and facing the pond again. Beside her, Diana did the same.

Diana broke the silence. "The Cup prize was high this quarter. Forty-five thousand unis, wasn't it?"

"Yeah." Where was Diana going with this?

"I heard your signing bonus was low. Most people get around fifty thousand unis. Didn't you get a little more than half that?"

What was this nonsense? Diana probably knew Kira's bonus down to the penny. "Well, most people aren't about to be foreclosed on when they sign up. I didn't have much leverage."

Diana turned toward Kira. "So, if you've saved a little over the past year, you could use your Cup prize to pay off your signing bonus and quit. That doesn't happen very often."

Kira stiffened. This would be harder than she thought. "Diana, I—"

Diana raised her finger. "If that's your decision, I'm OK with that."

"What?" Kira's tension turned into confusion. "All that work . . ."

"My job is to get my clients through gunfighting and on to whatever comes next. If I helped you buy your way back to the life you want, that's a win. Even if you never fight a real match."

"I'm not sure it's the life I want." Kira sighed and looked down. "I'll still have all that debt. I've been to the point where they were ready to send a property recovery team to take me away." She rolled her shoulders to clear the tension from remembered fear. "I don't want to be in that situation again."

"I can't tell you what to do about that. If you decide to be a gunfighter, I'll do my best to get you through. If you decide to leave, good luck and Godspeed. I want you to know that."

"Thanks." Kira weighed a possibility. "What does the AI say my chances are?"

"For twenty-six matches, you have a 59.12 percent chance of being alive after the last one."

"You know this off the top of your head?"

"It's been on my mind."

"What about Chloe?"

"51.48."

The next question was the most important one, the one Kira had never had the guts to ask, and it might be the one Diana wouldn't answer. Still, now was the time. "What's it like to pull the trigger on another person?"

Diana drained her wineglass and turned. Light from the windows played across her face. "Probably not as hard as it should be. A lot of the training is desensitization. Like when we tell you to imagine the targets and the mechs as real people. That's so when you go up against real people, it feels like shooting at targets and mechs." She shrugged. "It's a cheap mental trick, but it works."

Is that who Kira really wanted to be? Someone who could shoot people as if it was nothing? *Death's Angel.* "How is that

OK? I mean, killing them just so TKC doesn't have to pay the claims?"

Diana snorted. "That's just a matter of degree."

"What?"

"No matter what you think you're doing, and no matter who you think you're working for, you're turning somebody's life into somebody else's money. We're just unusually direct about it."

"How can you say that?"

Diana twirled her wineglass between her palms. "When I was an undergrad, I interned as an assistant archivist for a company being sued for contaminating water near their plants. Big, old, well-thought-of corporation. Made a lot of those 'most respected' lists. The contaminant was long-lived and hard to filter out. It caused cancers, neurological problems, birth defects, immune system disorders—the bad shit. They'd known about the risks for years. There was even a memo saying they shouldn't change the process because change would be expensive and they'd contaminated the water supply so thoroughly, stopping wouldn't reduce their liability very much."

"Didn't somebody blow the whistle on them? Didn't you? I mean . . ."

Disdain flickered across Diana's face. "That was my job. The archivist and I organized the information and turned it over to the lawyers representing people suing the company. It's called discovery."

"So, how did they not win? With all that in there?"

"They did win."

"So, wait. What?"

"They won a couple bellwether trials, scored some good-sized settlements, and then the plaintiff's lawyers called for group trials to determine final damages. The company convinced the court the cases were potentially different enough they should all be tried individually. That could take as long as forty years."

"Oh dear God."

"So, they went to sick people with life expectancy of five to fifteen years and said, 'You can wait for your day in court, or you can settle for pennies on the uni now.'" Diana folded her arms. "What do you think most of them said?"

Kira nodded. "I see."

"So, the plaintiffs gave up a chunk of their lives for a pittance, the shareholders got their profits, and the execs got their bonuses. Maybe the rest of us saved a little on kitchenware." Diana paced in the open deck. "In this job, we're dealing with people too stubborn to quit. People who won't accept the outcome of the process. Usually because they think they're being cheated—and to be clear, they're not always wrong. But we deal with them honestly, we don't hide behind a phalanx of publicists and lawyers, and we don't take cover behind a stack of legal briefs. We shoot at them; they shoot at us."

"So that makes it all OK?"

"It's legal, and it's what they choose. One way or another, it's always about turning lives into money."

"Well, I don't think a performance of *Hamlet* is going to kill anybody."

Diana made another one of those joke-that-only-she-got smiles. "And where do you think the money for that comes from? Who funds the grants, and what does it do for their agenda?"

Kira rubbed her temples. "This would be easier to figure

out if I knew whether you're my hard-assed fairy godmother or Mephistopheles."

"I don't think I offered you all knowledge in exchange for your soul."

"No. But I'd probably let it go for a lot less than that."

Diana smiled. "How about this? I'm not an angel or a demon, just a person trying to do right by the people who matter to me."

"That might be the scariest answer of all."

Diana zipped her jacket all the way up. "It's chilly. I'm going back in. Join me?"

Kira shook her head. "I've got some things to think about."

"Suit yourself."

Kira stared out over the pond. Split futures, like the two sides of the combat area. In one, she emptied her bank account, paid off her signing bonus, and went to live in the theater, like Erik in *Phantom of the Opera*. Working for Marla. How much pull did Marla really have with her board, and how long would it last? She'd only been on the job a little over a year, and Kira didn't know her all that well. Sure, they'd hit it off at the Shores of Superior Theater Fest and kept in touch, and she'd gone out of her way to offer the position. But still . . . Would Marla be able to keep the grant money flowing and protect Kira's special arrangement?

And, even if all that worked, would she find another job like it when the grant ran out? And another, and another, until she was forty-four, and her loan was all paid off. Then what? And what if there wasn't always another job? Then she'd have struggled and saved for nothing, and she'd wind up as a debt slave. Like the survival rates, it was the cumulative odds that killed you. She might pull off this transition, and the next one, but how many after that?

If she stayed, though? She'd have enough to keep her creditors at bay. With a little luck and some endorsement contracts, she might pay them off completely before she fought her last match. But every two weeks, someone would try to kill her. Unless she killed them first. But it was only another year. Maybe a little more.

Two more futures split from that one. In one, the day came when she was just a little too slow or not quite accurate enough, and she died. Chloe and Diana would come to her funeral. Maybe a couple of other gunfighters. She rolled that over in her mind. Odds of seeing that one play out were a little more than two in five.

In the other, she walked away free. Debts paid. Some money in her account. Free to go back to the theater or live any life she wanted to live. Only about a year from now. Nearly a three in five chance of that.

No debt. Not unless she counted the blood on her hands.

Kira's handset made a *ping* noise, interrupting her musing. High-priority personal message. She frowned and pulled the device from her belt. Eastbrook Talent Agency. Kira's breath caught. *Eastbrook.* How many times had she sent a picture and credits to them when she was in New York? Had she ever gotten so much as a "don't call us, we'll call you" generic response? She keyed the message to open.

Ms. Clark:

Congratulations on winning the Midwest Regional Cup!

As I'm sure you're aware, your accomplishments open a world of exciting possibilities, including endorsements, merchandising, and appearances. I'm Adrian Connell, and I'd like to be your guide to that world. Please use my contact information below to arrange a meeting at your convenience to discuss . . .

At the bottom, his personal contact info. Direct line. Handset number. Personal message address. The information they didn't part with until they were serious.

Her handset pinged again. Had she ever purged her high-priority senders list?

The Grace Masterson Agency, this time. No. Not just the agency. Grace Masterson herself. Same deal—congratulations, let's talk about your future, here's my personal contact info. From the founding agent. Kira put her handset back in its carrier. A buzz that definitely wasn't whiskey filled her head.

She turned back to the window. Inside the Lounge, the others sat around the big table. Claire's long-delayed nachos arrived, two plates of chips and meat and black olives smothered in gooey cheese. Chloe dug right in, Gary right behind her. Two guys from Lucky Pig had joined the group, talking and laughing. Diana arrived, bearing another Angel's Envy, and took her place. A dark-haired man in First Trust colors tried to sit next to Chloe, and she shooed him off. Because it was Kira's chair.

She didn't have to stand out here in the cold, a pathetic orphan with her nose pressed against the glass. That big table full of good food, surrounded by people talking and laughing, with the smell of cooked meat and spices in the air—there was a place for her there. All she had to do was go in and claim it.

She pulled her handset off her belt clip, called up Marla's contact, and tapped out a message: "Thanks for all you've done, but I guess I'm going to be a gunfighter."

She reviewed the message, hit SEND, and opened the door back into the Gunslinger's Lounge, where her friends and colleagues waited.

CHAPTER 12

During the coming match, Kira will fire from the last place on the field Niles will look, nullifying his advantage in draw speed and maximizing her advantage in accuracy.

When they walk from the start point to their kill boxes, she will slant left, entering her box nearly fourteen feet from the strikeline that marks the shortest distance. This will take her eleven paces. Niles, with longer legs, can reach his box in less than ten if he sticks to the strikeline. Completing his turn before she puts her foot down in her kill box, he will face the disorienting gray expanse of the Wall for about a second.

Assuming his trainer hasn't broken the bad habits apparent on his match vid, when the Wall clears, he will aim down the strikeline and sweep right, his gun tracking along with his eyes. When he duels citizens, this isn't a problem, because he's fast enough to correct his mistake before they can fire.

But Kira isn't some hapless citizen. In the second or so it will take Niles to recognize and correct his error, she will draw her weapon, stabilize her sights, and fire the shot that will end his life.

At least, that's the plan.

The judge reaches the part requiring a response. ". . . either of you wish to concede, or abandon this course of action?"

Kira answers with a clear "no."

Niles's refusal comes a fraction of a second later.

The judge touches his bench display. "I have recorded your intent."

Quitting is no longer even a theoretical option.

CHAPTER 13

From her position in front of the judge's table and beside Diana, Kira waited with her eyes fixed on the door to her opponent's changing room. If Rusty Cunningham took just two more minutes to step onto the dueling field, she'd win her first professional match on a forfeit.

In the waiting room, he'd denounced TKC as a bunch of greedy, cheating bastards and Kira as a freak and a bitch no man would ever want. But there'd been wide-eyed terror under the anger, and Kira had played to it.

When he'd exhausted himself on his rant, she'd calmly inquired what he'd done to prepare. He replied that he owned a small arsenal, had hunted since he was eight, and had spent two weeks training in a simulator. She'd responded with a raised eyebrow and obviously restrained amusement, which did nothing for his temper.

He'd started to wind up again when the receptionist sent them to the changing rooms. What had happened there? Had his anger doubled and redoubled on itself until it became incoherent rage that left him with quivering hands and clouded judgment? Or had the doubts hit, depleting his resolve and leading him to take the hallway door?

With just over a minute to spare, the entryway opened. Rusty hesitated on the threshold, blinking in the unfamiliar light and fumbling with the cloth belt of his dueling tunic. His name badge sat slightly askew against the Velcro holding it in place.

With some prompting from the ward, he found his way to his spot in front of the judge, placing him on Kira's right. Rusty's second stood a bit beyond him, dressed in jeans, a dress shirt, and hiking boots.

Rusty caught sight of Diana and sneered. "It figures you'd have some other whore holding your leash."

Kira turned to her second, flicking her thumb in Rusty's direction. "You're right. I'm going for the head shot on this one."

Diana said nothing, but on the edge of Kira's vision, Rusty flinched. The judge signaled for attention, and when everyone fell silent, he recited the cause of the action—something to do with an insurance payout for lightning damage—and the rules of engagement. Finally, he came to the part requiring their participation. "Do either of you wish to concede or abandon this course of action?"

Kira responded, "No."

After a moment's hesitation, Rusty said the same.

Kira put away any remaining inclination to view him as a person and thought of him only as a target.

"As judge, I have recorded your intent." He tapped the surface of his bench, entering that bit of data into the Association's recordkeeping system. "Your holsters and weapons have been prepared by the wards in the presence of your seconds while monitored by an Association AI. Do either of you wish to challenge these arrangements?"

Again, they both declined.

The lead ward spoke. "You may don your gear."

Diana came to the table with Kira, where their ward gave them the gun belt, holster, and gun, each randomly selected from the four sets laid out for the event. With Diana's help, Kira put the belt on, clipped the holster into place, and secured it to her thigh with a strap.

Kira ran through the tests with her ward. When she drew, the holster triggered a foul if she was outside the kill box and activated the motion sensor in the gun belt if she was inside. The sensor signaled a foul after only a few centimeters of movement, just as it should. If she fell or ran after drawing her gun, she would lose.

The ward confirmed the sensor's reset, making the unit ready for live operation.

With her preparations complete, Kira watched her opponent and his second struggle with the equipment. The ward hovered nearby, insisting they keep the safety on during the equipment checkout to protect everyone else. Rusty announced he would comply during the checkout, but he would leave the safety off during the duel to maximize his speed. Good. With some luck, he might hook his finger inside the trigger guard when he drew and shoot himself in the leg.

At last, he was ready.

The lead ward spoke again. "Assume your positions."

The seconds and EMTs moved behind the judge's table,

where a transparent shield protected them from stray rounds or a citizen determined to make a political statement. Kira and her opponent returned to their places on opposite sides of the centerline, facing the start point.

If Rusty killed her, he would gloat about it for years. She let that thought slip through her mind, without consideration.

The Wall went up.

On the ward's command, they walked down opposite sides of the barrier to the red circle. Kira put her toes on the edge of the marked area and waited, her back to Rusty and her face toward the kill box. She tightened her focus, letting all the extraneous parts of her world slip away. She had a duel to win.

The lead ward called out, "You may proceed on my count." After a pause, he spoke with a steady rhythm. "1 . . . 2 . . . 3 . . ."

Kira walked toward her end of the field, following the strikeline and matching her pace to the ward's cadence.

". . . 4 . . . 5 . . ."

She kept her breath regular and her mind focused.

". . . 6 . . . 7 . . ."

She picked a spot between the left boundary and the strikeline where she would enter the kill box.

". . . 8 . . . 9 . . ."

Kira adjusted her stride to place her pivot foot on the boundary line.

". . . 10 . . ."

The ball of her foot on the line, Kira executed a full rotation, ending when she faced the far side of the field with her foot planted in the kill box. The Wall disappeared. She pulled her pivot toe inside the box and drew, her hands meeting at waist level and her thumb flicking off the safety. Rusty stood a little off the strikeline, looking down at the dueling pistol he was extracting from his holster instead of looking for her. Kira brought her sights into alignment on his chest. He looked up just as her finger found the trigger and applied smooth, steady pressure. A flash, a bang, and the kick of recoil against her palms.

Rusty's pistol went off and Kira flinched at the noise, but there was no follow-up *crack* from a passing bullet. Wild shot. Rusty lay on the pseudograss, making no effort to get up. Was he embarrassed, or . . . Kira let the thought pass.

The assigned EMT and ward ran toward the prone figure in the kill box. On the judge's table, a tentative win light flashed on Kira's side. The EMT for her side of the field pointed to her, and she shook her head to indicate lack of injury. Freed from any immediate responsibility to her, he jogged off toward Rusty.

Kira reholstered her weapon and waited, hands on her knees and taking deep breaths. Across the centerline, Rusty still lay flat on the ground. He could get up any time now as far as she was concerned. She had her win. His EMT kneeled next to him, his arms active and posture focused. The other EMT and Rusty's second arrived. Kira's EMT joined his partner, kneeling beside the prone form in the kill box. After a brief exchange, the first EMT stood and unfurled a body bag.

Oh shit . . . A hollow sensation in Kira's abdomen, as if she'd been cored out. She took a slow, deep breath and let it all pass through. None of this had anything to do with her. She just showed up and did her job, same as anyone else.

"You may approach the judge, if you are able." The voice of the lead ward stirred Kira to action. The trek back seemed longer than the path she'd taken on the way out, even though the diagonal route was shorter. Diana greeted her with a pat on the shoulder. "Good job."

Kira nodded in acknowledgment. "Thanks."

Kira returned her gear to the ward. After a brief inspection, he set it on the judge's table.

An EMT arrived. "Ms. Clark, I need to examine you. There was a discharge on the field. Please raise your arms." The technician walked around her and patted her down, confirming her lack of injury.

The exam complete, Kira let her mind wander. She was done, except for the formality of hearing the judge's pronouncement. Technically, the presence of either the combatant or their second was enough to make it official, but unless they were injured, combatants were expected to stay. Kira mimicked Diana's pose: relaxed but alert, arms behind her, focused on nothing in particular and staying out of the way while others did their work.

Back in Rusty's kill box, the EMT who had examined Kira returned dragging a rolled-up stretcher behind him. After laying out the carrier, the two EMTs moved to opposite ends of the body bag, grasped the handles, and lifted it into place. When it was secure, they picked up the poles and shuffled Rusty's mortal coil off the field.

By long-standing agreement, producers never included any aspect of handling a body on match video. All but the most bloodthirsty fans found it too upsetting.

With the field clear, the ward directed Rusty's second back to the judge's table to hear the ruling. The man walked slowly, with his head down.

A stab of pain, like a runner's stitch, struck low in Kira's rib cage. She cleared it with a cleansing breath. *It's OK, it's OK, it's OK. We're all just doing our jobs.*

Kira assumed her place in front of the judge and Rusty's second shambled into the position Rusty had occupied a few minutes before. Was he crying? Who had Rusty been to him, anyway? Friend? Brother? Cousin? Kira focused on her boots. Everyone here chose to be here. They were all playing out the consequences of their decisions. Responsible adults.

The judge stood to make the match's concluding statement.

"As judge in this contest, I have inspected all reports pertaining to it, heard all appeals and objections, and observed the event in person. Based on these observations and reports, I declare this to be a fair combat under the laws of the United States and the rules of the National Association for Dueling. I declare the outcome to be a victory for TKC Insurance through their representative, Kira Clark. This judgment is final and there can be no further appeals."

DIANA SET THE DATA PAD'S DISPLAY FOR A CLOSE-UP OF KIRA'S toe on the kill box boundary line. "Did you realize how close you were?"

For the fourth time during the post-match debrief, Kira leaned across the tiny briefing room worktable to study the data pad. Flop sweat rendered her uniform damp and clammy, Chloe was waiting in the Gunslinger's Lounge, but Kira wasn't going anywhere until Diana said they were done. Best to come clean. "I knew I was tight, but I thought I had more room than that."

Diana tapped her handset. "Position awareness is on the agenda for our next session." She folded the data pad shut and put it away.

Hallelujah.

Diana shifted to a more conversational tone. "We have things to work on, but I meant what I said—that was a good debut. Your strategy was sound, you executed well, and you scored a clean kill. You stayed calm, too. Sometimes that's the hardest part." Diana reached into her gear bag. "Before I forget." She handed Kira a cellophane packet with an enamel pin inside. "Congratulations. You've earned it."

"Thanks." The word sounded hollow in her ears. Kira stared at the pin, a red circle with the black silhouette of a dueling pistol on it. Fastened to the collar of her Guild jacket, it would tell the world she was a proven veteran. At least, that's what it meant to Guild members. To others, it merely marked her as a proven killer. She put the pin in her purse.

Diana sat up a little straighter, then folded her arms and leaned across the table, her expression a bit too casual to be genuinely casual. "So, how was he in the waiting room?"

Kira straightened. "About like he was on the field—*total* asshole. Yelled at me the whole time, called me a bitch and I don't know what else. Went on and on about how badly he was getting ripped off and how I was part of it." Kira made a dismissive flick. "On top of everything else, he was gun fetishist. He kept rattling on about all the weapons in his gun safe at home, like that was going to help him on the field."

"So, an easy guy to shoot." Diana's expression remained a bit too focused.

"Oh yeah. When I was a waitress, I had to put up with that crap." Kira slapped the spot on her leg where the holster had been. "Today, I didn't have to."

Diana's muscles softened, and she backed off a little. "You drew a good opponent for your first match. Sometimes they're more sympathetic."

Kira mirrored her mentor's relaxation.

Diana continued. "Still, you took a life today. How do you feel about that?"

Kira shrugged. "It's like we said in training. He made a choice to come here. He could have accepted the arbitration ruling, but he took his chance and came up against me. Bad day for him."

Skepticism flickered across Diana's face. Was it because Kira was reciting Diana's own words back to her, or in spite of it?

Diana tapped her finger on the worktable. "If that's how you feel, well and good. But you don't have to wear the ice princess mask with me."

Kira managed not to respond with open derision. Where did Diana get off telling anybody to remove their mask? Her second had a more carefully-curated face than anyone Kira had ever known.

Diana let several seconds of silence unfold, which Kira refused to fill. With a small sigh, the older woman produced her handset. "I'm sending you the contact information for Loretta Davis. She's a private psychologist, but the Guild has her on retainer. She's covered by your dues. If you want to talk, she's there, she's free, and she's confidential." From the depths of her oversize purse, Kira's handset chirped to acknowledge new information.

"OK, but I really don't think I need it."

"Maybe not, but you're no longer unbloodied. Chances are you'll need it sometime. It can be good to have someone to talk to."

Again, the deliberate silence. Again, Kira refused to speak.

Diana put the data pad into her gear bag. "We're done. Your forty-eight hours off starts now. Be at Firing Point Four at noon on Wednesday and we'll do some work on shooting from the midpoint of your draw. Your next opponent might not be as slow." Diana's thumbs worked her handset, and Kira's device chirped again, affirming the appointment. Diana gathered her gear bag and opened the door. Kira grabbed her purse and followed.

"Any special plans for your first break?"

"Chloe and I are getting together for drinks at the Lounge as soon as I get cleaned up."

"Good choice."

Kira picked up her pace to keep up with Diana. "It's tough to make plans with anybody else when you don't know if you'll be alive or not."

"Get used to that." They stopped at the door of the locker room. Diana pointed down the hall to the cafeteria. "I'm going to snag an early lunch, then I've got a simulator session with Dave the rest of the afternoon. Enjoy yourself. You did well. And say hi to Chloe for me."

"Thanks. I will."

In the empty locker room, Kira sat on a bench and shivered in her still-damp uniform. It was over. She'd played Death's Angel for Rusty Cunningham, the staff of the match, and maybe a couple hundred people on the live vid feed. If nothing else, it provided some footage to support her agent's quest to find a sponsor. She'd followed up with forty minutes of Kira Clark, Dutiful Student for Diana. Now, she was done.

An image of Rusty's body flashed across her mind. He lay flat in the kill box, felled by her bullet. Wait. Not her bullet. Not *Kira's*. The projectile belonged to Death's Angel. The part required a quick, accurate shot, and she'd played her part. Don't like the outcome? Take it up with the director. Or maybe the writer. Not her.

So how come your hands are shaking?

She retreated into a focus-on-the-breath exercise. The first came in a ragged gasp that threatened to turn into a sob. So did the second. The third was better, smoother. Tension departed with the exhaled air. Gradually, the breaths became longer and more even. Passing through. It was all just passing through. When she finished, her breath and her heartbeat were both slow and regular. She opened her locker, shed the uniform, and wrapped herself in a towel. When she'd stuffed the uniform in her laundry sack, she extracted her shower kit.

It would feel good to be clean.

AT THE LOUNGE, CHLOE HAILED KIRA FROM A BOOTH NEAR THE bar. "Hey, I saw it on the feed. You were great!"

Kira grinned. "Thanks."

"What did Diana say?"

"She said it was OK. There are some things we'll work on, but she thought it was a good debut."

"She said the same thing to me, even though I didn't get a kill."

Kira shrugged. "You knocked your guy down before he even got a shot off. That's more than I can say."

Chloe made a face. "Like your guy had a real shot. The vid guys said he put it in the pseudograss five feet in front of him. That's not a shot, that's just going for the trigger too soon and getting hit."

A waiter appeared carrying a glass of amber liquid with a little ice. "Angel's Envy for Ms. Clark?"

Chloe grinned. "Just like you did for me." She raised her glass, the cherry still floating in the yellowish liquid of her whiskey sour. "What should we drink to?"

Kira lifted her glass to the same height as Chloe's. "To victory."

Chloe's grin broadened, and they clinked their glasses together. "To victory!"

Kira sipped and savored the liquid heat spreading across her tongue and down her throat. She took a second, longer pull from the drink, and the buzz made its way to her brain.

Before she could take her third sip, Jenkins entered and parked in his usual spot on the barstool farthest left. Kira studied the big, heavy redheaded man for a few seconds and turned to Chloe. "I'm still betting IT department."

Chloe eyed him. "I think he's a janitor over at the Guild's local office."

"That's all contract. They have a different union."

"OK, well, maybe he's one of the lawyers, then."

Kira laughed and snorted. "Stop that. You nearly made whiskey come out my nose."

No one seemed to know Jenkins's exact role. So far, they'd established that he wasn't a professional gunfighter, he never acted like anyone's second, and he wasn't a trainer. But he appeared almost daily, held down his barstool, spoke little, and ordered a steady stream of drinks and bar food before wandering out a couple hours later. He wasn't listed on the official roster of Guild staff, but that only covered officers, managers, and people who worked with members, like the shop stewards. Still, no one ever challenged his presence, so his mystery deepened with each appearance.

Kira looked over her shoulder again. "We could just walk up and ask."

Chloe wrinkled her nose. "He's mean to everybody and smells bad." Chloe's face brightened, and she pointed to a vid monitor off on the right. "Hey look, they're doing your replay already."

The match vid picked up with Kira standing in front of the judge, waiting for permission to put her gear on. Her opponent entered, and after Kira's crack about the head shot, he looked as if he was about to say something, but was cut off by the judge's signal for attention. The split view of the match showed Kira's opponent a little slower than her through every step. For the exchange of fire, they started with a shot from behind Kira and over her shoulder from a slight angle. On her muzzle flash, they zoomed in close on Rusty. During debrief, Diana said Kira's bullet punched straight through his heart and spine, and he probably hadn't even felt the pseudograss when he hit it. However, the slow motion on this view showed him feeling something. Shock? Disbelief? Fear? He might be reacting to the muzzle flash rather than the sensation of being struck, but he certainly realized what was happening. The camera zoomed back and up to show the work of the EMTs and the ward, with her on the inset, waiting.

The vid replay ended, and Kira held an empty glass. The alcohol made her head heavy and thick, as though she wore a protective helmet. She punched another order into the table.

"So, what do you want to do tonight?" Chloe sounded tentative.

Kira considered. What did she really want to do? Thoughts came. "Drink. Go out. Dance with unsuitable men far into the night."

Chloe fidgeted with her glass. "Well, I guess we can do that."

Kira scowled. "Don't overwhelm me with enthusiasm. What do you want to do?"

"Well, we haven't seen Desi in ages. I haven't even met his new girlfriend."

Kira rolled that over in her mind. One part of her pulled for the normality and domestic comfort of the visit. It was a work night for Desi, so they'd be doing nothing wilder than snacks and vid before turning in early. The other part of her pulled toward the clubs on Court Avenue—deafening dance music, strong drinks, and people she didn't know. Invisibility, oblivion, and no guarantees on where or how the night would end.

"Gunfighter's Long Island Iced Tea for Kira Clark?" The waiter hovered uncertainly, waiting for a sign. Kira raised her palm, and the waiter placed the drink in front of her.

Chloe frowned. "It's only three in the afternoon."

"I know." Kira took a long drink.

Chloe's frown deepened. "You're not going to last into the night if you keep this up. You know what's in those, right?"

"Triple sec, gin, vodka, tequila, and white rum, plus some flavorings so it doesn't kill you outright." Kira took another long drink. "Exactly what I want right now."

Across the table, Chloe fidgeted some more.

Kira pulled herself together, trying to be persuasive. "Look, we've been good the whole time we were in training. We deserve to cut loose a little bit. We're real gunfighters now."

And maybe that's why you want to be someplace where nobody knows who you are, and you want to drink until you forget what you've done. Kira quashed the thought and gave Chloe an expectant look.

Chloe shifted in her seat and looked at her hands. "OK, maybe you're right. Maybe we do deserve a little fun. We can at least see what's out there."

She'd have to drag Chloe into the evening, but at least Chloe was willing to be dragged. "Yeah. I heard Charlie's on Court is hot, even on weeknights. Let me finish this, and we'll go."

Kira hefted her drink. *I'm gonna shotgun this Long Island Iced Tea, and everything is going to be fine. Just fine . . .*

CHAPTER 14

"You may don your gear."

Reacting to the judge's order, the wards cross to the table's front, where they dole out equipment randomly selected from the four available sets. Diana and the ward both behave as if this is an ordinary match, instead of the highest-stakes duel in the past three years and the second-largest vid audience ever.

In response, probably just as Diana intends, Kira settles into the routine—fit the gun belt, set the holster, and keep a straight face during the little tickle on her thigh as Diana puts the stabilizing strap in place. Kira loads a bullet into the pistol's breech and closes the action, receiving both a satisfying click and a faint whiff of gun oil in return.

Her ward tests the sensors while Diana watches. The draw sensor and the motion sensor behave correctly, both inside and outside the kill box. The ward runs through it all on pure routine, right down to the reminder that if she reholsters before firing, she forfeits her right to shoot.

Set the safety, holster the weapon, and Kira's task is complete. The ward studies his readout and confirms the sensors have reset. Diana ratifies the results with her thumbprint.

At the judge's signal, the ward assumes his place on the sideline of Kira's side of the field. Diana makes her way to a spot next to the EMT, behind the plastic shield.

The lead ward's voice sounds rich and deep. "Please assume your positions."

Kira and Niles take their place in front of the bench, receive the judge's approval, and turn to face the start point.

The Wall splits the combat area in half from floor to ceiling. She won't see Niles again until she's looking at him over gunsights.

Her eyes are on the red semicircle of the start point poking out from under the Wall at midfield. She focuses on the spot, slows her breathing, and allows everything else to flow through her without giving it attention—the collective pressure from millions of eyes on vid, the vast financial implications, the life she wants, and the life she might lose. It all passes by and dissipates, leaving only her cold, deadly precision behind.

On his side of the Wall, Niles coughs and spits.

The lead ward intones, "Combatants, please advance to the start point."

Kira proceeds along the Wall, reaches the marker, and takes her position. Even with her toes on the outer edge of the circle, only a few inches separate her from Niles. Body heat pricks through her uniform, marking his presence. His breathing slows, and their breaths synchronize. Is he doing that on purpose? Or is she doing it unconsciously, her body responding to the simple, animal existence of another, without her mind's involvement?

For an aching moment, it's clear the dispute that brought them to this point has nothing to do with them. Their warm bodies and beating hearts are just chess pieces in a game between their em-

ployers, soulless legal entities with intellects as vast and cool and unsympathetic as an alien intelligence, watching the outcome with envious eyes.

God, was any of this worth it? Who was it all for, anyway? *Kira takes another breath.* Focus, focus, focus . . .

The moment passes, and the vision goes the way of all other extraneous concerns. Kira wills her consciousness to collapse, and her awareness tightens until it includes nothing but the field in front of her, the gun on her hip, and the opponent at her back.

CHAPTER 15

The senior dueling arena entrance guard was named Owen Johnson, and he informed Kira that Joshua M. Reardon, windmill mechanic and the seventh opponent of her career, had arrived about five minutes earlier. Owen probably wasn't supposed to tell her that. However, the parlor trick of catching the ejected cartridge in midair when she cleared her pistol had tweaked his interest. Reciting the Beretta tagline in the same husky voice she used in the commercial garnered the undivided attention of both Owen and the other guard on duty. Owen's partner completed the best search of her gear bag he could manage without taking his eyes off her and then handed it back. They both wished her good luck, and she gave them a small smile, a thank-you, and a wink in return.

Claire rounded the corner at a fast walk, wearing her second's uniform and lugging her gear bag. "Hey, Kira!"

Kira smiled and waved. "Hey."

Claire paused, catching her breath. "Can't stop long. I misread the notice. My match is on the other side of the building."

Kira nodded. Claire could have had her handset read the

door sign or map to her, but she seldom used the aid in public. Habits from a lifetime of concealing her dyslexia were hard to break.

When her breathing slowed, Claire continued. "A friend gave me four tickets for the Drake women's game on Thursday; her family couldn't make it. Chloe and Gary are in. Do you want to come?"

"Basketball?"

Claire shook her head. "I should uninvite you for asking that question."

Kira laughed. "Give me a break, I spent my winters in drama club." Kira adjusted her grip on her gear bag. "But sure, I'd love to come. I mean, if . . ." Kira angled her head toward the waiting room door.

Claire's tone became more serious. "You'll be there." She stood back a little and squared her shoulders. "Cut 'em down and walk away." As she spoke, she made the cutting hand gesture, ending with a thumbs-up.

Kira grinned. "Thanks."

Claire clapped her on the shoulder and resumed her trek. When she disappeared around the bend of the long hallway, Kira turned her attention back to her match. Joshua's cause-of-action information stated he had a flood insurance claim that may or may not be valid, while his public profile suggested he also had an overdeveloped case of righteous indignation and a wholly unjustified confidence in his skill with firearms. The clock above the waiting room door gave Kira twenty-seven minutes to convince him just how untenable his position was before they went to the field and she provided a conclusive demonstration.

The trainers hadn't said much about the waiting room, beyond the admonition not to let the encounter degenerate into a shouting match or scuffle that would get both parties ejected from the facility. Getting canceled and assigned to another date would screw up the TKC dueling schedule, and in the hierarchy of sins a gunfighter might commit, disrupting the delicate balance between Guild-mandated personnel availability and the relentless demands of Association-assigned dueling dates was right near the top.

For Kira, time with her opponent was an opportunity. Acting was all about getting an emotional response from an audience, and at a minimum, she could render her adversary uncertain and flustered. Perhaps today would be the day she finally produced an exceptional performance that would send her opponent to the exit rather than the dueling field.

Kira set her gear bag's strap on her shoulder and pulled her cloak over it. She adjusted her look, making her face and body hard and businesslike. Everything from her black trilby hat down to the tips of her low-heel boots served the impression of speed, organization, and lethality. Her scents were leather and maybe a little bit of sweat. No perfume. Nothing sweet.

She gripped the handles of the waiting room's double doors. Time for the most important show of the day, for an audience of one.

The draft she produced by pulling on the doors lifted her cloak. Perfect. The garment's crimson lining provided a dramatic backdrop for her black leather jacket and pants while also picking up the explosion of red ruffles at her throat. The hat, pulled low, obscured her face.

Joshua sat on the third chair of the left row, perfectly positioned to observe her entrance.

She strode past him, allowing only a glimpse of her face in profile. The maneuver both juxtaposed her appearance with the room's office-bland decor and denied eye contact. Kira focused on the receptionist's desk at the room's back wall. She was pulling this off.

At the desk, she turned enough to put her hands in her opponent's line of sight. She flexed her right, counting on the gesture to draw his attention, and followed up with a series of quick, fluid movements that removed her gloves and placed them in her jacket pocket. Demonstrating how quickly she could transfer her gloves from her hands to her waist should get him thinking about how fast she could move her gun in the opposite direction. She confirmed her identity with a thumbprint and, only then, turned to assess her competition.

Joshua wore a neatly pressed white shirt and plain black slacks, dressing up a little for the occasion, although his battered Cubs baseball cap didn't seem to fit with that decision. His round face and a scraggly red beard made him look younger than his thirty-four years. He also looked uncomfortable, pinned between armrests a little too narrow for his body. A new gym bag rested on the chair next to him. Its deflated look suggested that, like Kira's gear bag, it contained little more than a dueling tunic.

With a carefully practiced motion, Kira removed her cloak, put her bag on a chair, covered it with the cloak, and settled into the fourth seat down on the right, just a little closer to the receptionist and the changing room doors than her opponent. Back when Diana had been a gunfighter, duelists had been allowed to bring friends and family members along for support. That ended when a series of preduel brawls convinced the Association to bar everyone except combatants and staff from the waiting room. Too bad, really. Family members could be a professional's best allies in convincing a citizen to abandon the match.

She pulled her handset from her belt clip and checked the time. Twenty-three minutes remained before the receptionist called them to the changing rooms. Using her handset the way a hunter uses a blind, she pretended to read as she studied Joshua.

He had his handset out, too, jabbing the screen at irregular intervals. Probably playing a game.

"I can tell you're looking at me." He had a high, nasal voice for such a heavy man. His eyes remained fixed on his handset.

Kira let the hand holding her device fall across her knee and spoke in a matter-of-fact tone. "I'm studying my opponent."

He tapped the screen decisively. "Well, I'm studying you, too."

She sustained her businesslike manner. "That makes sense. We'll be trying to kill each other in a few minutes." He blanched at the word *kill*. Good. Fear led straight to the exit door. She studied him as if he were a prop or a bit of set design she wasn't sure about, increasing his tension with very little effort on her part.

He shifted in his seat. Was it the emotional pressure of her gaze or the physical pressure of the chair arms?

At twenty minutes till, the bolt to prevent late arrival fell into place with an audible *clunk*. Joshua jumped at the sound.

"That keeps people from coming in late." She nodded toward the door. "It still works if you want to leave." She let that assertion hang in the air. It would be best if he spoke before she said anything more.

After a minute or so, he lowered his handset and focused on her. "I'm right, you know."

She replied only by shifting her attention to his face and tilting her head, inviting a reply. Men usually thought they were winning if they talked more, and the more he talked, the more she would know.

He rubbed the bill of his cap and continued. "You people should have paid for my house. I paid my premiums, and you owed me for that. All this fancy talk about exclusions and un-covered causes and such don't change none of that. I don't care what the arbitrators say."

At last, a glimpse of his real motive. He'd be facing her bullet over a claim for about seventy-five thousand unification dollars, probably a bit more than two years of his income. In practical terms, that made no sense. His job provided decent pay and steady work. Even if he had to declare bankruptcy, at his age the loss should be survivable. The emotion driving him to risk his life was probably just righteous anger.

She gave him a slight nod and allowed some softness in her voice. Let him believe her aggressive, all-business demeanor was a mask she was letting slip. "I agree. What the arbitrators say doesn't matter to us now."

His face and shoulders sagged, and he sank into the chair. If he believed someone who mattered listened to him, he might see this as a practical issue rather than an emotional one. And in any practical calculation, facing her made no sense at all. "I un-derstand why you're angry. But you have to decide if the money is worth dying for."

He twitched at the word *dying*. A faint, painful stirring rose in Kira's chest. Pity. The emotion itself wasn't helpful right now, though she tapped into it to make her voice gentle and inviting. "Do you want to tell me why this is so important?"

His handset slipped. He caught it before it could fall and then fumbled as he put it in his bag. He hung his head and stared at his lap. Kira let the silence drag out. He'd feel the need to fill it long before she did.

Finally, he spoke. "Why would you do this to me?" He looked up at her, his face filled with equal parts pain and accusation. "I was a good customer for nearly three years. I always paid on time. I didn't try to cheat you. Now you say all this stuff about how the standard flood coverage wasn't enough and that I needed the expanded flood coverage." His look became positively mournful. "Why would you do that?"

She let her arms grow heavy and looked at the floor, her face a simulation of regret. "I can't do anything about any of that." Now, to make common cause and imply they had shared goals. "Today it's just you and me with a choice to make." She further softened her eyes and pose, showing him something she hoped looked like genuine sympathy, and watched for feedback. There might have been a slight trembling in his hands. She pressed on. "Is it worth it to us to fight this out? Or should we call it a day, go home, and live our lives?"

His shoulders stiffened and his head snapped up. "But I'm right," he said. "I have justice and I have righteousness on my side. That counts for more than all that stuff you think you know. Your bosses are crooks, and my mama always says the righteous shall triumph in the end."

His response sounded desperate, lashing out to defend a

core belief he felt slipping away. His use of *your bosses* rather than *you* was a good sign. He wasn't holding her responsible for his situation. Now, she needed to apply just the right pressure to shatter his brittle resolve.

He rubbed his cap again, fingering its stained brim like a worry bead or a rabbit's foot. The battered hat suddenly made sense. She could use that.

"So, why are you wearing your lucky cap?"

His eyes widened.

She tilted her head, again inviting a response.

He pulled off the hat, gazing at it as he spoke. "I wore this hat for every game of the playoffs and the World Series when the Cubs won. It worked for me then, and I'm thinking it will work for me now."

"So." She left a few seconds of silence before she continued. "Justice and righteousness alone might not be enough?"

He kept staring into his cap.

Let him think on that for a while and see what it did to his confidence.

She needed one more ingredient for this stew of fear, uncertainty, and doubt. "How many people have you killed?"

He pulled the cap to his chest and stared at her. "Wh-Why no one. I ain't never killed nobody in my whole life."

She assumed a look of world-weariness. "I've killed five." Strategic pause. "On the dueling field."

"How do you live with yourself?"

She produced a careless shrug. "It's my job, and I do it."

He stared at her in open-mouthed silence for a few seconds, and then lowered his gaze back to his lap.

She'd heard him, she'd made him question the efficacy of a just cause, and she'd demonstrated that though she might be a little reluctant, killing him was all in a day's work. Now she had to let it all simmer and see if he cracked.

Joshua raised his head and spoke in a low, almost menacing tone. "I know what you're trying to do. You're trying to make me quit. You're probably just as scared as I am. You probably made up all that stuff about them people you killed. You probably never killed nobody on the field. You just make 'em quit here, don't you? Well, let me tell you this: I ain't scared. I'm gonna fight you, and I'm gonna kill you. What do you think about that?"

The doof hadn't even bothered to read her profile. He didn't have the faintest idea what he was up against. The clock gave her about three minutes to let him know.

She let softness and compassion fall away, replaced by her hard, pitiless mask. When she spoke, it was in a cold, flat voice with a faint undercurrent of amusement. The Death's Angel voice. "Look, Joshua. There are some things we need to be clear about. Don't think we've had a moment in here and made a connection. We didn't. And don't think the pretty girl won't kill you. I will."

She stood, literally looking down on him, and nodded toward the changing room doors. "When we get to the dueling field, to me, you're nothing but a target."

He stared at her as if she'd split her cocoon and emerged, not as a butterfly, but as a bird of prey with slashing talons.

"TKC Insurance versus Joshua M. Reardon." The receptionist might have been announcing the next dinner party to be seated.

The randomizer assigned Kira to the left door. She passed

through it, refusing to look at Joshua. Had she pulled it off, or not?

It didn't matter. She powered through her routine. Her street clothes, gear bag, and handset went into the personal effects bin, replaced by her fitted dueling uniform and deliciously soft boots. When the fear came, she administered a self-hug and breathing exercise, and when it departed, she worked her way through her scene analysis. Until she left the field, she was Death's Angel: the cold, self-possessed, implacable killer. He was no longer Joshua, fellow human with feelings and value—he was just another place to put a bullet. Icy calm welled up in Kira's chest and spread through her body. She stepped into the scanner and let the device do its work.

Diana waited on the other side. With a flurry of hand signals, Kira confirmed her readiness and her belief Joshua might not show. Along with routine information, Diana conveyed Joshua had chosen a citizen as his second.

More proof he wasn't ready. Without the guidance of a Guild professional, he'd make all the first-time mistakes during the match and end up in a body bag. If she'd scared him to the exit door, she'd done him a favor, no matter how dire the financial consequences.

Kira took her place beside Diana in front of the judge's table. The opposing second, a brown-haired man dressed in slacks and a sport shirt, fidgeted on the opposite side of the centerline. He made furtive glances toward the door where Joshua should emerge. The EMTs and wards flanked the judge's bench.

A camera tracked Kira, its soulless glass eye staring out from its perch on the perfect white wall. Just how did Association techs keep the enclosure spotless when it had to absorb stray bullets and spattered blood?

The minutes dragged. Kira scuffed at the pseudograss with her boot.

The judge mounted his bench, and everyone straightened up and focused on him. He tapped at his display. "This readout shows that Mr. Reardon has made use of the corridor door in his changing room."

The neutral staff relaxed, but joy rose in Kira's chest. She'd done it. She'd pushed him into a forfeit. Even Joshua's second seemed to be breathing easier.

The final minutes ticked down, and the door to Joshua's changing room remained shut. When the clock showed zero time remaining, the judge signaled for silence. Out of respect for the moment, Kira stopped her nearly imperceptible bouncing on the balls of her feet.

"I declare this match to be a win by forfeit for TKC Insurance and their representative, Kira Clark. This judgment is final, and there can be no further appeals."

Kira turned to Diana, who clapped her on the shoulder. "Nice job."

Kira accepted Diana's congratulations, and looked back toward the field. No blood. No gun smoke. No body. Just a clean stage and a good payday.

HEADS TURNED AS KIRA ENTERED THE GUNSLINGER'S LOUNGE. EVEN without the cloak, left in her locker after her truncated debrief with Diana, the Death's Angel outfit garnered attention. It didn't hurt that an analysis of her forfeit was playing on the vid terminal right above the bar. From his manager's station, Steve greeted her before returning to the task of preparing his staff for the coming onslaught of the Winter Qualification Week crowd. Kira selected an empty booth and snuggled into its soft, dark, padded leather. A few quick taps on the tabletop, and her order for an Angel's Envy was in. She'd nurse that slowly while she waited for Chloe.

Chloe's quickmessage said she still hadn't gotten Diana's blessing on her range work, but she'd be down to the Lounge in half an hour or so. The plan was a quick victory drink and then home to change into Guild jackets for the Qualification Week after-party.

The vid screens that ringed the seating area pulled at Kira's attention. Most carried the wind-down of Qualification Week coverage, although there was less of that than usual. For the first time in nearly five years, no one from any of the Des Moines training complexes had been a contender for the Regional Cup. Under pressure from the patron's lack of interest, the Lounge's selection algorithm switched more screens to the citizen-on-citizen duels that made up the bulk of weekend matches. Some professionals enjoyed ridiculing the citizen combatants, especially when they both missed, forcing a repeat of the match. Kira had never found the contests funny, or even interesting. More like watching drunks trying to punch each other out in a bar's parking lot than anything else.

A replay of Gary's Thursday afternoon duel showed up, and Kira watched his bullet graze the shoulder of his balding, stick-thin opponent. The hit barely drew blood, but it did make the guy drop his pistol. Anticipating return fire, Gary turned sideways and put his arms over his head. The citizen tried to retrieve his weapon from the pseudograss but lost his balance and fell, triggering the motion sensor.

The vid showed Diana and Gary exchanging a congratulatory handshake, but if you knew Diana, you could see trouble coming in her expressionless face and stiff body movements. Over post-match drinks with Chloe and Kira, Gary confided she'd been furious during the debrief. She'd devoted almost the entire session to berating him, hammering on the fact that if his opponent had been a little less flustered or clumsy, he would have been standing defenseless in the kill box while the citizen had all day to set up his return shot. During the seven days after his Guild-mandated rest period ended, Gary faced sixty-three training hours and no break for the weekend.

On the nearest wall, Niles LeBlanc held forth in a one-on-one interview with a commentator. "The guy kept trying to talk to me in the waiting room, and I just kept smacking him down, like, 'No, y'all are not allowed to talk to me. You aren't good enough to talk to me.' Every time he'd open his mouth, I'd shut him down. By the time we got to the field, he was cowed."

Kira rolled her eyes. Aside from his drawl being a bit less pronounced, Niles hadn't changed much. The announcer wrapped up. "So, Niles, thanks for letting us in on some of the tricks of the trade. Lesson for today: verbal interruption can create physical intimidation."

Niles smiled indulgently and responded. "One word of caution there, Dan. It doesn't work with women. Not even I can get them to shut up." He and the host exchanged knowing laughs.

Kira clenched her jaw, noted the name of the host, and

fired off a message to her publicity coordinator. If the host ever made an interview request, she wanted him to know he wasn't getting the meeting and why he wasn't getting it. She might only be seven fights into her career, but she'd already generated enough interest that there was some crap she didn't have to put up with.

The waiter arrived with her drink.

Samuel, the Lounge's big Samoan bouncer, planted himself on a stool near the door. The Qualification Week crowd would start arriving soon. He waved through a group of young men in shiny new gray-and-blue EMR Trust jackets. Some of the smaller companies must be finishing their receptions already. The group didn't include a second or an instructor.

The new grads looked around the room as if they were trying to read a reference manual. After some consultation, they staked out a table near Kira. Several of them had trouble with the table's ordering function, and they dispatched three of their number to forage for drinks.

Those remaining rehashed their trials.

"So, how did you do on Friday?"

"Eight kills, man."

Kira cringed. Had it only been a little over three months ago that she'd referred to a hundred-point hit on a mech as a "kill"? Kira moved deeper into her booth, drew her drink closer, and pulled her hat down low. Maybe that would be enough to hold the unbloodied wannabes at bay.

The discussion around the table got louder. "Forty-five? You're shitting me. You got the rest on nonfatals?"

"Yeah, what've you got?"

"Sixty-three."

"Bullshit." The newly minted gunfighter detailed his record, while the pair nearest Kira held a heated discussion over a disputed match.

"Hey there, beautiful." A young man juggling three drinks stopped at the entrance to her booth. He had chiseled good looks, a broad chest, and a surplus of swagger.

Kira turned her head down to her drink and pulled her arms in, watching him from under the brim of her hat.

He absently passed off two drinks to his tablemates and sat down opposite her in the booth. Evidently not a top scorer in the "Reading Nonverbal Cues" unit.

"I haven't seen you around. You must have been in one of the other qualification groups, right?"

Add an *F* in either "Observation and Awareness" or "Etiquette." A new graduate would obviously be wearing a brand-new gunfighter's jacket without a first-match pin. It was possible no one had explained the rules for approaching veterans to him, but it was more likely he was seeing nothing but "blonde girl."

Or maybe just "prize."

He looked at her expectantly. She let the silence drag out while assigning another failing grade, this one in "Taking the Hint." Getting rid of him before Chloe arrived would take active measures. Keeping her head down, she responded. "You might say that."

He brightened. "I'm with EMR Trust. I got fifty-three kills on my final." He was clearly trying to decide if she was impressed or not, then dredged for a question. "So, how many kills do you have?"

Kira straightened and pushed her hat up to reveal her face. "Five."

He didn't recognize her.

Instead, he looked both smug and embarrassed. "Well, five is pretty good. You must have made it in on nonfatals. That took some serious shooting."

She took a sip of her drink, eyed him over the glass, and used the Death's Angel voice. "I only count the ones that bleed for real."

Shock crossed his face, and a chorus of poorly stifled guffaws sounded from the adjoining table.

Kira remained silent until his ears and cheeks turned a shade of red that was almost cute.

"You can go now."

"OK." He followed his whisper with a hasty retreat to his fellow graduates.

On his return, the ridicule of her young suitor was merciless.

"'Oh, five, that's pretty good.'" The high, sotto-voice recreation provoked a storm of laughter.

"That was Kira Clark, you twig!"

"Hitting on Death's Angel. What's next, genius? Seducing the guild master's wife?"

The mockery had only died down a little when Chloe arrived. She slid into the booth and nodded toward the adjoining table. "What's with them?"

Kira smiled. "Oh, just some new guys learning you can die places other than the dueling field."

CHAPTER 16

The moment the changing room door snapped shut behind her, Kira crashed into the chair and buried her face in her hands.

Fuckitall . . . Fuck it all . . . Fuck. It. All.

Gabriel Hernandez was way too damn stubborn for his own good, and now he and his kids were going to pay for it. Yes, it was tragic that his wife had died in the damn house fire. Yes, TKC was probably avoiding payoff on the property claim through some sort of shitty, underhanded maneuver, and yes, it would be terrible that he and his four children would have to keep living in a two-bedroom apartment and he wouldn't have anything of value to leave them when he was gone. *But . . .* why, oh why, oh why couldn't he see past his own ego and understand that getting himself killed on the dueling field was going to make every single damn thing about this situation worse? Much, much worse.

Kira had done her level best in the waiting room, but the short, wiry man had just sat there and shrugged off every appeal she'd brought to bear, from subtle sympathy and I'm-only-telling-you-this-because-I-admire-your-courage counsel to her colder-than-dry-ice parting assertion that if preserving her life meant taking his, she wouldn't hesitate to do so. At one point, she'd even gone so far as to explain how her parents' untimely deaths had led to her current predicament, and told him he would be putting his kids in the same situation. Nothing worked.

Intransigent bastard. This is what they meant when they talked about people "too stubborn to accept the outcome of the process." He'd lost, and yet he refused to quit. Now it was Kira's job to deal with him.

So suit up and do your damn job.

Kira stood, pulled off her jacket, and worked through her changing room routine.

At least this would be good for her image. Her last four fights had been no-shows, and it was about time to let the fans see some action. Convincing the guy from Louisiana she was a demon who would both kill his body and consume his soul had been a great piece of work, but it happened out of view in the waiting room. Except for the receptionist, all anyone saw was Kira, Diana, and the guy's second listening to the judge declare a forfeit. Gunfighters with a lot of cancellations got higher ratings—intermittent reward was a helluva drug—but she did need to pay off occasionally.

She sighed and faced the clock. Eleven minutes left.

What if she didn't kill him?

During yesterday's simulator session, she'd posted the fastest draw times of her career. What if she used the extra time to take careful aim at the shoulder instead of the heart?

She didn't have to guess what Diana would say: *"Seconds*

have a technical term for gunfighters who don't shoot to kill. We call them 'corpses.'"

Still, if Kira could put a round through his right shoulder while he drew, the resulting spasm would almost certainly make him drop the weapon. Even with the doubtful assumption he could get the pistol off the pseudograss without triggering his motion sensor, he'd be trying to fire through great pain with his nondominant hand. No way in hell that would work. Even after repeated drills where she tried to fire while the shock suit mimicked an injury, Kira was lucky to score a hit one in five times. An untrained citizen? No chance.

Though the maneuver wasn't risk free. Even though she planned a more solid shoulder hit than the one Gary managed a few weeks ago, Diana would probably respond with the same mix of rage and a punishing training schedule. If she figured out Kira avoided the kill shot on purpose, her reaction would be even worse. Still, weighed against Hernandez's life and four orphans . . .

Distracted, she nearly fumbled the final ID check inside the scanner.

On the field, Diana announced the status of Mr. Hernandez's second by making a fist and bringing it to her thigh. A Guild professional. Her index finger extended from the fist. A first-rate one at that. One more sign: *Be careful*.

Hernandez hadn't seemed like the type to hire professional help.

She went through the drill—declaration of intent with the judge, equipment checkout, and finally, standing beside Hernandez, waiting for the Wall to go up. He wore his holster on his right leg—no surprises there. She made up her mind on the way to the start point. She'd give herself one extra beat to align on the shoulder, then take whatever shot presented itself, fatal or not.

Back-to-back, with only the hologram of the Wall between them. She breathed, focused, and visualized herself turning and firing. Following the lead ward's count, she marched down the strikeline, deviating just a few feet to the right at the end. She completed her turn, and a fraction of a second later, the Wall blinked away. Kira drew and found Hernandez a little to her left. She brought the gun to bear, let the sights stabilize on his right shoulder, and controlled her breathing to make the shot perfect . . .

His muzzle flashed. Pain flared in her right thigh, followed by a sharp crack from the bullet's shockwave. Her body tensed in a spasm. Her head struck the pseudograss and her vision blurred. Her gun was gone, dropped during the fall. Pain exploded through her upper leg and spread to her hip. She turned toward it, sitting up to get a good look at the damage. Bright red blood spurted from a rip in the inner thigh of her uniform.

Holy fuck. An artery.

Memory from self-care class: blood loss from a severed femoral artery could cause death in four minutes. She put her palm against the spot and tried to bear down.

A shadow. The clatter of a dropped kit.

"Lie back, Ms. Clark."

She kept pushing down, the blood still spurting under her palm.

A hand pushed hers aside. The voice was firmer, louder, and more insistent. "I said, 'Lie back.'"

Kira flopped back, and strong hands moved her leg and pressed on the inside of her thigh. The EMT flexed as he applied all his strength to stanching the flow, muscles bulging beneath the blood-spattered blue sleeves of his coverall uniform. Another shadow and the clatter from another dropped kit.

Kira gasped. Even through the uniform, the pseudograss rubbed her skin like a steel-wool scrub pad. Her heart raced. She tried to control her breath by count, but her body rebelled, interrupting the exhale to demand more air. Pain spread from where the EMT bore down.

Diana, kneeling beside her. "Hey, it's going to be OK."

Kira grabbed for her hand.

The EMT let up and tore the leg of the uniform away for better access to the wound.

On her thigh, nitrile gloves pinched hard at the surface and deep pain radiated from the wound as the EMT brought his weight to bear again.

The other EMT was on his handset, barely audible. ". . . femoral artery . . . conscious . . . not sure . . . trying to save the leg . . ."

Kira pushed up on one elbow and reached toward her wound and the EMT. "No!"

The EMT holding the wound barked at Diana. "Keep her *still*!"

Diana slid behind Kira and wrapped her arms around her. She spoke softly. "It's OK, it's OK, it's OK. My leg got torn up worse than this in Iran. I've still got it."

True enough, though Diana's leg required constant exercise to keep it limber and it was a mess to look at.

Kira leaned back into her second's chest, and Diana adjusted her grip. The change both enfolded Kira and held her arms to her sides. The EMT who'd been on the phone knelt and unwrapped a tourniquet kit. He reached across Kira's left leg and brought the strap around her right, while the other EMT continued to apply pressure to the spot where she'd been hit. The second EMT wound the torque bar until the strap was snug, then faced Kira and Diana. "This is going to hurt, but it's the best thing."

He directed his last look at Diana. Her grip on Kira tightened.

The medic turned the torque bar, and the tourniquet strap became a band of fire. Kira arched her back and sucked breath through clenched teeth.

Diana whispered to her. "It's all right, baby girl. It's all right. The ambulance is coming."

The tentative win light flashed on her opponent's side of the judge's table. When she tried to focus on it, it was surrounded by fog. Tunnel vision. Hypoxia symptom. She was going to pass out. Fuck. How much blood had she lost?

The pain in her leg became throbbing agony, and her vision narrowed further. When she focused on the EMTs, the rest of the arena vanished into the haze of her deteriorating peripheral vision. Diana's grip became closer and warmer.

The ambulance gurney arrived. A rush of cool air as Diana moved away, and other hands lifted her. A pinprick on her bicep. The words, "Something for the pain." Who said that? Someone held her hand fast while someone else drove a needle into her inner elbow. Straps bound her arm to the support. One of the EMTs held a bag of purplish fluid above her. Blood. It was blood. Someone else's. Not as bright red as hers, but still good. It must be very, very good.

Diana took her hand. Bright red smears marked the places where Kira had touched her, mostly the sleeves. "I'll finish up here. I'll be along as soon as I can."

Kira managed a weak wave as the ambulance crew took her away.

Everything was terribly foggy.

And then it was dark.

CHAPTER 17

"Proceed on my count." The lead ward calls cadence.

"1 . . . 2 . . . 3 . . ."

Kira chooses the exact point where she will enter her kill box.

". . . 4 . . . 5 . . . 6 . . ."

Steady breaths, relaxed hands, even pace.

". . . 7 . . . 8 . . . 9 . . ."

She aligns her foot so the final step will land on the very edge of the box boundary.

". . . 10 . . . 11 . . ."

Left boot planted, she pivots and reaches for her weapon. Her right foot stops just inside the boundary, the Wall comes down, and she pulls her left toe into the kill box while drawing her pistol. Her hands come together at midbody, prepared to rise and aim.

The muzzle of Niles's weapon flashes.

Shit. Shit! SHIT!

A hard punch to her gut announces the hit; burning pain confirms it. Kira bends and braces her left elbow against her knee for support. Her breath comes in gasps.

A distant part of her mind screams: What happened? What

happened? What happened? Did Niles break the pattern? Had she been slow? What?

She moderates her breath and calms the mental screaming. What happened no longer matters. The only important question is how she'll respond.

She lifts her tunic to examine the wound. It's a crappy hit. The entry point is about belly button height and well to the right of center. All told, it's at least a foot from her heart, maybe more. Another inch or so and it would be a clean miss.

He probably didn't bother to stabilize his sights when he swung back toward her, and then jerked the trigger and shot low to boot. How the hell is it that Niles can half ass everything and still make it work?

The fluids leaking from the wound are purplish rather than red, with no sign of spurting. It isn't an arterial hit, although it's possible he's nicked a kidney or the lower lobe of her liver and she's losing a lot internally. Probably nothing worse than a perforated colon, though. Even untreated, it would take her days to die from that, and she'll be on her way to the hospital as soon as the match is over. Kira puts her hand on the wound and the fluid wells between her fingers, though she can't tell if it's venous blood or the remains of yesterday's lunch. Maybe a little of both.

The pain worsens. She looks for Diana. Her second is out from behind the transparent barrier and leaning on the judge's table, as close as she can get until both pistols have been discharged or somebody falls. Diana says nothing, but nods toward Niles, as if reminding Kira of unfinished business.

Kira is alive, she's upright, and she holds a pistol.

The match is still winnable.

CHAPTER 18

The scene on the hospital vid monitor made Kira's chest hurt. It showed her sprawled across her kill box, Diana holding her still while two EMTs worked on her leg. The chyron said "Fallen Angel" and the analysts chattered, dissecting every aspect of her loss. More than a full day after the match, this was still apparently the biggest story in gunfighting.

One definite casualty was the aura of invincibility she'd cultivated over the past ten months. At least nobody called to ask about it. Of course, that might only be because her handset was still locked in her personal effects bin back at the arena, waiting to see if she died or not, and the hospital wouldn't give her a loaner. Or rather, they wanted to charge fifty unis for it, which amounted to the same thing.

No one had come to visit her, either. Despite her promise on the field, Diana hadn't been there when Kira came out of surgery. With a full day of lying in bed behind her and visiting hours about to end, she hadn't heard from Chloe, or Gary, or anyone.

A rap on the door. "Ms. Clark?"

The nurse's thick black hair matched his mustache.

"Come in."

He lowered her bed's side rail and examined her wound. He swabbed away some drainage, made some notes in his data pad, and changed the bandage. After another consultation with the data pad, he adjusted the drip rate on her IV. "I've upped the rate on your QuickHeal. That should get you out of here a little faster." He folded the pad shut and faced her. "Do you have any questions?"

Kira pushed herself a little more upright. "Has anyone stopped to visit?"

The nurse looked away. Why was he so uncomfortable?

An attention-cough came from the door, emitted by a big man in a red-trimmed Association uniform. He carried a slim briefcase. "You've been isolated until you and I have had a chance to talk."

His face was vaguely familiar. Where had she seen him? The greasy-looking red hair, soft, round face, and watery blue eyes fit somewhere, but where?

He held up his handset, displaying the official Association seal. "I'm Deputy Investigator Arnold Jenkins from the Association for Dueling. I've been assigned to your case."

Jenkins. The barfly from the Lounge.

Holy fuck. Jenkins was a shark. Chloe would never believe it.

"Wait . . . If you're Association, why are you always at Gunslinger's instead of Libra's?"

He smiled an indulgent smile. "Investigators have access to both. You'd be surprised at what you can learn listening to people talk after their third drink." He put his handset back in its carrier. "And Gunslinger's has a better selection of IPAs."

Jenkins placed his briefcase on the foot of the bed and opened it. "I'd like to discuss your match with Gabriel Hernandez, but first I need to ask: Do you want either Guild representation or legal counsel present for this interview?"

A lawyer would cost something, and the deductible on the hospital stay was going to eat into her cash reserve enough. Waiting for a Guild rep would mean a reschedule, and it would be that much longer before she could talk to anybody. Besides, if Hernandez had somehow cheated, or even if they thought he might have cheated, the faster that story got out, the better it was for her. "No, I'm fine."

The nurse addressed Kira. "You've got water there if you want it." He pointed to a carafe on the overbed table. "Hit the call button if you need anything else."

Kira thanked him, and he left.

Jenkins reached into his briefcase and withdrew a data pad and omnidirectional microphone. He set them up on Kira's overbed table and ran what looked like a sound check.

"Now, Ms. Clark, will you please repeat your consent to recording this conversation and state that you've waived your right to have legal counsel or Guild representation present?"

He hadn't asked if it was all right to record the conversation before, but she let it go. It would be good to get this over with. "Sure. It's fine if you record, and I don't need a representative."

Jenkins nodded. "Ms. Clark, in your own words, can you tell me about the events leading up to the match?"

Kira sat up a little straighter in bed. "Scheduling made the assignment ten days ahead."

"That's normal at TKC?"

"Yes."

"Did you change your training routine once you knew Mr. Hernandez was your opponent?"

"Diana set the simulator mechs to be about his height, and quick."

"Did you know Mr. Hernandez has four children?"

"Yes, I saw them on the profile and we talked about them in the waiting room."

"That's interesting." Jenkins paused and made a note. "Were you aware his children's mother is dead as well?"

"Yes. We talked about that, too."

Jenkins kept fiddling with the data pad. "Your parents are dead, aren't they, Ms. Clark?"

"Yes."

"How old were you when they died?"

"Nineteen."

"Do you think of yourself as an orphan?"

Heat flushed in her lower neck. "I . . . I guess. I don't think about it that often."

He studied her for a few more seconds, and then looked down at the data pad, where he made a note. "Did you try to communicate with Mr. Hernandez before the match?"

Kira frowned. "We're not supposed to do that."

"But did you?"

"No. Why would I do that?"

Jenkins ignored her question. "Did he try to contact you?"

"No."

"What about Jacob Carver?"

"Who?"

"His second."

"I don't know him."

"He's a Guild member."

"I don't see the freelancers much."

"But you could have seen him at Guild meetings or in the common areas of the arena. Maybe the Gunslinger's Lounge?"

Kira shrugged. "I suppose. Like I said, I don't know him."

Jenkins consulted his data pad, made a few notes, then returned his attention to Kira. "Very well. Can you tell me about the match and the waiting room?"

"There isn't much to tell. We got there at about the same time, we went through security, and then we talked in the waiting room."

"What did you talk about?"

"Like I said, his wife, his kids. How bad it would be for his family if he died."

"Why were you talking about that?" Jenkins's eyes narrowed.

Kira looked at him as if he'd asked why she'd loaded the gun. "I wanted him to fixate on the risks and quit."

"That's something you normally do?"

"I always try to talk them out of it—that's the best outcome for everyone." Kira looked rueful. "He wouldn't give me a chance."

"How's that?"

"He just kept repeating about how TKC owed him, and how he had to see this through for his family."

"Do you think he was right?"

"About what?"

"About TKC owing him?"

Where was he going with *that*? A textbook response was safest. "I don't really know. By the time we get to the waiting room, people with way more information than I have made a decision. I'm just standing up for it."

Jenkins seemed disinclined to pursue that angle and focused on his data pad. "So, that's the waiting room. You go through the changing room, where you're alone, and then out on the field. There, we have video." He tapped the data pad, and an image from the dueling field cameras appeared on the room's vid monitor. It zoomed in on Kira and Diana meeting outside the changing room door. The image zoomed to Diana's fist and froze. "Tell me what's happening here."

Kira swallowed. "Diana is telling me he's got a Guild second."

The image advanced to Diana extending a finger.

"She's telling me he's good."

"Who is?"

"The second."

Jenkins grunted and made some more notes on the data pad. The image switched to Kira's response signs.

"Tell me about these."

"I'm telling her I'm ready and my opponent is determined."

"Because of what he said in the waiting room?"

"Right."

Jenkins chewed on his cheek and made more notes. He let the images play until Kira drew her pistol. At that point, he halted the playback and brought in a close-up of Kira with a two-handed grip on the dueling pistol, looking over the gunsights. "Tell me what you're thinking about, here."

"I'm thinking about firing."

"What's taking so long?"

"What?"

Jenkins made an impatient gesture. "Up until now, you're half to three-quarters of a second ahead of him. Here, you hesitate. It's like you're waiting for something."

She should have expected that question. The commentators had certainly been going on about it.

"I had trouble stabilizing my sights." The lie was both harmless and small.

Jenkins shifted inside his uniform, becoming more upright and tighter. He squinted at the screen. "While you're hesitating, Mr. Hernandez fires."

He let the video run again. Kira's leg buckled and she fell, her face twisting in agony. Jenkins froze the image.

Jenkins looked a little distracted. But it was like he was *trying* to look distracted. Kira shifted in the bed, her muscles tensing. On the monitor, her heart rate jumped, and Jenkins's eyes flicked up to read it. He tapped something into the data pad.

"How tight a pattern do you normally throw, Ms. Clark?"

She tried to match his nonchalance with her own. "I can usually put ten bullets in an eight-inch circle. I can get it down to six inches if I'm having a good day."

"With a two-second draw-to-hit clock?"

"Right."

Jenkins killed the vid image, then looked up from the data pad. "Tell me again about when you were notified Mr. Hernandez would be your opponent."

He went through the details, stopping to question her about different parts of the story, supplying new facts, such as her drink order at a time when Jacob Carver was also at the Gunslinger's Lounge, and skipping around to ask about details at different times and places. He fired up the video again, starting in the middle, running forward and backward, asking for the same information in different ways and with different degrees of detail.

Kira pushed off the blankets. Why was it so hot in here?

Again, he stopped the vid on the frame where she stood with her gun drawn. "You've got an opponent coming into firing position, and you're taking half again as long as your average time in the simulator." He pointed to her gun on the image. "I'm going to ask you again, Ms. Clark: What are you waiting for?"

"I'm waiting for . . . Oh, fuck it. I'm waiting to get a good shot." It was technically true—she wanted a good shot at his shoulder.

"A good shot? Your gun is up and aimed. All you have to do is pull the trigger and you'll hit him in the chest."

Kira sighed. "I wanted it to look good." She waved toward her bandaged leg. "Look, it was a boneheaded mistake, and I paid for it, OK?"

Jenkins sucked on his cheek again, squinting at the image. "All right, let's go through this again. There's a few points I need to clear up."

Kira frowned. "I just told you what happened. Why do you even think I'd let myself get shot like that?"

Jenkins paused, then spoke as if he were addressing a very slow student. "If you know you're going to get hit, where are the best places?"

Kira frowned. "Upper arms. Shoulders. Outer thighs."

"Why?"

Kira made a dismissive gesture. "No vital organs." She resisted adding, *And quit talking to me like I'm the slowest trainee in class.*

Jenkins continued. "When someone is facing you in a two-handed stance, how large a target are the arms and shoulders?"

"Pretty small. But if he hits the inner thigh instead of the outer, I get . . ." She pointed to the bandages on her leg.

Jenkins nodded. "How wide are your thighs?"

What the fuck kind of question was that? "Wide? I don't know. Five or six inches, maybe?"

"You told me your shot pattern fell in a six-to-eight-inch circle against a two-second clock, correct?"

"Right."

"What if there's no clock?"

"No clock?" Kira frowned. "When I practice just mechanics and aim, I can get it down to a two- or three-inch circle."

"So, from your own experience, you know that given enough time, a well-trained marksman can shoot accurately enough to hit either the inner or the outer thigh at twenty yards." Jenkins paused, as if assessing her response. "And you know that Mr. Hernandez had an excellent trainer."

The room became much, much warmer.

An hour and a half later, the water pitcher was empty, Kira's sheets and gown were damp with sweat, and the pain in her injured leg spiked with every heartbeat. She ran her hand over her neck. The muscles were rock hard.

Jenkins returned the microphone to his briefcase, calm as if he'd just completed a presentation on disability insurance. The data pad went in next, and he zipped the case shut.

"Thank you for your time, Ms. Clark. I'll be in touch if we need anything further from you."

He turned and left, shutting the door behind him.

Kira flopped back in bed and looked at the ceiling.

Sweet Jesus, how much trouble am I in?

CHAPTER 19

Kira entered the control cab of Simulator Twenty-Three. Diana glanced at the system clock. "You're late."

Kira flinched. "I'm sorry. I guess I lost track of how long things take while I was in the hospital."

Diana sniffed and kept working at the control panel, but said nothing.

Kira pulled a dueling pistol from its mount by the door, checked the chamber, and put it in her holster. At the control panel, she presented her wrist and Diana gave the simulator control over Kira's shock suit. The system administered a confirming tickle on Kira's bicep. Diana set the shock level to 50 percent.

Kira frowned. "Half? What happened to 'twenty percent is good training'?"

Her trainer ignored the question.

Irritated, Kira pushed her point. "I thought you might take it easy on me my first day back."

Diana worked some additional controls as she replied. "You thought wrong."

It was time to acknowledge the elephant in the room. Kira took a deep breath. "I heard about Gary. I'm sorry."

"You're sorry all over the place this morning, aren't you?" At least Diana faced her when she said it.

Kira folded her arms across her chest and looked at her feet. "I know it's hard for you to lose a client, that's all."

Diana let out an exasperated sigh. "You sound like Howard." Despite the exasperation, her faced softened a little as she said her husband's name, as if hearing it made her a little bit happier. Or in this case, a little less angry. "I appreciate your concern, but I put on the jacket and I made the call. It's part of the job. I'm OK."

"You made a casualty call this morning?" Kira frowned. "I thought Gary's parents lived in Arizona."

"They do. I went to see his sister last night. She's not technically next of kin, but they were close. I owed her the visit."

Kira kept her voice steady. "What did she say?"

Diana shrugged. "She cried. Then she yelled at me. Pretty normal reaction."

"I'm s—" Kira stopped and gathered herself. "That must have been hard for you."

"Everyone grieves their own way."

But what about you, Diana? How do you grieve?

Kira shifted her stance. "Look, I just want to say—"

Diana's face hardened. "I said, 'I'm OK.' That means, 'I'm OK.'" She tugged at the sleeves of her uniform, pulling them farther over her wrists. "Now quit goldbricking and get down to the field. We've got work to do."

KIRA PUSHED HERSELF UP FROM THE FLOOR OF HER KILL BOX. The shock simulating a hip-shattering hit had forced her down on one knee, and she stretched her right leg to relieve the tightness and pain. Two hours and six matches into the session, it was clear Diana mourned the dead by pushing the living to the edge of physical endurance. Kira's gait rolled a little as she made her way back to the judge's table.

Her trainer's voice came over the earpiece. "So, what happened there?"

Kira tossed her spent brass into the case bin. "I was too slow." She picked a fresh round from the ammunition rack, loaded her pistol, and closed the action with a soft click. "The mech was ahead of me, so I should have gone with point-to-aim instead of waiting for sight alignment."

"Very good. Same settings. Let's try that again."

Kira holstered her pistol and took her place beside the mech.

In addition to setting the shock factor at more than twice the normal training value, Diana had cranked the mech's performance so high it responded like a professional gunfighter in top form. So far this morning, Kira had yet to inflict more than a superficial hit, while the mech had sent simulated rounds through most of her vital organs, leg bones, and spine. At least it hadn't killed her outright yet.

Kira walked to the start point and stood back-to-back with the mech. Marching to the cadence of the recorded ward's voice, she entered the kill box well off the strikeline, turned, drew, and fired. The kick from the recoil hit at almost the same instant as the sting on her shoulder from the mech's shot. Her mechanical opponent staggered, but didn't fall. After building to a crescendo of scalding pain, the burn in her shoulder subsided.

God damn. This is getting old.

Diana asked for Kira's self-critique and supplied a few points of her own. Kira asked for dispensation to get a drink of water, Diana granted it, and Kira pulled a bottle from the cooler under the judge's table. Diana called her back before she'd gulped down even half the liquid.

Kira set aside the water bottle and reloaded her weapon. She ached from the hits she'd taken, and there were undoubtedly more to come. Yet, she took her position and waited for the simulation to resume. All too soon, the recorded voice rang out.

The session became a blur of pain and frustration. She wanted to quit. She wanted Diana to let up. Neither one was going to happen. It was just barely possible she'd keep her job after walking off the field in a snit, but Diana would forever regard her as a person who folded under pressure.

She altered her route to the kill box, focused on the speed of her draw, and made the fastest turns she could manage. Again and again, the mech defeated her, and the suit punished her with a painful jolt.

When the clock showed noon, Diana announced they'd work through lunch, although she did allow Kira to devour two protein bars and wash them down with a bottle of energy drink before resuming the session.

The day's eighteenth match left Kira doubled over in the kill box, trying to mitigate the pain of a simulated gutshot. When the burning sensation finally stopped, Diana rattled off about boot placement and rotation timing or some damn thing. Kira half listened to the instruction, said something noncommittal in response, and walked back to the judge's table when Diana told her to jog. At the table, she flung her spent brass in the general direction of the case bin, jammed a fresh cartridge into her gun, and shoved the weapon into her holster. She stood with her arms folded across her chest, waiting for the recorded ward's voice. In the earpiece, Diana admonished her to "straighten up." Whatever the hell that was supposed to mean.

On command, Kira marched down the field with the mech, stood at the start point, took her ten paces to the kill box, turned, and prepared to fire.

Agony blossomed in her chest—a fatal hit. She dropped the gun and wrapped her arms around herself, desperate to reduce the pain. Her vision blurred, she squeezed her eyes shut, and the torment continued.

When the shock finally stopped, she was down on all fours.

Diana's voice came through the earpiece. "So, what just happened?"

Several pithy replies popped into Kira's head, but she remained silent.

Diana's voice again, still calm. "Say again? I didn't quite catch it."

Kira trusted herself to whisper. "I lost."

"Say it again."

Kira let anger flow into her voice. "I said, 'I lost!'"

"Again."

Despite the lingering pain, Kira rose to her feet and shouted toward the control cab. "I. Fucking. Lost. OK?"

"What happens when you lose?"

Diana's voice contained the faintest flicker of something gentle. Compassion? Sadness? A vision interrupted Kira's search for a smart-ass response: her body, crumpled like a discarded gum wrapper in the kill box, with a dark stain spreading around it as her life bled away through a nine-millimeter hole in her chest.

Kira hung her head and spoke just loud enough for the throat mic to pick it up. "I die. When I lose, I can die."

This time, the voice in her ear held the tiniest bit of warmth. "So, what keeps you alive?"

Letting her voice go flat, Kira gave the expected reply. "Fast walks, fast draws, and straight shots."

After a long silence, Diana spoke. "OK. That's enough for today. Put the gear away, police your brass, give me three slow laps, and meet me in Conference Room F."

KIRA HESITATED AT THE DOOR TO THE CONFERENCE ROOM. WHAT was she walking into? The door's tiny window revealed Diana at the room's worktable, focused on her data pad. Kira opened the door and dropped into the opposite seat. Diana remained engrossed in whatever she was reading.

Hunger gnawed at Kira's stomach. The air conditioner kicked on and poured cold air from the ceiling. The shock suit and uniform, soaked with sweat from the session, grew clammy and stank. As the chill settled in, knots formed in Kira's abused muscles, and her body began to quiver.

Diana wrote something on the pad with a stylus, tapped the device a few times, and then wrote something else. Kira moved her chair, scraping its legs across the tile floor, and planted her elbows on the table with a thud.

Diana ignored her.

The air conditioner kept pouring out cold air, and Kira's legs stuck to the chair's cooling plastic through her sweat-drenched pants. Her jaw began to tremble. Soon, her teeth would be chattering. What was Diana still so mad about?

The stony silence dragged on, punctuated only by the occasional tap on the data pad.

She wasn't going to let Diana end things like this, if that's what this was about. If Diana wanted to assign Kira to another trainer, there had to be some kind of discussion. Kira's voice nearly cracked as she spoke. "Look, Diana, I know I'm supposed to shoot first. OK? I get it. You can let it go."

Diana looked up, as if noticing Kira for the first time. She put the data pad on the table, sat back in her chair, and studied Kira over steepled fingers. "It's not what you know that keeps you alive, baby girl." She paused and sharpened her focus. "It's what you can remember at the right time."

Kira sagged into her chair. "God damn it, Diana. I'm sorry, I—"

"Don't be sorry. Be better."

Kira hung her head. She wanted to cry, but she wasn't going to. Not where Diana could see.

Her trainer's voice remained cold. "I'm going to a funeral this weekend. I can't afford to screw up another Saturday by going to yours."

Kira's stomach knotted with more than hunger. "Do you really think I'm that bad?"

"Not when you're paying attention. Not when you're on it." Diana held up the data pad and pointed to a graph of Kira's performance. "Do you know you got faster later in the day? At least when you weren't screwing around and throwing a tantrum."

Kira looked at the floor.

"Aside from that, you kept improving." Diana put the pad down and faced Kira. "So, baby girl, what's the lesson?"

Kira looked down at her hands. That hid the anger in her face, but not her voice. "Shoot first or die."

Diana relaxed and sat back. "That's right. Never forget they're shooting at you, too. When you aim, settle for good, because waiting for perfect can kill you."

Kira kept her head down. "I knew what I needed to do when we started. Believe it or not, nearly bleeding to death did make an impression."

Diana snorted. "It's too easy to treat that as a one-off and go back to old habits." She tapped the data pad. "Now, though—I think you know it in your bones."

The knot in Kira's stomach loosened.

Ever so slightly, Diana's tone softened. "Listen, everyone knows you're the Queen of the Waiting Room. I love that. The company loves that. A win where your opponent takes the door is a risk-free win, and we'll take as many of those as we can get. But"—Diana folded the pad open again—"you have to back that up with performance *on* the field. I've scheduled some time tomorrow morning with a physical therapist. You've got a catch when you rotate right, and I want them to look at it. Then I want Ross to work with you on draw speed in the afternoon. I've got

Firing Point Seven reserved. Work on shooting from both the right and the left. It may be time to use that."

She punched her data pad, and Kira's handset chirped in acknowledgment.

Diana continued. "I sent you the full schedule. There's a bunch of firing range work with specialists to get you built back up, then we go into the simulator. I hope you don't have plans for the weekend."

"I was going to go to the funeral."

"I allowed for that."

Kira made a face and sighed.

A note of irritation crept into Diana's voice. "They're only giving us five days to get you ready for a fitness assessment. We're stretched thin, and losing Gary makes it worse. It's another two months before we get any new graduates." She drummed her fingers on the tabletop. "Now that the Review Board closed the investigation, they want you back on the field."

"So, I'm clear?" Why hadn't Diana told her that before now?

"Yes, you're clear. They've looked at Jenkins's report and chosen not to go forward. From what I can tell, Jenkins tried to convince them you waited to fire so Hernandez could hit you in the outer thigh and give you an excuse to miss. Instead, Hernandez either double-crossed you or botched the shot. It's plausible, given the evidence."

"Then how come I'm in the clear?"

"No motive. Even with open access to your financials, he can't show a payoff. He pushed the idea you did it so the Hernandez kids wouldn't be orphans, but apparently the Review Board didn't find that credible."

That was good for the case, but what did it say about her?

Diana wrapped up. "No evidence of prematch communication, and the fact you nearly died does weigh in your favor."

"At least I got something for all that blood."

Diana looked disgusted rather than amused. "See that you don't need it again. Jenkins may close this one out, but he'll be watching you. Go clean up and get some rest."

"He can watch all he wants. I didn't do anything wrong."

"You say that like it matters." Kira stared, but Diana just shrugged. "He thinks you've escaped this time, but he'll be looking for the chance to snag you again. Don't give it to him."

"OK."

The briefing should have been over, but Diana clearly wasn't ready to end it. She pressed her hands together and fixed her gaze on Kira. "I understand what you were trying to do. You shifted your aim from his chest to his shoulder because you didn't want to kill him."

Kira kept her face blank.

Diana studied Kira for a few seconds before she resumed. "Understand you don't have that luxury. That's part of what today was about, too."

Kira responded with the smallest of nods.

Diana shook her head. "Dismissed."

Kira left. When the briefing room door shut behind her, she allowed herself a sigh of relief. Getting back into Diana's good graces would be a long-term project.

Staying alive long enough for it to happen might be the hard part.

KIRA ENTERED THE GUNSLINGER'S LOUNGE AND STOPPED TO savor the smells of old leather, polished wood, and strong beverages. Just a quick drink to relax, maybe some nachos on the side, and then home to pack her lunch and sleep. Leave it to Diana to assume 6:30 a.m. was a perfectly normal time for a physical therapy appointment.

Kira picked a booth and found herself facing a vid screen showing a replay of Gary's last match. He stumbled a little coming out of the turn, taking an extra second or so to stabilize and orient himself before he drew. By the time Gary's weapon cleared his holster, his opponent had already drawn a solid bead on him. Gary fired when his hands came together at midbody; a desperation shot. Slow motion showed his muzzle flashing a few tenths of a second before his opponent's bullet struck. Gary staggered as the projectile buried itself in his abdomen. Across the field, his opponent twisted in agony as Gary's round tore into his lower chest. Both fell to the pseudograss, but the motion sensors gave the match to the citizen.

The screen split, showing the activity in both kill boxes. Diana was useful—calming Gary, handing implements to the EMT, and assisting the technician to do what could be done for the wound. The citizen's second mostly sat by helplessly, repeating, "You're going to make it," until it became irritating. The scrolling text said Gary died later that night, after surgery failed to halt the blood loss from a damaged kidney. The citizen was still hospitalized, but expected to recover.

A shout pulled Kira away from the video. "Hey, Jack's in a bleed-off!"

People gathered in front of the big screen over the bar. Some of the sets on the wall changed to show the match and the sound came on. The screen's left-right split displayed Jack Basinger, a gunslinger in the orange-and-blue colors of Consolidated Trust, on one side and a citizen in beige on the other.

Jack tore his tunic, using it to improvise patches for the holes in the front and back of his upper chest. His second and an EMT stood nearby, poised to help, but waited for a request from Jack. A few feet back, the ward watched the group, his stun rifle slung over his shoulder and his hands on his transponder. If either the second or the EMT touched Jack, the ward would key the transponder and the system would treat the touch as if it were a fall.

On the opposite side of the screen, the other EMT and the citizen's second positioned themselves near their man, with their assigned ward watching over them. The citizen gasped and shifted as he tried to position his hands to stop the fluids escaping from an abdominal wound. The second, dressed in a Guild freelancer's black-and-white, responded to the crisis by kneeling low and counseling his client. Only the sweat on the second's brow, rendering his dark skin unnaturally shiny in the field lights, betrayed the intensity of his concern. The field mic either wasn't picking up what he was saying, or the vid producer wasn't running it.

A shout came from the crowd in front of the bar. "C'mon, Jack! You can outlast that dirtbag."

On the screen, Jack shifted his stance and adjusted his grip on the front chest patch. He wavered.

Another voice came from the crowd. "Jack's got the worst of it. He's not going to make it."

"I've got a hundred that says he will."

"You're on!"

"One-seventy says you're full of shit!"

"Put your money down. I say Jack stands through."

The bartenders found themselves pressed into service as bookies, accepting cash and the markers that identified the bets from the surrounding crowd. The group grew in size and enthusiasm, some shouting for Jack, others for the citizen. Nearly every screen displayed the match.

At the table next to her, a gunfighter from Hounsfield & Associates watched the nearest screen with wild eyes. He shouted and pounded on the table as if it were the final minutes of a soccer game instead of a life or death struggle.

Kira stared around the room. People stood throughout the Lounge, cheering or booing with each shift in either contestant's fortune. Acting as if this couldn't be them or someone they knew as soon as tomorrow.

"What the fuck is wrong with you people?" Had she said that out loud? The noise level made the question irrelevant.

The pounding and shouting became louder as both combatants began to sway. Kira paid her bill and fled through the main door, leaving half her drink and an untouched order of nachos behind.

CHAPTER 20

Kira's gut burns, sweat soaks through her uniform, and her heart races. Her stomach demands the chance to throw up, but that seems like a bad idea. At least until she gets this shot off.

The motion sensor keeps Niles in place, but he's turned his shoulder toward her and uses his arms to cover his head.

Kira pushes through the pain and comes upright into a range-perfect two-handed shooting stance. She tries to align the sights. Instead of a gentle figure eight motion, the aiming dots jerk and wobble with each new twinge from her abdomen or tremor in her arms. It will be pure luck if she hits him at all, much less in a vital area. Sticky warmth spreads down her thigh and touches her calf.

She lowers her arms and braces herself on her knees. Her mouth is dry, the uniform clings to her skin, and she shivers. The gun feels awkward in her hand, as if it's suddenly become too big and too heavy. She smells like a raw steak starting to go bad.

The commentary plays in her head.

"Stan, this should be an easy shot for one of the Guild's most accurate marksmen. I wonder what the problem is."

"Niles is getting the benefit of that hit. That wound isn't

going to get any better, so if she can't get a shot off now, she's finished."

If she misses, it's over. She falls to the pseudograss, the EMT takes care of her, and she wakes up in the hospital. To what? Long-term injuries, possibly. Joblessness and foreclosure, certainly.

And then what? Small parts assembly until she's crippled by carpal tunnel? Twelve-hour days of sewing, picking fruit, or mopping up toxic waste and nights of sleeping in an open barracks until the morning she can't wake up? Maybe one of those skeevy "personal services" gigs where the services get really, really personal. In all cases, her life used up and wrung out for someone else's benefit, and then discarded like an old rag.

She has one failure-proof shot left. She can put the pistol in her mouth and pull the trigger, cheating her creditors of their prize.

Kira stares at the gun and lets the possibilities spool out in her mind while fluid oozes down her leg.

To die: to sleep; no more; and, by a sleep to say we end the heartache and the thousand natural shocks that flesh is heir to . . .

A small stab of pain, the dying complaint of some clutch of cells in her abdomen, reminds her she doesn't have time to be Hamlet. Fog already obscures the edges of her vision, and she needs to do something before she passes out. Putting her own brains on the back wall will be original, and she'll never hear anyone say she failed.

OK—Ophelia it is.

CHAPTER 21

Kira zipped her Guild jacket up to her throat and shoved her hands in its pockets. Her handset showed the vehicle as more than twenty minutes away, but waiting on the sidewalk in front of their apartment gave her and Chloe a chance to enjoy fall before harsher weather arrived. Like the party they were about to attend, it was a way to celebrate their continued presence among the living after nearly fourteen months as gunfighters.

The event wasn't billed that way, of course. The gathering, held at the venerable 801 Steak and Chop House atop Des Moines's tallest building, honored all the members of their gunfighting class who fulfilled their twenty-six-match commitment to TKC. It was an expensive place, but the Guild local could afford to splurge. There were only seventeen of them left to feed.

Chloe's face scrunched up as she punched numbers into her handset. "OK, how can there be only seventeen? We started with eighty-one."

Kira stretched, and tried to remember. "Two traded right after graduation."

"Got that."

TKC's Contract Adjustment Division doubtless wished they could have those back, but the roster had seemed flush at the time. Kira thought some more. "Five guys paid off their signing bonuses and quit."

Chloe nodded and punched the numbers in. "Yeah, they bailed after they got hit."

"Not Perkins." Kira laughed a little. "Just hearing the bullet go 'crack' when it passed his ear was enough."

"Oh right."

"Holst and Singh, medically retired." One was bedridden. The other lost an eye but, incredibly, survived. "Steve Escher, still on leave."

"Do they think he'll finish?"

Kira's shrug hit the limits of her jacket. "Spinal regen is tricky. It'll be six months before they know anything."

"So that's fifty-four, then." Chloe stared at her handset.

From their class of eighty-one, fifty-four deaths in the line of duty. Could she remember them all? Tory Phelps had been first, taking a bullet straight through the heart during his initial match. Cabot Anand was the most recent. They'd delayed the party until the Saturday after Thanksgiving so he could finish, but he ended his twenty-sixth match with a bullet in his spleen and bled out on the way to the hospital. In between? Too many to even remember their faces. Not to mention the ones that weren't in their class. Though in the last year, only Gary's death had breached the charmed circle surrounding Diana's clients.

Chloe returned her handset to its carrier. "Maybe we're all out of our heads."

"You mean about the extensions?" Throughout August and

September, TKC had offered fat bonuses to anyone about to complete their required service if they would commit to an additional six matches. Kira grabbed it right away. Chloe a bit later. Adrian Miles, who talked about craps tables and commodity trading with equal abandon, ignored the advice of his second and committed just before the offer closed.

Kira shivered again. There had to be something less morbid to talk about. "So, what did the engineer say about the foundation?"

Chloe sighed. "He told me it's going to take another ten thousand unis to get it in good enough shape to rent." She shoved her hands into her jacket pockets and looked down at the sidewalk. "That's on top of the five thousand I already spent."

"Ugh. That's too bad. I still think the duplex is a good idea."

"The only idea I have, so I gotta run with it."

"You'll get it fixed up and it'll work. It's just gonna take a little longer."

"I suppose so." Chloe looked down the street, as if she could turn away from the topic and make it vanish.

Kira tried again to lighten the mood. "It's only six matches, five to go for you. Maybe not even that."

Chloe waved Kira's assertion away. "Six is what we just signed up for."

"Yeah, but if one of us takes the pro fight, you really think they'll hold us to six? Besides, the purse will be big enough you can just buy your way out."

That's what being rich meant, after all—you could just buy your way out of your problems. The richer you were, the bigger the problems you could buy your way out of.

Kira squeezed her friend's shoulder. "If I win, I'm taking you with me."

"Maybe." Chloe shivered a little. "Diana says you hear about five pro fights for every one that happens. Companies don't like to do it."

"Yeah, but if you win it, you're not just free, you're *rich*." Kira conjured a vision of the winner's purse in her mind. It looked like a pile of glittering gold coins, a treasure that would free her from all her worries. Diana would remind her a dragon guarded that golden hoard—to claim it, she'd have to beat another professional gunfighter.

Chloe pulled herself further into her jacket and sounded even more morose. "I guess we'll see."

They stood in silence. Kira racked her brain for a happy topic, something to cheer up Chloe before the driver arrived. If not actually happy, just getting her to think about something besides dead gunfighters and crumbling foundations might be enough. "Are you going to invite Danny to Thanksgiving?"

Chloe smiled. "Nah. I think it's too soon to let Mom grill him. We deserve some fun, first."

"Oh? And just how much fun are you planning to have?"

"Cut it out. You sound like my brothers." Chloe blushed a little.

That was an improvement, but it would be a mistake to push it further. Chloe had been dating Danny less than a month.

Even in the November cold, the sidewalks still hosted a fair number of people darting in and out of the shops on Ingersoll Avenue. A property recovery team in blue body armor rounded the corner and headed in their direction. Kira lowered her eyes and fought the urge to pull out her handset and check the status of her loan. Of course it was current. She'd checked just this morning, and she had activity alerts, and . . .

A young, blonde-haired woman in a too-large brown jacket broke into a run. In response, the property recovery team took up pursuit, and people on the sidewalk scrambled out of their way. The woman ran into the street, gambling there weren't any human-controlled vehicles in the traffic flow. The drivers, controlled by the traffic grid, avoided her with fluid swerves. One of the team members touched something on his belt, and the woman fell to the pavement, thrashing and screaming. The two blue-clad men took up positions on either side of her, and her writhing stopped.

Something squeezed Kira's forearm. She looked down to find her jacket unzipped and her hand inside, reaching for the gun in her shoulder holster. The pressure on her forearm came from Chloe's hand, and her friend's eyes pleaded as much as her voice. "Kira, you can't . . ."

Still standing in traffic, the team cuffed and shackled the woman, then hoisted her up. She sobbed as the specialists frogmarched her to the sidewalk on the far side of the street.

Kira relaxed her arm but couldn't move while Chloe maintained her grip. "It's OK. I'm not going to do anything."

Chloe let go, but kept her eyes fixed on Kira. Kira withdrew her hand and zipped the jacket back up. Chloe softened a bit.

They watched as an official white van arrived, its rear doors opened, and the specialists loaded the woman into it.

When the van pulled away, Chloe turned to Kira. "I know that was hard, but we're just a couple of fast guns, and those guys"—she pointed to the property recovery team—"those guys are banks and cops and big companies and . . ." Chloe paused, searching for words. "They're, well, shit, they're everybody. You and me can't fight everybody all by ourselves."

Kira wrapped her arms around her chest and struck the bulge of her holstered pistol beneath her jacket. She caressed it, savoring its hard bulk and the implication of power. "I know. I've just never seen a binder work before." She'd read about the implant, of course. Spare, clinical prose described the binder as a device placed in the base of the spine and wired to the sciatic nerves. When activated, it produced the painful, debilitating spasm they'd just witnessed, but no long-term effects—at least not any effects anyone without a binder regarded as important. That allowed it to be used as often as needed. Normally, it was keyed to a coded signal, so if a confined person got too far from their workplace, pain forced them back. No telling exactly how the woman had beaten that, but there were ways. The binder could also be triggered on an ad hoc basis, as the team had done. There wasn't any way to avoid that. Not that anyone ever talked about, anyway.

If Kira's future came down to a choice between wearing a binder and fighting a dragon, the dragon fight looked pretty damn good.

Her handset sounded, and a two-seat, copper-colored vehicle pulled up to the curb in front of them. Its doors opened, folding back like the wings of a beetle. Chloe and Kira slid into their places, and their ride prattled its thanks for their business and directed them to buckle up.

"I wasn't trying to draw back there." Kira faced Chloe, who responded with a side-eye.

"Don't try to tell me you just had to scratch."

Kira looked down at her knees. "No. I was reaching for the gun. But I didn't want to use it. I just wanted to feel it. To know it was there. I think it's kind of like when you cross yourself when you're in trouble."

"Hmph." Chloe clearly needed some convincing on that point.

Across the street, the property recovery team relaxed and broke out cigarettes, a small celebration after their catch. Chloe was right about everybody backing them. Everybody with power, anyway.

The driver played its second warning message on fastening her seatbelt, and Kira buckled in. Satisfied with the safety of its riders, the vehicle eased away from the curb. Across the street, one of the specialists touched the side of his helmet, talking to someone via an earpiece. He said something to his partner, and they stubbed out their smokes. A driver pulled up beside them, and his partner jogged to the door on the far side of the vehicle, as if eager to chase down the next runaway.

Kira tore her eyes away and slid down in the seat. For now, she was on the right side of all that. If she missed a couple payments, though, they'd come for her, and her gun would be every bit as useless as Chloe thought it was.

The driver entered the high-speed section of the traffic flow and raced into the gathering darkness.

CHAPTER 22

Something was loud. Really, really loud. A sizzling noise. Kira turned, and everything hurt. Mostly her head. But also her joints. And her back, even though she lay on something soft. Dry mouth. She tried to wet her lips with her tongue. They tasted awful. Where was she? This didn't feel or sound like the hospital. But she hurt more than enough.

"C'mon, baby girl. Time to wake up. It's Sunday."

Oh hell. I'm on Diana's couch.

Kira rolled to a sitting position and cradled her head in her hands. "God. What is that racket?"

"Pancakes frying. If you think that's loud, wait until I start laying out the plates."

There ought to be a special-purpose curse a hungover night owl could hurl at a cheerful morning person, but Kira couldn't think of one. Instead, she opened her eyes. On the other side of the living area, four stools stood before a pass-through counter. Beyond the counter, dressed in a dark red housecoat, Diana worked the pancake griddle.

Kira pushed herself up, trying not to move her head any

more than absolutely necessary, and crossed the twelve miles or
so separating her from the kitchen area. When was the last time
she'd been this hungover? Using the serving bar for support,
she climbed onto one of the stools and looked up and down the
counter.

"C'mon, Diana, don't fuck with me. Where's the coffee?"
Her voice came out even rougher than she'd expected.

Diana produced an empty cup and a full decanter from below the counter. "Here you go."

"Thank God." Kira seized the decanter and poured. Holding
the cup with both hands, she drank with the reverence of a sup-
plicant imbibing communion wine. She sighed as she finished.
"That's good. Thank you." She poured a second cup but took
only one long sip before setting it down.

Diana shouted toward the bedrooms. "Breakfast in five!"

Kira winced at the decibel level. Diana, ever the believer in
the instructive value of pain, had probably done it on purpose.
By the time Kira finished another therapeutic gulp of coffee,
Howard marched down the hallway in flannel boxers and an
oversize T-shirt, scratching his belly with one hand and holding
his handset in the other. He was a little taller than Diana, and
broad shouldered. The puffiness of recent sleep made his face
look even softer and friendlier than usual.

Diana grinned and put a full cup of coffee in front of her
husband. He grinned back and they kissed. Diana set up the
decanter for a refill and went back to supervising the pancakes.
"OK, we're ready." She looked toward Kira. "Can that stomach
of yours take something solid?"

"I think so. That smells good."

"Well, you did leave most of whatever you ate last night in the toilet."

Embarrassment added itself to Kira's physical miseries. "Oh God. Did I make a mess?"

"No. You're as accurate in the bathroom as you are on the dueling field. Cleaned up with one flush. Thanks to the gunfighter's cut, I didn't even have to hold your hair out of the way."

Howard shuddered. "Can we have a new subject? I was planning to be hungry."

Diana doled out plates and put the first round of pancakes and sausages on them, following up with butter and warm syrup before rounding the counter and taking the stool next to Howard. With everything and everyone in place, Kira nibbled tentatively at her food. Diana cleared her plate with measured efficiency, while Howard plunged in with real enthusiasm.

As they finished, Diana poured another round of coffee.

Howard pushed the empty plate away. "That was a great breakfast, Di. Kira and I will get this cleaned up."

Apparently, people who crashed on the couch uninvited and stayed for breakfast did not receive a guest's immunity from housework. Fair enough.

Kira slid off her stool and winced as her heels struck the floor. Her hangover recovery had a long way to go.

Diana poured another cup of coffee for herself and got comfortable on her stool. That the person who cooked didn't clean up and the person who cleaned up didn't cook was such a consistent rule of the Reynolds household that Kira had never heard them discuss it.

Howard ran an AutoSponge over the pancake griddle,

slowing over the dirtiest parts so the device had plenty of time to break down and absorb the organic compounds. In its wake, the cooking surface was spotlessly clean, the cauterized remains of the food digested and swept away. Kira stacked plates in the dishwasher.

Without breaking his concentration on the griddle, Howard spoke. "So what brings you here this morning? Looks as though you had a rough night."

What had happened last night? Chloe had left the party early, spending the night at her parents' place so they could travel to a cousin's wedding first thing in the morning. Diana and Howard had bowed out early as well, leaving Kira, a Guild steward whose name she couldn't remember, and a couple guys from the class to drink, talk, and toast departed class members. Somewhere in there, she got very drunk, and everyone else paired off or headed home. Then she'd come here. Why had she done that? The driver could have taken her back to her apartment and she could have spent the night in her own bed instead of on the Reynoldses' couch.

"I'm not sure, really. I wanted to be someplace safe, and I didn't want to be alone. I'm sorry if I intruded."

From her perch across the serving bar, Diana entered the conversation. "Chloe told me about the property recovery team."

Kira gathered the glasses and put them in the dishwasher. She didn't have to look at anyone while she did that. "I guess that might be part of it. I knew about binders, and teams tracking people down and all that, but seeing it happen in front of you is . . . different."

Diana switched to her slightly-too-casual voice. "Are you OK with your loan?"

"Oh yeah. I'm current, I've got a couple payments in savings in case there's a hiccup with my pay deposit or something, and I've knocked off a big chunk of principal since I started drawing a full salary and getting endorsement deals and everything."

"But not paid off." Of course, Diana would cut straight to the main issue.

"No." Kira rearranged the glasses. "Not paid off."

Howard washed the AutoSponge. "So, just how large are those debts of yours, anyway?"

It was a rude question, but Howard asked it innocently enough. Kira had always begged off when Diana tried to get into details, but maybe that was a mistake. She glanced at Diana and took a slow, deep breath. "As of the last payment, I owe 189,865 unification dollars."

If Howard intended to conceal his shock, he did a bad job of it. "How did you do that? That's more than our mortgage."

Kira pulled in on herself. What must they think of her? Irresponsible, foolish girl who'd gotten in way over her head. But maybe she'd avoided this long enough. Maybe there was no cure but to tell the whole story. Get it out there. She took another deep breath. "Well, the year I started college, my dad went in for gall bladder surgery, and he got one of those resistant staph infections. Mom probably wasn't very good about isolation, and she got it, too. By the time I came home from school, they were both in one of those quarantine things at University Hospital in Iowa City."

The units looked like the "bubbles" used to protect people

with compromised immune systems from the outside world, but in this case, they protected the rest of the world from patients infected by untreatable, ravaging bacteria.

"It went on for weeks, and in the end, we couldn't even hug to say goodbye." Kira stopped working. Her heart pounded, and she wanted to run away. She kept talking instead.

"Then they showed me the bill. It was literally more money than I'd ever seen in my life. They took everything—all my parents' savings and their retirement money, the life insurance, and my college money and everything. They even took the house and some stuff that really belonged to me." Resentment welled up in Kira's chest. "The Dickens collection was supposed to be mine. It was from my grandma."

Diana spoke up. "Even if they cleaned out your parents' estate, they couldn't stick you with that bill, could they?"

"No, they couldn't. But I was at Paget College, which is like thirty-five thousand a year tuition and another twelve for room and board, and I'm flat broke. I mean, *nothing* but a couple hundred in my checking account, my clothes, and the stuff in my dorm room." She rubbed her upper arms, as if she could scrub away old indignities. "They had me talk to the financial aid people right away, of course. They offered me a nice break on the tuition, even a little on fees, but the big thing they offered was—"

"Loans." Disgust tinged Howard's voice.

"Yeah, loans." Kira steadied herself. "I understand it looks irresponsible as hell now, but I was nineteen. I'd just lost my parents and my home, and if I dropped out of school, I'd lose all my friends and my future, too. So I signed."

Diana frowned, as if she were trying to follow the story and keep the math straight in her head at the same time. "So then what happened?"

"I wanted a career in theater, and I wanted an MFA. I believed in myself, I believed in my talent, and I believed that if I did what I loved, the money would come." Kira paused. At least they didn't laugh out loud. "There was no one to stop me, and so I just kept going to school and signing loan contracts. Then I borrowed more to live in New York. Even in a walk-up with four other girls and a bathroom down the hall, the bills pile up when you aren't making anything. I did stuff that was supposed to be good for my career and that paid by exposure." She shook her head.

Howard scratched the back of his neck. "Even so, I don't see how you could possibly spend that much."

"Oh, a lot of it isn't what I spent. The whole time you're in school, interest is piling up. Every time you convert the loans and refinance, there are fees. I never had cash, so of course they roll those into the principal. A service, you know?" Her voice was bitter. "Then, when you have trouble, there's late fees, and penalty interest that compounds, and default waiver charges." Kira raised her left hand in a helpless gesture. "And then there's so much. The only way I had any hope of getting out from under it was to consolidate it all and get the interest rate down. And the only way to do that was if I offered a lifetime services contract as security. I knew there were risks, but I could make the payments and the interest rate wasn't too bad, even for somebody with my crappy credit. I got an office job with a bank, and I thought I could handle it. But the principal was up over three hundred fifty thousand unis." Kira stared at the floor. "Then, I got laid off, missed a couple payments, and my interest went up over 25 percent. There was no way I could cover that."

Kira resumed filling the dishwasher. "I got the call telling me foreclosure was in progress, and I should plan to wind up my affairs and report to a collection point"—she gasped, but steadied herself—"to get a binder installed." Her hands shook as she put the silverware in the rack. "Then this ex-boyfriend told me about an opening for a gunfighter. Dad taught me to use a gun when I was a kid, and I'd just finished a play where I worked with the armorer, so I thought I could do it. But the main thing was that the signing bonus was enough to get me current." Kira closed the dishwasher and began the start sequence. Had she added the soap? She opened it to check. She had. She closed it and started the machine again. "I figured I'd have it all paid off after I got my twenty-six matches in, and then I'd be free, but . . ." She fell silent.

"Interest." Howard's voice was full of sympathy. "Most people forget about interest."

"Yeah. I'm always shocked at how much it eats up." Her shoulders sagged as she continued. "I guess I haven't always been good about putting vid fees and merchandising and stuff against the loan because sometimes . . ." She shifted her weight. "Anyway, I'm twenty-seven matches in, and I still owe all . . . all that." She looked back and forth between Diana and Howard. What was she expecting? Sympathy? An idea? Nothing was forthcoming except attention, so she continued. "That bonus for the next six matches helped, but at this rate, I have to fight at least another thirty-two matches. That's fifty-nine. Nobody can do that. Not even what's-his-name, the guy who stuck around for all those years. He died on number fifty-six." Kira leaned against the pantry door. "But how else can I make enough money to keep up my payments? It's not like I can just declare bankruptcy and wipe this out. If they foreclose, it's over. You're one of the Bound."

"OK, if they foreclose, they control your life, but that only lasts until they've gotten enough out of you to pay it off, right?" Diana leaned on the counter.

"Oh no. Once you're Bound, that's it. They own you. There's even this thing where if they sell your contract for more than the loan, the bank gets to keep all that, because it's 'surplus earnings.' You're just stuck." Kira's voice broke. "They can put on all these bullshit 'maintenance charges' for what it costs to feed and care for you, and charge that against the value of your work. And of course, they get to say how much maintenance is and what your work is worth. When I could afford a real lawyer, she said she'd never heard of anybody being released unless they were too old or too sick to do anything." She hung her head. "They get to control your whole life. Where you live, what you get to eat, if you can get married, if you can have kids, everything." Unbidden, anger flowed into her voice. "When I read my contract, it looked like there were all these protections, but my lawyer says they're meaningless if the contract holder goes to court and says they 'impede access to the value of the contractor's work.'" She quivered. "It really is a lifetime thing."

Kira straightened up and faced Diana. "I have to get this paid off before things get to that point. That's why I want the pro fight. I don't know how else I'm going to get out of this." She choked out her final words. "I really don't."

Diana got off the stool, entered the kitchen, and embraced

Kira. Her voice was gentle and motherly. "It's OK. We'll find a way through this. I don't know what it is, but we'll find a way."

Kira began to cry. Diana held her until she got the worst of it out. When the sobs subsided, Diana pointed to the dining room table. "Come. Sit. We'll talk."

Kira accepted a box of tissues proffered by Howard, and Diana steered her to the table. Diana took a chair across the corner, leaning in close.

"OK, here's what I know: The pro match *is* going to happen. The stockholders have to be informed first, and they're still working on a public announcement, so don't say anything about this. And while they haven't settled on the size of the purse yet, it's going to be big."

"Big enough to pay me off?"

Diana sucked at her teeth. "Yes. Big enough. Probably with some left over. Maybe a lot left over."

Kira squirmed with frustration. "So, that's what I want."

Diana took Kira's hands in hers. "OK, here's the other thing I know. For a professional, you're slow. Super accurate, but slow. When you go up against a citizen, it doesn't matter much. You can outdraw most untrained people. But with a professional on the other side of the Wall . . ."

Kira straightened in her chair. "We could work on speed."

"We could." Diana edged closer. "We could also work on other things."

"Like what?"

"Well, there are some big citizen matches coming up. If you keep shooting reliably, I can get more of those for you. Big purses will help."

Kira muttered, "Maybe."

"Not just locally. TKC is stretched thin right now, and there may be some travel. When Higgs and Grafton retire next month, you'll have the best record in the region. That makes you an easy sell for a big purse. Plus travel bonuses."

"Travel would be OK."

"You could do it more often if you'd accept an alternate second for the trips. That way, they only have to schedule around one of us being gone."

Kira shook her head. "No. I don't want anybody but you standing on the field with me."

"Not even Claire? She's good, and she likes you."

"They hired Claire already?"

TKC management had addressed their run of bad luck on the dueling field by shaking up their roster of seconds. Diana convinced them to hire Claire away from First Trust.

"They're still haggling over seniority points and vacation, but it's going to happen." Diana continued her pitch. "We could also set up a lockbox to send your other earnings straight to your creditors. I've had clients do that. It can make a huge difference."

Kira waved in Diana's direction. "But we're still talking about a year or so, right?"

"Probably. Hard to say until we dope it out with real numbers. But maybe we can whittle it down enough you could carry the balance on a second's salary. Maybe even a ward's."

Kira looked out the window. "Do you really think my luck can hold that long?"

Diana paused, then spoke slowly. "I think the odds of your

luck holding against a bunch of citizens are better than the odds of your luck holding against another professional."

"Does your friend the AI agree with that?"

Diana's fingers tapped on her forearm. "It's very difficult to assess the outcome of a single match. The error bars are huge. But against most of the United Re stable, you're better off taking your chances with a bunch of citizens."

"When do we know who it is?"

"Normal rules between corporations are that they announce their choices simultaneously. Once we know, it's too late to do anything about it."

Kira folded her arms and looked down, turning inward. Her voice was soft, barely audible. "OK, we'll try it your way and see how it goes."

Diana squeezed her shoulder. "Good girl."

CHAPTER 23

Kira adjusts her grip on the pistol and sneaks a glance at the sidelines. Both Diana and the ward are focusing on her. She has to get the pistol to her mouth fast and pull the trigger before the ward understands what she's doing and stops her with his stun rifle. On-field suicide isn't covered in the rules, but the ward will probably decide to intervene immediately and parse the nuances later. Diana stands upright and frowns, as if she's guessed Kira's thoughts.

When you're down, you can quit, keep doing what you're doing, or do whatever it takes.

Is taking her own life quitting, or doing what it takes?

No question how Don Myers will spin it. He'll tell everyone that if he'd been selected as TKC's champion, he would have at least taken the shot on the company's behalf instead of wasting it on himself. Each commentator will have five explanations for the True Meaning of her death before her body stops twitching.

And then there will be Niles. He'll mug his way through the post-match press conference, unharmed and full of fake modesty. He'll close with one of his infuriating little smirks and some quip about hysterical females on the dueling field.

Well, fuck all THAT!

A surge of anger takes the edge off Kira's agony and sharpens her focus. There has to be a better way out of this, a way to go down swinging.

Her right side isn't helping her—too much pain, too many tremors, and not enough stability. Kira transfers the pistol to her left hand, swings her blood-soaked right leg behind her, and faces Niles sideways. Shifting weight to her left leg, she extends her gun arm and locks her wrist, keeping her elbow slightly loose. She cups the pistol grip like a C-clamp, disengages her thumb, and brings her right fist to her chest for stability.

No doubt there's pandemonium in the commentary booth. Surprise, motherfuckers! I'm not right-handed.

There it is. The sights move in a nice, even circle, centered on the side of Niles's chest. Even under the best circumstances, hitting the heart from the side at this distance takes a lot of skill and a little bit of luck, but it's still her best shot. A near miss could still sever his spine, puncture the trunk artery, or rip a big enough hole in his lungs to make breathing impossibly difficult. She thumbs off the safety, brings the front sight into sharp focus, and gives the trigger a slow, smooth pull. The recoil is perfect, and Niles staggers.

But he doesn't fall.

CHAPTER 24

Chloe shoved the ottoman out of the way with her foot, and eased Kira into the apartment's recliner. "Sit here. I'll get a cold pack." Chloe bustled off to the kitchen area, leaving Kira alone with the numbness on the right half of her face. Was it left over from the punch, or the Long Island Iced Teas? Whatever the source, it was being replaced by a deep, throbbing pain threatening to become much worse. Kira popped the recliner back and accepted the soft, cold, gel-filled bag when Chloe returned. So much for celebrating the second match of her extended contract.

The entrance chime called for attention, and Chloe sprang to the door. Who the hell was she expecting after eleven on a weekday?

"Hey, Claire. Thanks for coming." Chloe ushered in their friend. Claire wore a wrinkled T-shirt and sweatpants, and her hair was arranged in the loose, two-strand braid she used to keep her extensions from tangling overnight, rather than the more complex French braid she wore during the day. She must have just rolled out of bed. Why had Chloe called her?

Claire set her purse on the coffee table and withdrew a pair of blue nitrile gloves. She snapped them on and stood over Kira like an examining physician. "Care to move that thing and give me a look?"

Kira moved the cold pack, and Claire winced. "Wow. That's quite the shiner. He must have landed one hell of a punch."

Chloe must have decided they needed someone with more than basic first aid but didn't want to involve Diana or the emergency room. Claire was a good choice—seconds got decent trauma training—but Chloe could have asked. Kira wasn't all that drunk.

Claire bent down and pressed several spots on Kira's face. Kira flinched, but Claire seemed satisfied. "I don't think anything's broken. Teeth OK?"

Kira opened her mouth, and Claire poked with her gloved finger. "It looks good in there."

Claire straightened up, and Kira put the cold pack back into place. It both numbed the pain and blocked any judgment that might be in her friend's face.

Claire issued her instructions in a calm, matter-of-fact tone. "Get down to the dispensary first thing tomorrow and get a shot of QuickHeal. Get in for an eye exam as soon as the swelling goes down." Her voice became a little more distant. "When are you off leave?"

"Diana wants me back at 6:00 a.m. on Thursday." Kira's voice sounded ragged and hoarse.

"Stay quiet and keep it on ice until then, go back for a second round of QuickHeal as soon as you can, and the swelling should go down enough that you won't miss any work." She leaned down toward Kira again. "What's that?"

Kira raised her chin in response to pressure from Claire's finger. In the part of Kira's vision that wasn't blocked by the cold pack, Chloe arrived with a mug of what smelled like tea.

"That bruise looks like—"

"He was choking her." Chloe's voice sounded pained.

"So why did he stop?"

Chloe looked down. "I sort of drew on him."

"Did you—?"

Chloe shook her head. "No. He let go when he saw the gun pointed at him."

"Cops?"

Another shake of Chloe's head. "No. But we aren't going back to Ozzie's any time soon." She glared at Kira. "I *liked* that place."

Claire gestured for Chloe to take a seat on the sofa. "I think I better hear the whole story on this."

Chloe held out the tea, and Claire pulled her gloves off to accept it. Kira put the recliner upright and tried to focus. Her face throbbed. Exactly what had happened? Most of the evening was shrouded in fog.

Claire remained standing and turned to Kira. "Start right after the match."

"I debriefed with Diana, got cleaned up, and went to the Lounge."

"Gunslinger's?" Claire absently rubbed the tea mug, but her voice was sharp, like Jenkins during an interrogation.

"Yes."

"So then what happened?"

Kira groped for words. It was so hard to remember, and Claire wasn't going to let her be vague.

Chloe spoke up. "We met when I got off work."

"At the Lounge?"

"Yes."

Claire's attention shifted from Chloe back to Kira. "Then what?"

Kira struggled. "I guess we decided . . ." She really couldn't remember.

"How much did you have to drink?"

Kira looked up at the ceiling. "I don't know." *What a pain in the ass.* "I suppose I had a Gunfighter's Long Island when I first got there."

"OK."

Kira turned to Chloe. "Then you got me the Angel's Envy."

Chloe looked embarrassed and addressed Claire. "It's what we get each other after a win."

"What else?" The question was for Kira.

Kira shrugged. "I really can't . . ."

"You had another Long Island before we left."

Claire responded with a small head twitch.

Thanks a whole fucking lot, Chloe.

Time to take control of the story. "Chloe wanted to play pool, so we took a driver to Ozzie's."

"Did you have any more to drink there?"

Kira spoke before Chloe could answer. "Just a couple beers." Kira took the pack off her face. "We were there to play."

Chloe slid forward on the sofa. "There wasn't an open table, so we put down our quarters and said we'd play the winner. The guys said, 'Sure.'"

Claire took a drink of tea. Her face emerged from the cup with a puzzled expression. "OK, so how do we get from that to one of them taking a swing at Kira and choking the life out of her?"

Kira made a helpless shrug. That was the fuzzy part.

Chloe glared at Kira again. "I didn't see it start. I was up ordering cheese sticks when I heard this big commotion, and when I turn around Kira's busted a pool cue over this guy's head."

Claire's focus was entirely on Kira now. "So, what was all that about?"

Kira squirmed. "Look, I can't remember, OK? He hit me pretty hard. You said that. But I'm sure he had it coming. He probably grabbed my ass while I was trying to shoot or something."

Anger tinged Chloe's voice. "He was like a foot taller than you and a hundred pounds heavier and he was pretty much all muscle." Fear replaced the anger. "He could've killed you."

Claire paced. "OK, so you went out after a match, got drunk, and picked a fight with a guy who could beat the crap out of you. Were you carrying?"

Kira nodded. "Oh yeah. Diana drilled that into us."

Claire stopped, fixing Kira with a look of pure incredulity. "You're a gunfighter, you've got a pistol, and you defend yourself with a pool cue?"

"I don't know. I told you, I don't remember this all that well."

Claire sighed and shook her head. "So, tell me about your match today. Who was it?"

"Elaine Thomas."

"What was she like?"

Kira tried for a flat, neutral tone. "About forty. Tall, thin. Tough target, but slow."

"What was she there for?"

Kira stared at the floor. Memory pressed in. She took a deep breath and forced the words out. "Stage four ovarian cancer. TKC denied payment for the treatment. She said she'd die one way or the other." Kira squeezed the cold pack. "I guess she must have put her pivot foot in the kill box, because she was still turning when the Wall came down. There was time to set up the shot and put the bullet right through her heart." Kira's voice caught. "It was quick." Kira closed her eyes, but Elaine's image wouldn't go away. "Diana said she probably didn't feel anything."

Claire pulled up the ottoman and sat across from Kira. "Something tells me the part of today you want to forget isn't hitting the guy with the pool cue."

Kira looked up at the corner of the room. "It's the same for her as anyone else. She had a choice. It's legal. We . . . It's sanctity of contract. It's what everyone agreed to." She trembled. "I did my job."

Claire moved a little closer. "OK, now say all that again, but this time, look me in the eye and make it sound like you mean it."

Kira gathered herself. It was a part, it was a role, it was a speech. She could play it.

Instead, something in Kira's mind cracked, and she flopped back in the chair and pulled the ice pack over her eyes. Claire had no damn right to do this to her.

Claire stood again. "Tell me about the match before today."

Kira let out an exasperated sigh. Claire wasn't going to leave it alone, and there was no way to get her out of the apartment; Chloe had called her. Kira didn't move and responded in a monotone. "A no-show. Ryan-something. I scared the shit out of him with the Death's Angel routine, and he left before we went to the changing rooms."

"What did you do after that?"

"I took the Deep Rail up to Minneapolis. I had a friend with a part in *A Funny Thing Happened on the Way to the Forum* at the Chanhassen Dinner Theater. It was fun."

"Did any of that fun involve drinking?"

"Bev doesn't drink much. I think I had a glass of merlot with dinner."

Claire nodded. "OK, what about the match before that?"

"Another no-show. He took the door in the changing room."

"Afterward?"

"Chloe and I went out for pizza."

Chloe brightened a little. "We ate at that deep-dish place."

Claire cracked a smile. "That's the only real pizza." She turned her attention back to Kira. "Drinking?"

"Beer with the pizza. Maybe two."

"The rest of the break?"

"We mostly hung around here. I had to look at some potential posters, and I did a vid chat with some fans."

Chloe agreed, and Claire went on. "How about the one before that?"

Kira lifted the pack off her face and stared at the ceiling. "Adam Spector. His brains ended up on the back wall."

Chloe jumped in. "One of the wards threw up."

Kira shot a hard look at her roommate. They all could have done without *that* particular image.

Claire paused, as if making a mental note, and fixed her eyes on Kira again. "Afterward?"

"I went to a party."

Chloe addressed Claire. "That was the one where she tried to sit in the window and chug a fifth of bourbon without choking. Then this second from Consolidated Trust dragged her back in, and she yelled at him."

Kira sat up and scowled at her roommate. "He shouldn't have grabbed me like that . . ."

Chloe's voice rose. "It was a fourth-floor window. You could have fallen out and broken your neck." Her face hardened as she looked at Kira. "He just put his arm around your waist and pulled you off the edge."

"He made me spill bourbon all over—"

Claire quieted them and continued her questioning, going backward through Kira's match schedule, asking about each opponent, the outcome, and what she did afterward.

"His name?"

"The Consolidated Trust guy—?"

"The next fight."

"Oh. Grant Perkins. Middle-aged and pissed off about a claim for his boat."

"A boat? He was willing to die for a damn boat?"

Kira pressed her face into the cold pack, which was now merely cool. "He was pretty adamant about it, yeah."

"What happened?"

"Hit to the upper chest, and he went down on his butt."

"Afterward?"

"Nothing. I had a couple drinks and went shopping."

Chloe piped up. "That was when you fell getting out of the driver, twisted your ankle, and scraped your hand."

God damn it, Chloe. Was this what being tattled on by a younger sister was like? Maybe she hadn't missed much by not having siblings.

Claire took a big drink of tea, and then broke the silence.

"OK, I think that's enough for you to see the pattern." She looked to them for confirmation. Chloe responded with a vigorous nod, while Kira rolled her eyes. Or rather, eye. Claire sighed. "When you kill somebody or hurt somebody on the field, you go out and get drunk and wind up hurting yourself. Can we all agree to that?"

The last question had the well-worn sound of something the speaker repeated too often. Claire's gift for statistical inference meant she often saw things clearly that others saw only vaguely, if at all.

Kira threw the cold pack on the floor. "Look, maybe you're right. Maybe I do take it out on myself when I shoot somebody. So the fuck what? Nothing's more dangerous than being on the dueling field in the first place."

Claire folded her arms across her chest. "Are you seeing a counselor? Diana should have given you a name after your first match."

"She did, but . . ." Kira looked away. "I never felt the need."

"Has Diana asked you about it?"

Kira snorted. "Diana asks me about everything—how much I sleep, what I'm eating, if I'm seeing anybody or not. Not that any of it's her business."

"It *is* her business—literally. But never mind that—has she specifically asked you about the counselor?"

"I guess."

"You know if she makes it mandatory, she has to report that. It can be part of a fitness assessment."

Kira sneered. "Oh, come on. They aren't going to force me out. Not with my record. They just signed me up for an extension, and they want to wring every win out of me they can get."

"How many fights do you have left?"

"Four. But I'm negotiating another extension. I'm not quite where I need to be yet."

Claire sucked on her teeth. "That's not good. How many more do you need?"

"I don't have to tell you that." *Who the hell did Claire think she was? She might be a second, even a TKC second, but she wasn't Kira's second.*

Claire stepped closer. "Kira, for some people, the longer they do this job, the easier it gets. It's like they get a callous on their feelings. For other people, it hurts more every time they pull the trigger, like a bruise that keeps getting hit. I think you're in that second group, and I think you need to talk to somebody about that. What was the name Diana gave you?"

Kira responded with an irritated shrug. "Somebody-Davis. It's on my handset."

On a nod from Claire, Chloe rose and held out Kira's handset.

"Go ahead and make an appointment." There was compassion in Claire's voice, but a hard steel undertone as well.

"It's OK. I'll do it. I just don't want to do it right this minute. My head hurts." Kira pulled the thoroughly warmed cold pack off the floor and put it against her face.

Claire and Chloe stood together, unmoving and staring at Kira.

Kira laughed. "Hey, you two should see yourselves. You look like you're doing an intervention on an alcoholic."

Chloe glanced toward Claire, who kept her eyes fixed on Kira.

Kira's chest tightened. "Oh, come on. You don't think . . ." She tossed the pack aside and stood. "No, I'm not, and you can't come in here and act like . . ." A hollow, sinking sensation hit Kira's stomach. Her mouth went dry.

Claire spoke. "For the record, I'd say you're a problem binge-drinker rather than an alcoholic, but I also think that's one of the first things you should talk to Dr. Davis about." She nodded toward Kira's handset, still in Chloe's outstretched hand.

Kira took the device. "I can't believe this. You're acting like I can't handle my life." She raised the handset over her head. "I'm not going to do this while you stand there and watch me. I just won't."

Claire spoke again. "It's not my job to run to Diana and report all this, but if she asks me what I know, I won't lie for you."

Chloe crossed her arms. "Same for me."

Kira's heart pounded, and her throat tightened. She had no choice, but it was just to get them off her back. She took the handset and tapped out an appointment request. Seconds later, Dr. Davis's office scheduling 'bot responded with a confirmation. She turned the handset toward Claire. "There."

She could tap the speaker button and spare Claire the trouble of reading the appointment. The display's black text on white background, oddball font, and abbreviations would be hell on Claire's dyslexia. But why shouldn't she suffer a little? She sure wasn't sparing Kira any embarrassment.

Claire leaned toward the screen, squinting. Kira let her

struggle for a few seconds, then relented and pushed the READ button. It's not as if she had so many friends she could afford to burn one out of sheer spite. The handset quoted the appointment in its clipped, English butler voice.

Claire leaned back and relaxed. "Next Tuesday. That's good." She turned to Chloe. "Make sure she keeps it and call me if she doesn't."

"Don't worry, I will."

Kira ground her teeth.

Claire's face became soft and full of sympathy. "I know that wasn't easy, and what you've got ahead is harder, but it's what you need to do. I hope you can see that."

Kira managed a sharp nod. "OK."

Claire took her purse off the coffee table, and Chloe walked her to the door. She left without saying goodbye.

When the door closed behind their friend, Chloe faced Kira. "I meant what I said about making sure you keep that appointment."

Kira tossed the gel pack back in the freezer. "I know you did."

Chloe watched her with sad eyes but said no more.

Despite the pain building in her chest, the lump in her throat, and exhaustion covering everything, Kira managed to keep it together long enough to extract a fresh pack from the freezer and make it out of the kitchen. Once in her room, she locked the door, embraced her pillow, and sobbed.

CHAPTER 25

Kira stood in Firing Point Three, her back to the target, waiting for the start signal. The chime sounded, she pivoted, planted her foot, pulled her toe inside the firing line, and drew, focusing on the movement of her right arm. The sights stabilized, and she fired. Last round of the set. She checked the clock. Chloe's twenty-eighth match would start in less than five minutes.

Kira called up the results hologram, which presented a comparison between her arm movements and an idealized, "most efficient" model. She'd kept her deviation from the model in single-digit territory and shaved almost a tenth of a second off her average draw-to-hit time. She keyed up the target results. Though not important for this particular drill, they looked OK, too.

A warble sounded from her handset, letting her know match coverage was about to begin. Kira buzzed the specialist she was working with. "Hey, Mike. This is Kira. I'm going to take a break. Chloe's up."

A couple seconds of silence followed. Probably Mike checking her results.

"No problem. Let me know when you're back at it. Same drill on the left hand."

"Sure thing."

Kira placed her pistol in the rack, pulled the ear protectors down around her neck, and grabbed her purse and water bottle. Past the outer door, Kira found only a handful of open tables in the break area. She spotted an empty one out near the edge, plunked down in one of the chairs, pressed her earpiece into place, and projected the video feed from her handset onto the wall.

The image showed the administrative area for the match. Diana and a ward tested a gun belt, pistol, and sensor. Across the centerline, the other second and ward concluded their examination of the ammunition. Tests complete, the judge asked for the seconds' consent to continue. Kira shifted in her chair. The other second was a Guild professional, and that was never a good sign. The chyron identified him as Jacob Carver, the same guy who'd coached her opponent when she got hit. Kira took a sip of water, relieving the dryness in her mouth.

Chloe emerged, and flashed her hand signals—*I'm nervous. Opponent prepared.*

In reply, Diana signaled the field was OK, and the second was a first-rate professional. She also gave Chloe a warm smile and a final signal—*control the Wall.*

No way to know what bit of intelligence Diana based that recommendation on. Faced with a longer-legged and well-trained opponent, exploiting the "last foot in the kill box lowers the Wall" rule made sense. Although Diana might be doing nothing more than calming Chloe's nerves by giving her something to focus on.

Chloe's opponent emerged—an athletic, gray-haired man dressed in a smart, fitted dueling tunic. He conferred briefly with his second, breaking it off when the judge rose and called for attention. They rolled through the rituals of consent and equipment checkout, and the Wall went up.

From a perspective above and behind the judge, the cameras watched the combatants march to the start point and turn back-to-back. Once they were in position, the vid went to split screen, showing the track of each combatant from a vantage point above the Wall, but at a low enough angle to show their bodies rather than the tops of their heads.

Both of them departed from the strikeline, Chloe veering to her right and the citizen veering to his left, but not quite as far. The citizen entered his box first and executed a smooth turn and draw. Camera perspective shifted, now watching from above and behind him as he faced the hologram's featureless expanse. He swung his gun along with his eyes, his only display of poor technique so far.

Chloe planted her pivot foot on the edge of her kill box and executed her turn, bringing the Wall down when her traveling foot landed inside the boundary. She spotted her opponent before she completed her draw and brought her gun to bear. He swung his gun toward her, and both weapons fired.

The citizen staggered back, clutching his chest. Chloe jumped, but remained standing. When the EMT pointed to her, she shook her head. The tentative win light flashed on Chloe's side.

Kira let out a long sigh and sagged into her chair. Chloe was another step closer to being done.

KIRA BURST IN THE APARTMENT DOOR, BEARING A PINT OF PICKET
Fence Dairy Raspberry Ripple ice cream she'd picked up on sale.
It would make a good victory gift for Chloe, substituting for a
glass of Angel's Envy. "Look what I got—"

Loud sobs cut her off. Kira locked the door behind her and
followed the sound down the hall to Chloe's room. Her roommate lay on the bed, her face buried in a pillow.

Kira pushed aside a tissue box on the nightstand to clear
enough room for her package and sat on the edge of the bed.
"Hey, what's wrong?"

She put her hand on her friend's back. Chloe shuddered and
turned to face Kira. Blotches covered her swollen face. "After the
debrief, I went to confession."

"OK." Kira handed Chloe a tissue.

Chloe accepted it and blew her nose. "And Father Pierce was
there. He said . . . He said . . ." Chloe burst into tears again, and
Kira waited it out, presenting another tissue when the sobs came
to a halt.

Chloe began again. "Father Pierce said I was"—Chloe's face
scrunched up with the effort of recalling the words—"'obsti-
nately persevering in manifest grave sin' and I couldn't come up
for the Eucharist during Mass anymore." Chloe pulled herself
up on her elbows. "I mean, how can he even say that? I always do
my penance, and I say the Breastplate of St. Patrick before every
match, and I light my candles and my whole family prays for me
and . . ." Chloe sank back into the bed.

"Because you're a gunfighter?"

"Yeah." Chloe blew her nose again. "Somebody decided . . .
something." She sighed. "I guess I didn't really get all that. But

anyway, it's changed, and now the church says I can't be forgiven if I keep doing this."

Exactly how Chloe managed the contradictions between her faith and her life was an ongoing mystery to Kira. But Chloe had always knelt in a confessional, spoke her sins out loud, and did her penance, while Kira sat in an office chair and told Dr. Loretta Davis about being angry with her dead mother and noticing where her body carried stress. Then Kira and Chloe both went out and did their jobs.

Only maybe this time, it wasn't going to work for Chloe.

Chloe started again. "If they'd said that at the beginning, I wouldn't have done it. I mean, they didn't say it was *good*, and I get that, but we all do stuff that isn't good, and that's what confession is supposed to be for, you know? And now it's like they've changed the rules and I'm stuck." She buried her face in the pillow again. "What am I gonna do?"

Kira rubbed her friend's back some more.

"Well, the Guild says you've got at least forty-eight hours all to yourself before you have to do anything. When does Diana want you back?"

"Not until Friday at noon."

"OK. That's some time."

Chloe propped herself up on one elbow. "Danny wants to go to Colby's Country Cabins tonight."

"The new ones out on Lake Panorama? With all the trails and everything?"

"Yeah, those. He got some kind of deal because it's the first week in December."

"That might be just the thing. Get out of town, clear your

head, go for some walks, really talk things over." Danny was probably no better at theology than Kira, but he seemed to be good for Chloe. Maybe that would be enough.

"I suppose."

On the nightstand, Chloe's handset buzzed. She picked it up. "Oh, crap. There's a bunch of messages. Danny says he's going to be here in twenty minutes."

"Are you packed?"

Chloe looked around the room. "I was going to do that when I got back from confession, and then . . ." She tapped the handset, and it displayed her face. "Jeez. I look like a mess. Maybe I should just call and tell him to forget it."

"Look, you hop in the shower, clean up, and get some makeup on. Finish packing. I'll chit-chat with him in the living room until you're ready, OK? If I get really desperate, I'll feed him some of those brownies I made over the weekend. They'll go good with the ice cream."

"Oooh, ice cream." Chloe swung her feet to the floor. "Thanks. That'll help. You're a good friend."

Kira squeezed Chloe's hand. "Hey. Like you said in the beginning, our chances are better if we stick together."

CHAPTER 26

"Damn!"

Kira drops the pistol and tears at her tunic until she has a patch of fabric to stanch the entry wound. Niles is still standing, but he's no longer her opponent. Pain, blood loss, and gravity will determine the outcome of the match.

Behind her, the ward's voice sounds. "Please remember if anyone touches Ms. Clark while Mr. LeBlanc is standing, she will be disqualified."

The EMT kneels directly in front of her. "Ms. Clark, do you wish to receive medical attention at this time?"

Kira shakes her head, and the EMT steps away.

Diana kneels in his place. Her face is drawn, but her voice is firm and upbeat. "Looks like this will take a little longer than we thought. How do you feel?"

Kira continues her self-exam, feeling her back for the exit wound. "Pretty good for somebody who's been gut-shot."

Diana grins. "Fair enough. Let me take a look." She rises and walks around Kira, her hands behind her back to suppress the human urge to reach out to another body in pain.

Kira's fingers find a small gash topped by a flap of muscle.

Diana's voice, from behind. "That's your exit wound. Wad the tunic up and put some pressure on it."

Kira complies, but the awkward angle makes it difficult to press very hard.

Diana kneels in front of her again. "I don't think he hit anything vital. You might lose some colon, but you can barely call yourself a gunfighter if you've got all the guts you started with." Diana examines Kira's fluid-soaked leg. "Blood is going to be the problem."

Kira pants. "How much do you think I've lost?"

Diana's brow furrows as she surveys Kira and the pseudograss beneath her. "Hard to tell, but it always looks worse than it is. Maybe a cup or two?"

Kira nods. Diana is probably bullshitting her, but maybe it doesn't matter. She should be able to lose about two pints before passing out.

Kira's heart races, and the fog moves closer.

Diana looks over her own shoulder, toward Niles's side of the field. "You got a nice, solid hit to the chest. He won't last long."

If she'd managed a truly solid hit, Niles would be down and they wouldn't be having this conversation. Kira bends a little to get more comfortable, puts more pressure on her wounds, and groans.

"Not too hard, baby girl, you don't want to damage anything." Diana bends down for a close look at Kira's torso. "Is it time to use your tunic as a wrap-around?"

Kira shakes her head. "I don't want to let up. I feel like I'm going to lose a lot if I do."

"Too bad. You could get a sports bra endorsement deal."

Kira chuckles until a stab of pain cuts her off. "Don't do that."

Diana nods. "It's OK. You're tough and you know how to stand through. This is going to be fine." She looks across the field again and offers her assessment in the same voice she might use to report the morning weather. "He's doubled over, but that won't help a chest injury. I bet he's got a collapsed lung." She turns back to Kira. "Just a few more minutes."

Kira shifts her stance and adjusts her grip on the fabric covering her wounds. It feels as if someone has driven a red-hot iron bar through her abdomen, but Niles can't feel any better than she does.

The commentators must be milking the hell out of this. Closing the first professional match in two years with a bleed-off is like something from a producer's wet dream. All over the country, people are fixated on their screens, pounding on tables, and screaming for her or Niles to fall. The Gunslinger's Lounge is probably worse than the rest of the city put together.

Diana leans close to Kira's ear and speaks softly to avoid the field mic. "How bad is it?"

Kira swallows hard. "I can't see the walls anymore."

CHAPTER 27

Kira flicked off the vid monitor, got up from the sofa, and paced to the fridge. How many times had she made this trip tonight? With Chloe out at Lake Panorama with Danny, the apartment seemed huge and dead. Something like hunger gnawed at her stomach the way the emptiness gnawed on her psyche. It was probably good that Diana's lockbox arrangement sent the royalty check for the last batch of posters straight to her creditors. Otherwise, the temptation to pull some unis onto her handset for shopping might be overwhelming.

Diet Coke. Apples. Leftover lasagna. Nothing in the fridge looked good. She didn't want more popcorn, either. At 10:00 p.m., it was too late to go out for coffee on a Wednesday night, even if she were willing to change out of her sweat suit and slippers for the chance to be around people. She should pack it in and get some sleep. With a match on Friday, she had a big day in the simulator coming up.

A sharp rap on the door. Who knocks instead of using the chime? And who the hell visits at this hour? Kira pressed the external monitor. Diana's face filled the display. She crowded the camera enough Kira couldn't see if anyone else was there, but not so close she couldn't see the collar of Diana's Guild jacket. Kira's chest tightened.

She opened the door, and found Diana accompanied by Michael, Chloe's oldest brother, looking awkward in the out-of-fashion gray suit he usually wore to Mass. Whatever this was, it wasn't good news.

"Can we come in?" Diana's question was matter-of-fact.

Kira stepped back from the door. "Sure."

"It's best if you sit." Diana's poker face was as perfect as ever, but instead of moving with her usual athletic grace, she seemed to push her body through each motion.

"Why?"

"Kira, sit." The calm quiet in Diana's voice demanded instant obedience.

Kira perched on the recliner, while on the far side of the coffee table, her visitors sat on the sofa. Michael drew back, his eyes a little wild, and let Diana take the lead. She spoke slowly, as if she were measuring the effect of each word on Kira before going on to the next. "We're sorry to tell you this, but Chloe is dead."

The tightness in Kira's chest became a fist crushing her heart. "What?" It was a ridiculous thing to say, but Diana looked patient, as if she expected it.

Diana spoke again. "Chloe is dead. She died earlier this evening."

"No." Kira shook her head. "She's on her forty-eight-hour break. She's with Danny at some cabins up by Lake Panorama. That's why she's not here. She's fine."

Diana and Michael exchanged a glance. Diana spoke again.

"This will be very hard to hear, but the man she was with is not Danny Jones. His real name is Walter Smith. He killed her."

"Killed her?" Kira's voice sounded high and ragged, but what Diana said didn't make any sense. How could Danny not be Danny? How could anyone have murdered Chloe?

"Kira," Diana continued in a calm, steady voice. "I'm sorry."

Something cracked, and the reality of what Diana said flooded in. Kira shuddered. "H-H-How?"

Diana reached out and took Kira's hand in hers. For the first time, deep sadness showed in her face. "Listen, I don't like being the person to tell you this, but you deserve to hear it from Michael and me rather than seeing it in the news, OK?"

Kira nodded, but said nothing.

"Walter Smith is the younger brother of Quentin Smith. Chloe killed Quentin in a duel last November. Walter forged some ID and a public profile so he could get close to her. He got her to go off one of the trails around the lake, and then he shot her."

"Shot her?" Kira's voice ran off the high register, stopping just short of a shriek.

Cold, bass fury poured out of Michael. "He made her kneel and shot her in the back of the head."

"Oh God." Kira's eyes stung. She shuddered and folded in on herself. Not just the idea of Chloe dying, but dying like that—not even putting up a fight. Not to mention dying at the hands of a man who'd sat right here in their living room a couple hours ago, talking and eating Kira's brownies as if he didn't have any agenda beyond a tryst in the country. Kira struggled for air, and her heart pounded.

God, how could she have missed it? She could read an opponent's intent in the flick of a finger or the twitch of an eyebrow, and yet she'd sat within feet of murderous rage and saw nothing. And Chloe had died. Died because Kira told her the trip was a good idea.

It was too much. Kira dissolved into sobs. When she stopped, Diana sat on the arm of the recliner, her hand on Kira's shoulder. Michael stood beside her, holding a towel from the kitchen.

Kira uncurled a little, facing Michael. "I'm so sorry. This must be so much harder for you."

Michael nodded and handed her the towel. "I've had a little more time." Tears welled in his eyes.

Kira sniffed and wiped her face.

"The good news is he's in custody." Diana's voice remained astonishingly calm. "A couple kids out on a night hike heard Chloe and Walter arguing. They had the presence of mind to call 911, and one of them caught most of it on handset video."

At least Chloe had argued. That was something.

Diana went on. "When the police arrived, he hadn't cleaned up and he still had the gun. During questioning, he blew up and said he did it for his brother. That's a confession."

Kira squeezed her eyes shut. That much hatred, directed at Chloe. Could've been directed at her just as easily. She shuddered again.

She stood, pulling at her sweat suit. Diana and Michael stood with her. Kira looked back and forth between them. "I-I'm not sure what to do, here." She faced Michael. "If you want to come get her stuff—" She caught herself. "Wait. That's ridiculous, isn't it? That's not why you're here."

Stop talking. Stop talking. Stop talking. You're making every-thing worse.

Helplessly, she looked at Diana. Surely she'd know what to do.

But it was Michael who took Kira's hand in his. His eyes were wet. "What we need to do now is cry. All of us, together. That's why I came. We're all coming to Mom and Dad's house and we're going to cry for Chloe tonight. We want you to come cry with us."

Kira stood and threw her arms around him, squeezing him tight. "Oh, thank you. Thank you, thank you, thank you."

CHAPTER 28

Nothing felt right. Beneath the Death's Angel regalia of cloak, hat, and black leather, overnight grit and oil clung to Kira's un-showered skin, and body stink vented up from the collar of her blouse. Definitely not the way she wanted her first gunfight after Chloe's death to begin. There was nothing for it now, though. Standing at the doors of Waiting Room Two, she repeated her breathing exercise, forcing the exhale to last twice as long as the inhalation.

It wasn't helping.

There was no way this could end well, an opinion she'd shared with the scheduler who summoned her just before 7:00 a.m. for an 8:00 a.m. match. In tones that managed to be both apologetic and firm, he explained both Tom Bucknell and his backup, Stan Casey, were suffering from severe stomach flu. He stiffly described the tertiary, Jim Watson, as "indisposed," which probably meant roaring drunk or hopelessly hungover. He went on to note that the two-week exclusion Diana negotiated for Kira after Chloe's death expired yesterday afternoon, and since the company faced a forfeit for failure to appear, one-hour notice was deemed sufficient under Guild rules.

Kira hated everyone involved. Especially Watson.

She attempted the breathing exercise again without success. The clock over the door gave her three minutes before the outer lock closed and she forfeited as a no-show.

She channeled all her anger and frustration into her appearance, hardening her face and body. Forget fake empathy or a slowly building sense of menace. She'd blow this one out of the waiting room on a blast of sheer, undiluted terror. Kira yanked the double doors open and propped them apart with outspread arms. Silhouetted in the doorway, she'd look like a raptor swooping in to claim her prey. *Fear this, bitch!*

Inside, a dark-eyed, curly-haired young woman greeted Kira's entrance with an excited grin, as if she'd caught sight of her favorite vid star in a restaurant. Her mouth formed a soundless *wow*.

Could this day possibly go any further off the rails? Kira fought down the impulse to retry her entrance and nearly stumbled as she made her way to the receptionist's desk. From there, she assessed her opponent. The woman's profile gave her age as nineteen, but she looked younger and softer—more like a teenager or even a pre-teen than an adult.

Kira checked in and picked a chair close to the door, far from both her adversary and the receptionist. If she could collect herself for a few minutes, she could figure out what was going on. The bolt to prevent late entry closed with its distinctive clunk.

Kira jerked and turned to the source of the sound. When she turned back, the young woman sat directly across from her.

Her opponent leaned across the aisle, a conspiratorial grin on her face. "Ms. Clark, I am so excited to meet you."

Excited to meet? What the hell was this? A fan? In the waiting room?

Before Kira could respond, the girl—there was really nothing else to call her—pulled an autograph album from her bag. "Will you sign?"

Kira's mouth dropped open. "S-Sure."

"Use your red ink! That's the best!"

OK, what were the rational possibilities? Among poor children, developmental delays, even serious ones, often went undiagnosed and untreated. Was that what she was seeing?

Kira's cousin Matilda had a cognitive impairment that caused people to mistake her for a teenager well into her twenties, and Matilda always got the best care available. If she'd been left without support, would she be like the person facing Kira right now?

Kira fumbled in her bag for a pen. One with her signature red ink. The girl's T-shirt, shorts, and sandals were cheap, massproduced designs, patterns several years out of fashion. Scrupulously clean, but worn, as if they were part of a very limited wardrobe. Possibly bought used.

Kira steadied herself and accepted the book. "Who is this for?"

"Sabrina. She's my next-youngest sister. She's a fan, too. But not as big a fan as me."

Kira signed, "All my best," returned the album, and leaned across the aisle with her elbows on her knees. It was time for an adult to take control of the situation. Kira made her voice serious without being harsh. "Look, you understand why we're here, don't you?"

The girl's expression became sober, and she nodded.

"All right. Here's what I know: Only one of us is going to walk off the field, and I'm going to do everything I can to make sure it's me."

The girl started to smile again, then suppressed it. Kira's eyebrow rose.

The girl looked embarrassed. "I'm sorry. I was just thinking how cool it is to get to see what you do in the waiting room. Everybody says you're great at it, but you never get to see this part on the shows."

Kira scrubbed her hands across her face. Somehow, she had to convince this impervious innocent how high the stakes really were. The girl apparently believed this was like a serial vid, where they'd all be back for the next episode, no matter what. What was her name? She'd read it in her public profile on the ride to the arena. She just needed to remember. Kira closed her eyes and cleared her mind. Finally, it came.

"Lotila."

The girl turned and smiled, basking in Kira's attention.

"Explain to me why you're here. Why didn't you accept the arbitration ruling?"

Lotila looked at the floor. "I can't. If I accept the judgment, I won't have any money, and I won't be able to make my payments, and then I'll be a debt slave. Forever and ever."

A giant hand squeezed Kira's heart. "You signed a lifetime services contract?"

The girl nodded.

"Why did you do that?"

"We all did. Daddy and Sabrina and me. Mama got really sick and couldn't work, and I couldn't find any work and Sabrina couldn't find anything and, even though Daddy was working, it wasn't enough. We had to eat. We had to keep the apartment. Then we saw this vid ad about how we could get lots of money if we just promised to pay it back, and if we didn't, then they would get work for us, and it sounded pretty good at the time, so we did it. We all did it, and we figured when Mama died, her insurance policy would cover it all, right? And then when she died, the company said we hadn't paid like we were supposed to, but we did; we just sent it to the wrong place, and it took Daddy a while to figure it out, and by the time it got straightened out, they said the policy was canceled, and we took it to the arbitrator, and they said the company was right and there wasn't going to be any money."

The torrent of words ended, and a torrent of tears began.

Oh holy hell.

Lotila had watched her mother die, slowly. Had she stayed at the hospital room, pretending to read a book, but really praying for a miracle, hoping it was all a dream, or begging for anything that would let her feel her mother's hug again? She'd stared into the same financial abyss Kira had and made the same bad decision—betting her freedom on finding enough money to pay it all off.

Kira took the whimpering girl's hand. "Listen. In a few minutes, they're going to call us. When they do, I'm going to the field and I want you to go out that door right there and go home. When you get home, let me know, and I swear to you,

I will do everything in my power to make sure they can't foreclose on you."

Lotila looked up, eyes swollen. "Can you pay my debt?"

Kira bit her lip. "How much is it?"

Lotila squirmed for a few seconds, and then said, "Seventy
thousand unis."

Kira almost groaned out loud. That was more than her
entire cash reserve and her next two months of salary, combined.

Regret settled like a rock below Kira's sternum. "No. I can't.
The truth is, I'm carrying a lot more debt than that, and if I don't
make my payments . . ." She trailed off.

"But, Kira, if you can't help yourself, how can you help me?"

Kira sagged in her chair. "I don't know. But there has to be a
way for you. There just has to." Less than ten minutes remained
on the clock.

What happened if neither representative showed up? What
if they walked out the door together? The answer, from Kira's
first month of training, floated up in her mind like letters rising
through mist: "In the event neither duelist appears on the field at
the appointed time, the decision of the arbitration panel stands."
Of course it did.

"Kira, I'm sorry, but I have to try. I have to do this. I'm going to be really sorry if I kill you, but if I don't, then what happens to my sister? It has to be me or her, because the policy was
for Sabrina and me. Mama said she wouldn't sign her insurance
over to no man, not even Daddy—"

It was a straw, and Kira grasped at it. "What does your
father say about all this?"

Lotila drew herself up. "Daddy said no. He said I couldn't

do it. But I know my rights. I'm over eighteen and he can't stop me. Like it says, 'Everybody gets their shot.'"

Kira's long-simmering hatred for the anonymous copywriter who created the Association's slogan rose to full boil. If they ever met in person, the bastard would die the most painful death Kira could devise.

"What's your father doing now?"

"He's my second."

Kira's breath stopped in her throat. If someone handed her a script saying the villain would shoot a child while the child's widowed father watched, she would have rolled her eyes at the overkill. And yet, here she was.

Lotila's voice continued. ". . . said if he can't stop me, he'd help me do the best I could. I'm going to the field for me, Sabrina, and Daddy."

Kira clasped Lotila's hand. "Listen to me, Lotila. *Listen*. It's already too late. If you go out on the field, you are going to die because I am going to kill you. If you die, TKC won't pay. Do you understand?"

Lotila looked stricken. "Kira, don't *you* understand? I have to try. I may not have much of a chance, but I have to try. If we don't get the money, then they'll foreclose on all of us, and the social people will come and take Lucas and Delilah, and then we won't be a family anymore and—" She burst into tears again.

Kira released Lotila's hands and flopped back into her chair. There was no way to change Lotila's mind. If, when Kira's parents were dying, she'd thought a duel might save them, or even help them escape financial ruin, she would have taken the match in an instant, and she would have been impossible to deter.

Kira closed her eyes. The sobbing girl seated across from her would go to the field. Once she got there, Kira would kill her. This would be another performance of "Death's Angel on the Dueling Field." It wasn't her; it was her character. The script, written by others, dictated the character's choices.

Kira thought through her scene analysis.

What was Death's Angel literally trying to do? *Win a duel.*

What action was she going to perform? *Teach someone a lesson.* She'd show Lotila and everyone else that the dueling field was no place for the innocent or the unwary. This was a life-and-death matter that couldn't be trivialized.

It's as if—

The question blew Kira out of the exercise. There was no getting around the real answer:

It's as if I'm doing the shittiest and most evil thing I've ever done in my life.

Even if she survived, Lotila's defeat would consign her father to foreclosure, leaving her younger siblings with nothing but extended family or foster care. Not to mention foreclosure for Lotila's next-youngest sister.

If Kira wasn't damned already, she would be when this was over.

She waited until the receptionist was preoccupied with something on her desk, and then bent down close to Lotila. "Are you a good shot?" She pulled back to gauge the look on the girl's face.

"Pretty good. I've been practicing."

Kira clenched and unclenched her jaw, and then leaned

close again. There was no way to know how sensitive the devices monitoring the waiting rooms were. Kira brought her voice to the lowest possible whisper, directly into Lotila's ear. "If I miss when I fire at you, then turn sideways, do you think you could hit me in the leg when you shoot? Do you understand what I'm saying?"

Again, she pulled back to gauge the girl's reaction. Lotila's eyes got big, and she started to speak, but Kira raised a finger to her lips. Kira checked the receptionist again, and then spoke directly into Lotila's ear. "Listen, fixing a duel is a crime. I could not only lose my job, we could both go to jail, and then we'd both default on our contracts. Don't say anything about this to anyone—not your father, not your sisters, not your brother, not anyone. If you *ever* say anything, I will call you a liar to your face. Do you understand me?"

For the first time, Lotila looked frightened. But she nodded.

"TKC Insurance versus Lotila Sims."

Kira's throat went dry.

Lotila looked at the receptionist and then at Kira.

"Will the duelists please enter the changing rooms? The clock is running."

Lotila slowly gathered her things and slid out of her chair. Kira remained rooted to her seat as the girl walked to the receptionist, presented her thumbprint, and took the left door. When she disappeared into the changing room, Kira stared straight ahead and attempted a cleansing breath. A small piece of paper, some sort of card, lay on Lotila's chair. Something Lotila had dropped. Kira picked it up.

"Ms. Clark?" The receptionist sounded puzzled.

Kira came to her feet and stuck the card in her pocket. "Coming."

REALITY HIT KIRA AS SOON AS THE CHANGING ROOM DOOR SHUT behind her. She had just agreed to fix a match, the unforgivable sin of the dueling field. The recording devices probably heard it all, and her counter-party was a kid who could barely tell the difference between vid and real life. She shuddered at the tension in her chest. It was going to take more than a good self-hug to clear this mess. She paced the room instead.

There was no way in hell this could work. Even if Lotila didn't botch her shot, it would be far more suspicious than her loss to Hernandez. That meant Jenkins and the sharks would come after them. Kira might hold up under another onslaught from Jenkins, but Lotila would crack. She and Lotila would both go to jail, TKC would sue the family to recover the dueling payout, and they'd all meet to get their binders installed together, just before the auction. Fuck.

Clothes stuck to her clammy skin, like a net wrapping tight, and the smell venting up from under her blouse got worse. She peeled off the jacket and tossed it in the personal effects bin along with her hat. She flopped into the chair and undid her top blouse button to take pressure off her throat.

None of it helped.

She was going to jail. She was going to be Bound. Her whole career would be summed up with "cowardly cheater." She thrashed from head to toe, like a fish fighting a hooked line.

There had to be some way to get out of this, a clue or an opening somewhere. What was the thing Lotila dropped in the waiting room? She rolled her body enough to pull the card from her pants pocket, and found herself staring straight at the exit door.

She could take it. If she quit, the discussion in the waiting room became meaningless. She'd have a month or so when she could talk to the press freely before the bank foreclosed. She could tell people she refused to kill Lotila and go out on a no-ble note instead of a craven one. Maybe her sacrifice and honor would move some rich person to pay off her contract. She sniffed and shook her head. Shit like that only happened on vid, and even then, only in the sappy ones they showed at Christmastime.

If she was going to do this, she had to accept that slavery lay on the other side of the exit door. Delayed perhaps by public support and some good personal appearance fees, but inevitable in the end. Still, what other future did she have? Could she really stay alive long enough for Diana's plan to work? Better to take this route and hope the Auction Gods smiled on her sacri-fice with the reward of a decent buyer.

She stood and faced the door. The clamminess was gone, and a cool breeze from the air conditioner played across her face. A line floated up in her mind, and she spoke it. "It is a far, far better thing that I do, than I have ever done . . ."

She reached for the door, but the card popped out of her hand and fluttered to the floor. It was about the same size, shape, and weight as a playing card, with rounded corners and a light laminate finish. She picked it up. An ID number topped two columns of figures labeled "Time" and "Accuracy" that ran the length of the card. It was a range record from a quick-draw training gallery, intended to record and commemorate the visit. The times were as fast or faster than Kira's best sessions, with accuracy good enough to assure a hit, and often a kill.

An entirely new line of thought snapped into place.

Everything Lotila had done and said was intended to elicit sympathy and throw Kira off balance. It all came straight out of Kira's profile and public records. Anyone could see her parents were dead and she had no siblings. It was a short step from knowing that to a guess she'd be unusually sympathetic to the claims of family. The existence of Kira's lifetime services contract, though not the exact amount of her loan, was a matter of public record, as were her parents' deaths when Kira was nineteen—the same age claimed by Lotila.

Lotila had put on a helluva performance, playing the hapless innocent to the hilt, and Kira had fallen for it like a damn trainee.

She shoved the card back into her pocket and peeled off the rest of her street outfit, slamming the items into the personal effects bin. She yanked on the uniform pants and tunic, pulling the belt almost too tight. She stretched, trying without success to ease the tension in her shoulders.

Who'd put Lotila up to this, and what were they getting out of it? Had they planned the same stunt with Tom, or did they have a different story lined up for him? They'd probably set up something for every gunfighter eligible for the match. It wasn't that hard to figure out who you might be facing if you knew the Guild's rest period rules and kept an eye on the schedule.

Still, they must have anticipated they couldn't convince her to throw the fight.

Diana's warning played in Kira's head. *"Never forget they're shooting at you, too."*

Of course. Despite her innocent exterior, the card showed Lotila was a damned good duelist. And then there was the way she'd picked up her bag in the waiting room—a smooth, practiced motion that betrayed training of some sort.

Even if they couldn't convince Kira to throw the fight, they could hope to confuse her, slow her down, and make her reluctant to pull the trigger. Then darling little Lotila—who'd probably been drilling like crazy in a simulator ever since the case started—would be waiting as soon as the Wall came down, ready to pop off a shot as dangerous as the one Hernandez had used to sever Kira's artery.

Kira stopped to compose herself before she stepped into the scanner. None of this should show in her face or her posture. They needed to think she was still struggling with Lotila's situation, that she'd hesitate, and that she'd be slow.

Kira loosened her jaw and widened her eyes before checking her look in the mirror. A little slackness around the shoulders rounded out the presentation, making her look far more conflicted than she felt.

Now, for the right sign to give Diana. One she'd never used before: Left hand, thumb and forefinger in a circle, tilted out and the rest of the fingers pointing straight; move from arm beside the body to crossing the abdomen at waist level. That was it.

She stepped into the scanner and then onto the field. Diana approached, and Kira flashed her hand sign: *I'm being played.*

Diana signaled back. *Field OK. Citizen second.*

Kira responded: *Follow me.*

Diana's head dipped just enough to show agreement. She would support whatever impression Kira tried to create.

While the judge droned through the rules, Kira observed Lotila's second. He was a big man, well-muscled but beginning to go soft in middle age. He wore the same shabby and out-of-date clothes as the girl, the sort of thing you'd find at a thrift shop. Or a costume store. He might be her father, but he also might not be. Kira caught his eye and showed him her best imitation of pity.

Kira and Diana worked through the routine of putting on and testing the equipment with their usual efficiency, while the girl and her second displayed a convincing simulation of ineptitude. They fumbled with the belt so badly their ward had to do it for them.

The thing with the belt was a good bit. With a little less insight, and without the lucky break of finding the card, their act might have put Kira even further off her guard. The Wall went up, and Kira let her display of sympathy and uncertainty drop. Her calm, cold center took over, and it no longer mattered if it showed. They marched to the start point and turned back-to-back. Under her breath, Kira recited: "Make the box, make the turn, make the shot." In her mind, the girl Lotila disappeared and a range target took her place.

Kira marched straight down the strikeline with the lead ward's count, entered the kill box, turned, and drew. The Wall was up. She settled into a perfect shooting stance with a relaxed grip on the pistol, her eyes scanning the field, and the gun's safety off. When the Wall came down, Kira's hands brought the weapon into perfect alignment. A smooth trigger pull, a flash, and the recoil passed through Kira's forearms.

Lotila was still trying to pull her pistol from its holster.

The girl's mouth formed an *O* before she crumpled to the pseudograss. Kira's body was suddenly full of water, and her arms couldn't support the weight of the pistol. Had it all been real? Every bit of it? The lifetime services contract, the younger sister, everything? Even the father? Something settled on Kira's throat, making it impossible to breathe. Oh God. The father.

The big man ran across the field, but not as fast as the EMT. The two men knelt beside the fallen figure. There was some activity Kira couldn't make out, and then the second EMT arrived. Had she waved him off? No. He hadn't checked with her. There was only one shot. Lotila had not even cleared her holster, much less fired. Kira's stomach churned. An EMT stood and unfurled a body bag. The father wailed, filling the dueling space with the sound of his grief.

Kira wanted to run across the centerline to tell him it was all a mistake. She'd believed Lotila was conning her. She would've done something different if she'd known . . .

"You may approach the judge, if you are able." The lead ward sounded like he was a thousand miles away. Kira moved to holster her weapon, succeeding on the second try. Head down, she walked to the judge's table. Diana's greeting and the judge's statement melded into a blur. The only part that penetrated the fog was: "this judgment is final and there can be no further appeals."

Protocol kept Kira at the judge's table, despite a desperate desire to go shower. It was going to take a lot of hot water and soap to remove the filth from her skin.

The judge addressed Lotila's second.

"Mr. Sims, I see here Lotila was covered by a lifetime services contract. Do you want to receive the death certificate yourself, or would you prefer the Association provided it directly to the contract holder?"

The man raised his head, confused. "My other daughter and I still have them . . ."

The judge's voice was gentle. "Mr. Sims, I understand. Those contracts are unaffected, but Lotila's is canceled by her death."

Kira's gorge rose. She ran for the exit door, desperate to be out of sight when her scanty breakfast made its return appearance. Behind her, Diana shouted something, but Kira couldn't tell what it was.

CHAPTER 29

Kira pushes to stand nearly upright so she can see what's happening to Niles for herself. In addition to being bent over far enough to test the limits imposed by the motion sensor, he's obscured by his second, the EMT, and the ward. He coughs violently, and his second reaches out to steady him.

Kira straightens a little more. "Hey, did you see—"

Diana is off her knees and on her feet, pointing across the field and addressing the ward. "That was contact. I call foul."

The ward says something into his mic in a low, urgent voice. After a few seconds, he responds to Diana. "The ward in place says no contact."

Diana shakes her head. "I want a judge's ruling. Now."

The pain pulls Kira down before she can see more. "What's happening?"

Diana kneels again, still exuding calm but unable to banish an excited edge from her voice. "That's one hell of a screwup, but it's our ticket out of here. Hang on until the judge rules, just in case."

The news floods through Kira like anesthetic, numbing her pain. She's going to get out of this. She'll fix whatever Niles's bullet has done to her body, and everything her creditors have done to her life. All she has to do is stay on her feet.

She adjusts her stance, ready to face the challenge.

CHAPTER 30

Kira entered the Gunslinger's Lounge, and the sparse, mid-morning crowd fell silent. People might have stopped talking because of her soiled uniform, the faint whiff of vomit about it, or her look of unrestrained fury. Maybe they'd watched the whole thing play out on the vid screens. It didn't matter. Lotila's unfurled body bag burned in Kira's retinas, and the bereaved father's wail echoed in her ears.

She crossed the Lounge by the shortest possible route and mounted a barstool. Steve Olsen, the assistant manager, waved the server away and stood in front of her, his hands braced against the bar's mahogany surface. He started to say something but stopped when he got a good look at her face.

"Jack Daniels. Straight." She paused. "Make it a shot."

Steve produced both a bottle and a shot glass from beneath the bar, filled the glass, and set it in front of her. He refused eye contact.

Kira tossed back the whiskey and tapped the glass on the bar. "Again."

Silently, Steve poured.

Kira downed the shot and tapped the bottle. "Tell you what, just sell me that whole thing."

Steve hesitated, and Kira stared him down. In the end, he slid the bottle to her, and she poured herself another shot. The scattered buzz of conversation resumed.

A flash appeared in the mirror behind the bar. The main door had opened, and Diana's silhouette filled the entrance. Still in her second's uniform, she duplicated Kira's track across the Lounge, shoved a stool out of the way, and planted herself in the space. Again, the room fell silent.

"Do you care to explain why you're skipping your debrief and getting shit-faced in company colors?"

Kira downed the shot. Heat from the drink fused with the heat from her anger. She turned to face her trainer.

"She was a goddamn *kid*, Diana. She was a sweet, gullible, wonderful little *girl* and I put a bullet through her heart, all for the greater glory of T fucking K fucking C Insurance."

Diana folded her arms. "So, what are you going to do about it?"

Kira pointed to her bottle. "I'm going to drink this until I'm numb. Then I'm going to hunt down the biggest, meanest, ugliest, dirtiest man I can find. I'm going to straddle his chair and shove my tits in his face and tell him to take me home and do whatever he wants with me. If I'm too damn drunk to make it out the door, I'll settle for Jenkins down there." She jerked her thumb toward the redheaded investigator at the far end of the bar.

Diana paused a few seconds before she replied. "So, when you wake up tomorrow with a sore head, a sorer ass, and a mouth that tastes like a monkey took a crap in it, how will things be better? Who will you have helped? Answer me that."

Kira looked at the floor. "I don't know who I'll help, but the person who killed Lotila Sims will get what she deserves." Her voice trailed off, finishing in a mumble.

Kira grabbed the bottle, started to pour another shot, and stopped. Other possibilities existed. Possibilities Diana could give her. She stared straight ahead as she spoke. "I want out."

In the corner of Kira's vision, Diana responded with a curt nod. "You still owe the company three matches on your contract extension, but if you pay the penalty, we can work something out."

"That's not what I mean, and you know it. Put my name in."

Diana leaned back. Although her face remained perfectly composed, her body language and the tension in her voice betrayed her shock. "For the intercompany match?"

"It gets me out, and I don't have to do anything worse than shoot somebody who's just as dirty as I am."

"Except maybe die trying."

"That sounds good, too."

Diana bent down close, her face only inches away. "OK, baby girl, if that's what you want, I'll put you in for it. But I need to see you cleaned up, showered, and in Conference Room B in fifteen minutes." She pointed at the whiskey bottle. "Don't bother to show up unless you can be straight, sober, and at the top of your game for the next three weeks. Got it?"

Kira put steel in her voice. "Got it."

Diana slapped the bar and stood upright. "I'll be waiting." She left the Lounge without looking back.

Kira remained on the barstool. She wasn't going to trail out behind Diana like a whipped dog. She could sit here for a minute, preserve some dignity, and still have time to shower and make the meeting. She could even have another drink if she felt like it. Her hand brushed the bottle. One more shot would be about right to take the edge off being trapped in a tiny room with Diana.

She checked the ornate brass clock above the bar. Less than eleven minutes remained. If she took another shot, she might as well heft the bottle and suck it down straight until Jenkins looked good.

She closed her eyes and breathed. On the stage behind Kira's lids, Lotila crumpled to the ground like a marionette with her strings cut, shock and betrayal on her face.

Kira could drown that vision right now, or she could hold it in her head while she arranged her life to ensure she'd never see anything like it again.

Pushing herself away from the bar and off the stool was harder than she expected. She caught Steve's eye and pointed to the bottle. "Keep that for me."

KIRA'S DAMP, SLOPPILY COMBED HAIR ITCHED, HER BLOUSE stuck to wet spots on her torso, and her outfit looked as though it had been wadded up before being worn, but she entered Conference Room B with two minutes to spare.

Diana looked up from her data pad, her voice hard. "Feeling better?"

Kira sat, hitting the chair with enough force to make it scoot back from the worktable. "No."

Diana pushed the data pad to one side and focused on Kira. "What the hell happened to you out there? You told me you were being played, shot your opponent, ran off with no explanation, and now you're telling me she was just a kid."

Kira folded her arms across her chest. Where to start? "In the waiting room, she told me if she didn't win the duel, they'd foreclose on her and her family." Kira shuddered. "I was ready to throw the match. We even talked about it."

Diana raised an eyebrow. "Go on."

"As soon as I thought about it, I knew it couldn't work. I was ready to take the door." Another shudder ran through Kira's body. "Then I thought she was feeding me a line to slow me down or get me to quit."

Kira stared at the floor.

"What changed your mind?" Diana still sounded like an interrogator.

Kira pulled the range card from her pocket and slapped it on the desk.

Diana picked it up and glanced over it. "This is amazing, but it's not how she performed on the field."

"Turn it over."

Diana looked at the other side of the card, where the range logo was almost obliterated by the words *Tom Bucknell*, scrawled in heavy black marker. Diana's brow furrowed. "I don't understand."

"It was a goddamn souvenir." Kira's voice came out ragged,

as if she were ready to cry. "It must have fallen out of her auto-graph book when I signed it."

Diana didn't move, but when she spoke, her voice was softer. "She had you sign her autograph book? I don't know what to say."

Kira's shrug nearly reached her ears. "There's nothing to say. She was a fan."

Diana took a deep breath and leaned on the table, her hands folded and her focus on Kira. "I realize it was bad. There are things that happen on the field nobody likes. We all do things we regret, sometimes very deeply. But everyone who was there chose to be there."

"Choice." Kira spat the word. "Death, slavery, or murder. That was my *choice*. Lotila's, too." She glared at Diana.

"It's the way things are."

Kira rubbed her nose on her sleeve. "Then how come I feel like a piece of shit?"

"Probably because you're still a decent person." Diana paused. "I've had clients who could have walked away from the field to-day, cleaned up, debriefed, and gone out to celebrate without a second thought. In some ways, they're easy to work with, but they always scared the hell out of me." She shook her head. "You aren't like that. You try to ignore what you're doing, but you leave a piece of yourself on the field every time, and sometimes it's a big piece."

Kira sagged in her chair. "I don't know if I have enough pieces left to keep going. I really don't. I feel like I'm going straight to hell, and I'm not even sure I believe in it."

Diana took a deep breath and squeezed her hands together.

"Try to hear me when I say that while I know what you're feeling right now is terrible, I also know it's survivable."

Kira curled in on herself. "There's no way you can know that."

Diana leaned closer across the table. "All right, it's true that if anyone tells you they know how you feel, they're talking shit. Even if the situations are identical, the feelings are different." Diana paused again, as if to weigh her words before speaking them. "But I am going to tell you that you aren't the only person in this room who shot a kid in front of her parent."

Kira responded with a puzzled frown. "What are you talking about? There's nothing like this on your kill list."

"I'm not talking about dueling. I'm talking about southern Iran. Some little village—I can't even remember the name. After we secured an area, they had us use female troops for house-to-house searches." Diana sighed. "Scrambled the hell out of assignments, but they told us it offended local sensibilities less."

Kira uncurled a bit. This was more than Diana had ever said about her time in the war.

Diana continued. "Anyway, there were never enough women, especially officers, so I'm out there constantly, filling in for squad leaders even though I'm running a staff. Eventually, I get to the point where coffee to wake up and whiskey to sleep isn't enough. But, when you're a wounded war hero, medical people will give you things you really shouldn't have." A rueful smile crossed Diana's face. "I learned to use that."

Kira blinked. Diana as an out-of-control addict seemed both cosmically wrong and completely inevitable.

Seemingly oblivious to Kira's expression, Diana went on.

"One day, we go into this house. It's run-down, even by local standards. The place looks as though it's barely holding together, the door doesn't close right, and the roof's a mess. My translator's trying to explain to the lady of the house we just want to look around and make sure there are no weapons. She's being difficult and the squad is getting jumpy. Then this bag of rice falls in the corner of the kitchen and something's moving toward us. Before you can blink, I've got my sidearm out and I'm firing."

Diana held her breath steady. "Turns out to be the lady's daughter. She's eight. She was hiding behind the rice bag, got scared, and decided to run to Mom. We do the whole first aid thing, but it's useless. She was a tiny kid to begin with, and I put two rounds in her chest. She was probably dead before she hit the floor."

Kira stared. "So, what happened?"

"Shooting the kid was bad enough. When my drug tests came back positive for unprescribed stimulants, it was worse. Riots are breaking out all over, people are getting killed on both sides of them, and we had to call off an offensive just to put the lid back on. The locals are screaming for justice, command needs a guilty party, and there I am with a gun in my hand and shit running through my veins. The court martial was just a formality."

"So that's your manslaughter conviction?"

"I pled down to that." Diana sagged a little. "It probably should have been murder, but my friends hired a good lawyer." She looked around the room. "When I got out, I became a gunfighter. There aren't a lot of employers who don't care if you've killed someone."

"I guess I thought . . ." Kira trailed off into silence.

"It's not a story I tell a lot of people. And not just because the details are still theoretically classified."

Maybe Diana did know what it was like. Kira faced her mentor. "Does it get better?"

"No. But eventually, you notice it less."

Kira stared at the floor again. "I'm not sure I can live with that. I know I can't keep doing what I'm doing."

"I think you'll be surprised at what you can live with."

Diana probably did have it worse. In her trainer's mind, embarrassing the Corps, derailing the offensive, and getting Marines killed during the riots probably weighed on her just as heavily as the girl's death, if not more. *But still* . . .

Kira moved to the table and begged. "Diana, you have to put me in for this. I have to get out."

Diana's face remained calm, but tension practically radiated from her shoulder muscles. "You're wrong about that. Neither one of us *has* to do anything."

Kira slumped. "You thought I was going to stay in the Lounge and drink it away, didn't you?"

"I knew that was a possibility."

"But I'm here."

Diana sighed. "Yes, you are."

"So that means I'm ready."

"It means you want it. That's not the same thing." Diana rubbed the bridge of her nose. "This isn't a good time to make this kind of decision. Take your forty-eight hours off. Go see Dr. Davis and have her help you sort it out. Then come back, and we'll talk."

Kira's throat tightened. How could Diana be so obtuse?

"Will you listen to me? I can't *do* this anymore. I can't keep killing other people to keep myself safe. I can't drive them into slavery to keep myself out. I can't come up with a good enough story to make that OK. I just can't do it." She put her elbows on the table and cradled her head. "I know you keep saying it's legal, but just because it's legal doesn't mean it's right."

Diana reached across the table, her voice full of sympathy. "My first couple days in the brig, I just wanted it to stop. I would have signed an agreement calling for my own execution if the Marines had put one in front of me."

"And you've got the wrists to prove it."

Diana pulled at her uniform sleeves.

Kira continued. "One of the girls I roomed with in New York tried to kill herself when she was in school. I know what the scars look like when someone's serious and knows what she's doing."

Diana responded with a few seconds of silence, then she spoke in a firm, gentle voice. "Then you know when I say this passes, I know what I'm talking about. Take your time off. Let it cool. Decide with a clear head."

Faced with an unfavorable decision, Diana was angling for delay. A good strategy, but Kira wasn't going to succumb. Not today. She had to stand her ground, push back, and make Diana see things her way for a change. Kira searched for a lever big enough to move her second and keep the conversation going. "Tell me what the payoff is." Kira straightened as her memory of the Gunfighter Rights session became clear in her mind. "The Guild *requires* you to tell me the estimated payout for all prospective matches."

Diana scowled, but after a long pause, she opened the data pad. "They're still arguing with the Guild, but they've agreed the total value of the dispute won't be considered any less than 275 million unification dollars when they calculate the purse."

Kira's breath caught. "Good lord. Who screwed up and let anything that big slide into arbitration?"

"I don't know, but I'm sure they don't work here anymore."

Kira punched the numbers into her handset. Her breath caught again as the totals came up. "So, that's about eleven million for me, and a little less than three million for you."

Diana nodded in agreement.

"That's . . . that's not just paid off. Even after taxes and everything, that's rich. I could do anything I want."

Diana slapped the data pad shut. "You don't get to spend it if you're dead. You have to fight another professional for it." Diana leaned across the table, using her size to put weight behind her point. "That means you're not going to psych them out in the waiting room, and you can't count on outdrawing them on the field. They're going to show up, and they're going to be just as fast, just as well trained, and just as deadly as you are. And just as motivated by the purse." For a split second, Diana's weariness and fear showed in her face. "There's nothing from the AI, Claire's stats, or even the betting line that says your chances of walking away aren't equal to your chances of leaving in a body bag." The mask of calm determination dropped back into place. "If you're selected, the only way out is to resign. It's either the field or foreclosure."

"So, in other words, just another Tuesday." Kira managed a small smile.

Diana let out a frustrated sigh and focused on Kira with

an intensity that registered as physical pressure. "This is the last time I'm going to ask you—are you really up for this?"

Kira barely hesitated. "This job is killing me either way." She nodded toward the door and the Gunslinger's Lounge beyond, where her bourbon waited with her name on it. "Even if I can dodge the bullets for another year, I can't dodge the bottle. I'll pickle myself." In her mind's eye, a year of failure and humiliation stretched out before her, as alcohol and guilt consumed her life, her dignity, and whatever talent she might possess. "If I'm going to die, I'll take a quick, glorious end over a slow, miserable one."

Kira sat up straight, put her handset in note-taking mode, and faced her trainer; a professional dealing with a professional issue. "So, yeah, I'm up for this. What's the drill?"

After another long hesitation, Diana reached for her data pad. "They're looking for volunteers, but they're not limited to that. They're going to review all the records, listen to trainer's assessments, and draw up a short list this week. The selection committee will interview the candidates, then they'll get it down to three to five finalists, run that group through some additional tests, and make the final pick ten days before."

Kira nodded. "What are my chances of getting it?"

"Lots of variables on this one." Diana rubbed her chin. "But it's probably yours to lose."

"So not everyone is as pessimistic about my chances as you are."

Diana set the data pad aside and adopted her speaker-of-hard-truths tone. "This isn't going to be a rational decision. It's being made by scared little men in big suits who are more concerned about looking good than being right. You're our best-known gunfighter, you've got an exemplary record against citizens, and I'm sure you'll have the committee eating out of your hand when the interview is over. Unfortunately, none of that has any bearing on how you'll fare against another professional."

Diana paused, sizing up Kira's reaction. Backing out was still an option.

Kira spoke in a relaxed but firm tone. "It's still my best chance, no matter how they decide."

Diana nodded, her Marine officer reflexes almost visibly kicking in. She'd argued hard for her point of view, but even though the decision had gone against her, Diana would put her best effort into supporting it.

"All right. I'll list you as a formal volunteer as soon as we finish. That gives us extended simulator access hours, and we'll be using them. I want to see you in Simulator Three at 0600 on Monday." Diana made an entry in her data pad, closed it, and faced Kira. "Remember what I said. I need you straight, sober, and at the absolute top of your game, no matter what's going on in your head. Can you promise me that?"

"I promise."

"Good. I hope it goes without saying that I'll be working your ass off the entire time."

Kira grinned. "I wouldn't expect anything less."

"Good girl."

Diana stood, signaling the end of the session. Kira rose as well.

With their business concluded, Diana seemed to soften. She put her hand on Kira's forearm. "You've had a big day today. Are you OK?"

Kira hesitated for a few seconds before responding. "Good enough to go home."

Diana examined her carefully. "The Guild says the next forty-eight hours are yours, and I can't tell you to do anything, but I'd like it if you stayed in our spare room until it's time to go back to work. Howard or I will be around most of the time."

Gratitude manifested itself as an ache in Kira's chest. "Thanks. I think that's a good idea."

CHAPTER 31

Below Kira's perch on the catwalk opposite the control cab, the final moments of the day's last selection match played out on the field of Simulator Six. She leaned on the railing just a few feet from Diana, who maintained a laser-like focus on the duel below.

Felix García entered his kill box, turned, and drew with his customary speed. On the other side of the Wall, the mech completed the same actions, but just a split-second slower. Felix fired first, winging the mech and sending its shot wide. At the judge's table, Felix's second, Raj, raised his hands in triumph, though Felix's victory was not as impressive as the three clean kills Kira had scored earlier in the set.

Kira nodded in appreciation. Farther down the walkway, Don Myers and his trainer, Adam, watched their rival in stoic silence, while a few staff members standing near them applauded. The day's business concluded, Kira picked up her gear bag and joined the line to descend the staircase. When she reached the floor, she caught up with Diana.

"So, what do you think?"

Diana had her data pad open and tapped something into it. "Felix had a good set."

"I mean overall. Where do you think I stand?"

Bringing Kira's rivals to Des Moines for the final trials should have made it easier to assess their relative positions, but Diana pursed her lips. "The selection committee still won't say exactly what data they're using or how."

"Come on, you must have some idea."

Diana looked thoughtful. "Felix has the best speed, but he falls apart when the mechs control the Wall and change up their firing position. Don is inconsistent, but on his best days, he can beat anybody. My hand tally says you're the most consistent and you have the best overall score. But you've also lost to mechs set to emulate every probable United Re opponent in at least one match." Diana continued fiddling with her data pad as they walked. "Plus, we don't know how they're scoring your records against citizens or your interviews. It's all up in the air."

Kira sighed. The adrenaline buzz she'd allowed herself after the match was wearing off, replaced by frustration at the uncertainty.

Diana remained resolutely upbeat. "Word on the interviews is starting to leak out. I'm hearing the committee was impressed with you."

"That's good." Her meeting with all four members of the selection committee had featured a predictable mix of staff-developed technical questions asked by executives who didn't understand what they were asking, ham-fisted attempts to gauge her loyalty and motivation—she'd almost failed to cover her re-action when asked to describe her long-term goals—and inquiries that were just plain weird. Although she was rather proud of coming up with "a great blue heron, because they're patient, but fast and accurate" in response to the completely bizarre "What kind of animal do you see yourself as?"

Still, the vibe had been favorable when she left the room, and that was all that mattered.

They reached an intersection, and Diana closed her data pad, ready to wrap up. "Only three sets left. By this time tomorrow, we should know if it's you, Don, or Felix."

Kira leaned toward the hallway leading to the firing range area. "OK. I'm going to the range and try to shave a little off my draw-to-hit time before I leave."

Diana shook her head. "I can't go with you. Arjun took a swing at his weight trainer, and Claire wants to talk about it." Even though Diana's clients were temporarily reassigned to other seconds while she ran through the selection process with Kira, Diana's sense of responsibility persisted. "Besides, rest would be better."

Kira squirmed. "I don't think I'll get much rest if I go home right now."

Diana frowned. Sending Kira home was definitely on the table.

"If I go back to the apartment, I'll just sit there thinking about what I should be doing instead."

"All right. Put in a little range time. But get a good meal with some protein and eight hours of sleep, OK?"

Kira adjusted her gear bag. "OK. I'll do that."

KIRA LOWERED HER PISTOL AND SCOWLED AT THE DATA READ-out. Two hours in Firing Point One had produced sore feet from the concrete floor, an aching skull from the ear protection head-set, and no improvement in her draw-to-hit time.

She directed the computer to display impact markers, and a tight group of red *X*s appeared on the chest of the target projection. At least her accuracy was holding up. Maybe it was time for a real break. She put her pistol on the safety stand, put the range control computer on hold, grabbed her water bottle, and entered the break area.

Aside from the scattering of simple tables and plastic chairs, the space was as empty as a school cafeteria in summertime. She sat and pulled the headset down around her neck. Muffled shots sounded from Firing Point Four. When they stopped, a muscular, brown-haired man emerged from the access door. Don Myers. A shock suit peeked out from under his uniform sleeve. Like Kira, he must have come straight here after watching Felix, spurred on by anxiety over tomorrow's final set of trials.

He removed his headset and waved in Kira's direction. "Calling it a night?"

"Nope." She might have, but if Don was staying, leaving was out of the question. "Just taking a break before the next set." She took a swig from her water bottle.

Don ambled over to the vending area, picked an energy drink with the improbable name of Crunk, and pulled up a chair at Kira's table. "Big day for us tomorrow."

Kira took another deep drink from her water. "Yup."

"So, what are you working on?" Don's attempt to feign casual interest wasn't going well.

Kira fiddled with her bottle. "Better draw-to-hit time. How about you?"

"Quick-draw accuracy."

"Interesting." No point in tipping her hand any more than necessary to keep him talking.

He leaned forward and slid his chair closer to the table. "So, when do you plan to wrap up?"

No matter what time she gave, he'd stay later, just to prove he'd "outworked" her. She made a vague gesture toward her firing point. "I dunno. Whenever I'm satisfied with where I'm at, I guess."

"Me, too."

Annoying bastard. Kira drained her water bottle. "Well, we'd best get to it, then."

He pounded down the last of his Crunk and walked back to his station.

Back on the range, Kira instructed the computer to give her a set of ten against a fixed target. At the end of the drill, her average was one one-hundredth of a second worse than her previous round. She'd reached the point of diminishing returns, and it was time to go home.

Or it would be, if Don went home, too. It was petty, it was small, and she was absolutely going to stay at the range longer than he did, even if that meant they both saw the sunrise on the way home.

She left her weapon on the safety stand, uncleaned, and poked her head out the door to find Don doing the same thing. She stepped out and stretched.

He said something. Kira let the headset fall around her neck. "What?"

"I said, 'Packing it in?'"

She shook her head. "Nope. Just a stretch before the next set."

He hesitated a split second too long. "Yeah. Me, too."

Kira re-entered her station and told the computer to give her another ten shots.

She laid out the cartridges for rapid reloading, slapping them into their holders, and jammed one into the dueling pistol. She snapped the action shut and holstered the weapon. Doing the set one-handed would break things up a little, and if she were hit with a damaging shot that didn't knock her down, it might even be useful.

She narrowed her focus and blasted through the set: fire, empty, reload, holster, draw, fire, repeat. Over and over, until she reached for the next cartridge and her hand closed on air instead. All done. The sharp scent of gun smoke hung in the air, and haze obscured her view of the target. The ventilation system must be struggling. Her time remained the same, and her hit marks fell in a tight pattern, though just a bit to the left. Good enough.

She poked her head out the door and found Don halfway out his. He frowned. "If we keep this up, we're going to be here all night. Felix will smoke both of us just because he's had some sleep."

She stepped out into the common area. "Fine. Go home."

His annoyance deepened. "You know I'm not going to do that."

"Neither am I." Shoulders square, chin forward, wide stance. Take up space. Look big. Make it clear she wasn't going to back down.

He stepped out and let the door shut behind him. "Just give it up, OK? You know you're only in it for the dramatic value."

Muscles on the back of Kira's neck tightened. "What the hell did you just say?"

He spread his hands. "Oh, come on. You don't think you're a real contender for this, do you? They only named you as a finalist to get people's attention. You've got that whole 'Death's Angel' thing going, people have heard of you, so it adds some interest. The Association likes that, and TKC's willing to throw 'em a bone."

"I've got the best win-loss record in the whole company!"

He made a sweeping gesture with his arm. "Only because half your opponents don't show up. That's a sweet gig, and I understand why they keep you on the payroll. But this is a real match, and they're going to pick a real gunfighter for it, not somebody who just plays one on vid."

The muscles in Kira's neck tightened further, and heat rose in her chest. "I've got the best *on-field* win percentage in the entire damn region!"

"Pfttt. For the matches you've fought. It's easy to rack up nice stats when you barely need to show up for work."

Kira ground her teeth.

Movement in the simulator area tickled at her peripheral vision. Someone wearing a green service coverall propped the door of a control cab open. Kira licked her lips and stepped in close to Don. "OK, 'real gunfighter,' we've both got shock suits on. Let's grab a couple pseudoguns and settle this in a simulator."

He folded his arms across his chest. "They'll bust our chops for being in there without a trainer. Besides, everything's locked up for the night."

She pointed through the arch between the break room and the simulator area. "Four's open."

Don turned to where Kira pointed. When he looked back, he responded in a steady, low-pitched voice. "OK, let's go." He led the way and Kira followed, determined to keep up despite her shorter legs.

They climbed the stairs to the control cab, eliciting a burst of what sounded like Portuguese from the startled janitorial service employee. Don responded in the same language. Several seconds of vigorous conversation followed, punctuated by hand gestures. There was a brief pause while the wiry, brown-skinned man leaned around Don and took a long look at Kira. No telling what Don had said, but that looked like progress. A bunch of handset activity followed. A personal payment? When they finished, the custodian gathered up his supplies, adjusted the floor cleaner on his back, and paused to take another long look at Kira. Then he hustled out the door.

She punched a generic training ID into the command console and initialized the simulator. From their stand near the door, the pseudoguns chirped as the capacitors took a charge. "What did you tell him?"

Don waved in the general direction of the door. "I told him you got off on doing it in the control cab, gave him twenty unis, and asked for some privacy."

The muscles in the back of Kira's neck wound tight again, and heat flushed her face. "You miserable asshole! I'm not—"

Lacking a suitable conclusion for the sentence, she stormed toward the door instead.

Don spoke with exasperating calm. "Yeah, that's what I figured."

Kira stopped, her hand on the exit plate, and turned back. Don stood with his arms folded across his chest and his chin raised, wearing the look of a man seeing what he expected to see, and feeling smug about it.

"I knew you'd find some way to back out and make it look like it was my fault. You know you're going to lose when you come up against the real thing."

The heat in Kira's chest rose higher, but she hid it behind an expression of icy resolve. She took her hand off the door and walked back toward Don with a series of measured steps. When she arrived in front of him, she wore her best version of the Death's Angel face and spoke in a voice calculated to shave ten degrees off the room temperature. "OK, you want to have a gunfight? We'll have a gunfight. One match, ten yards each, one shot, standard scoring. Loser tells winner, 'You're the best real gunfighter in TKC.' Then he goes home."

Don scowled. "Sounds good."

"Sync your suit." In her head, she added: *asshole.*

Without taking his eyes off Kira, Don put his left wrist near the console pad while Kira punched in the commands that gave the simulator control over the shock generators in Don's suit. She repeated the process with her own, and the system confirmed its control with a low-powered tingle.

Don flashed a grin when Kira twitched at her test. Bastard. She'd give him something to grin about.

The sliders to set the strength and duration of the shocks displayed. Kira shoved both values to maximum and acknowledged the software's warning that the setting was dangerous for people with a heart condition.

Don pointed to the settings. "Oh, hey, that's just ridiculous. If either one of us gets a fatal, it'll take all day tomorrow to recover. Felix will walk all over us."

Kira gave her left eyebrow a strategic arch and injected as much condescension into her voice as possible. "Oh? A 'real gunfighter' is worried about getting killed by some poser?"

He stepped back. "You . . . You really are out of your mind, aren't you?"

Good. Let *him* be scared. Let *him* feel angry and frightened and wonder what was going to happen next.

"I've been told that." Kira removed one of the pseudoguns from its mount. She checked the safety, opened its action, and held it with the barrel pointed down. "Here."

Don glared at her, but he didn't move.

"Either take this thing or admit you haven't got the ovaries to handle it."

Don rolled his eyes and shook his head. "This is what you do, isn't it? Get a person so confused and frustrated they just quit." He snatched the pseudogun from her hand.

She walked back to the gun stand to retrieve hers. "I prefer to think of it as helping my opponents see the reality of their situation." She followed up with a cold, cruel smile.

A few minutes later, they stood side by side in front of the judge's table, their pseudoguns holstered, looking down the field toward the start point and waiting for the simulator to run the match script.

Kira absentmindedly scuffed her boot in the pseudograss. "You know, I don't always psych people out and get them to quit."

Don responded with a derisive snort.

"Sometimes I just get them so worked up they can't shoot straight."

Before Don could respond, the Wall came up, followed by the recorded ward's voice. They marched to the start point.

Standing back-to-back on the red circle, the carefully hidden heat in Kira's chest disappeared under a wave of icy calm. She brought her attention to a pinpoint focus and chose a spot half a meter to the left of the strikeline where she'd enter the kill box. She marched toward it with the lead ward's cadence and executed a perfect turn. The Wall was up. Gun drawn, she moved into a double-handed stance, legs bent. The Wall came down, and she spotted Don well to the right of the strikeline, through his turn but barely clearing his holster. Kira's front sight came into focus, and she fired. Don's weapon flashed, a desperate shot from midbody.

A burn flared in her upper right leg. A deep male scream and a burst of profanity furnished proof her shot found its target. Kira swore, dropped her gun, and braced her hands against her thigh. The burn intensified. She closed her eyes and strained, willing herself not to move beyond the limits set by the motion sensor. The outer thigh was a low-point hit. If she could remain standing, she'd win this. An infinite time later, the pain stopped, and Kira searched the other side of the field for her opponent.

Don lay flat on his back, breathing heavily. A win light flashed on Kira's side of the field. The scoreboard read: MYERS, 41; CLARK, 100.

She scooped up her pseudogun and walked toward her fallen adversary, limping a little. By the time she arrived, Don was on all fours, puking bile onto the field surface.

Kira stopped a few feet away. "You OK?"

Don sat back on his haunches. "For somebody who just got the shit shocked out of him, sure. I'm fine."

Kira nodded. "OK, say it."

"Say what?"

"What we agreed."

"What are you, a goddamn kid?"

Heat rose in her chest and face again, but this time, there was no reason to hide it. "No, I'm the winner of a gunfight. Now say it. You know damn well you'd make me do it."

He glared at her.

Without moving her arm from its relaxed position, Kira thumbed the pseudogun's reset, eliciting a chirp from the capacitor. Would the suit provide another jolt without an initialization message from the cab? He probably didn't know, either.

Don pushed himself to a standing position, spread his arms, and shouted to the ceiling. *"All right.* Kira Abigail Clark is the best goddamn real gunfighter at TKC Insurance." He looked down at her. "Happy?"

She smiled. "Yes, as a matter of fact, I am."

CHAPTER 32

The bile tastes worse than the chunks that came before it, and the contortions of her now-empty stomach add their own sharp spike of pain to the background agony in Kira's abdomen. She shudders and wobbles.

Diana again. "It's OK. It's OK. Good to get that out."

"Yeah, maybe." Kira lets her head hang. Fuck it all, that hurt. What was taking the judge so damn long?

She tries to look up again, to see Niles. She catches only a glimpse. He tries to straighten—maybe to get a look at her? He sways, his arms wrapped around his upper chest, and he only gets about halfway to upright before he sags down and staggers a little. He can't possibly last much longer.

But neither can she.

Fog narrows her visual range, and color washes out. Almost out of sight on her left, something stirs. A person. The ward? How did he get over there? Wait. Diana is talking to him over on her right, so it must be the EMT. But the EMT is short, and this person is tall and thin. And now there's another one. Shorter. Who the hell is letting people on the field, and where are they coming from?

She adjusts her hands, trying to minimize the blood flow from her wounds, and turns toward the gathering crowd.

Rusty Cunningham.

Canfield Harper.

Jason Armitage.

The first three people she killed on the dueling field. Kira sags, Diana takes a sharp, sudden breath, and Kira stabilizes herself.

"Diana, can you see . . ." Kira stops. Of course Diana can't see them. Her second doesn't have one foot in their world, not the way Kira does. They're coming for her. Kira presses down harder on her wounds. She isn't going to go. She'll stanch the flow, she'll be OK, it was just . . .

The crowd on her left gets bigger.

Santiago Rodriguez, who'd put a bullet within inches of Kira's head but hadn't lived through the mayhem her round inflicted on his liver.

Patricia Stevens, hair as red and wild as it had been on the day of the duel.

Jake Garn.

Reginald Dupree.

Roger Cummings.

Benjamin Lopez.

Elaine Thomas. Tall and elegant, wearing the dress she'd worn in the waiting room. Had they buried her in it?

Kira gasps and looks away. "No. I don't . . ."

Diana's voice, concerned. Far away. "You don't what?"

Kira squeezes her eyes shut. "I don't want to die."

"You won't, you won't . . ."

Easy for Diana to say. Her kill list isn't forming up next to her, getting ready to take her away. Kira looks again.

Oh shit. Lotila. She stands in front, autograph book tucked under one arm. Kira tries to wet her lips and faces the growing sepulchral crowd. "I'm sorry. I'm sorry . . ."

As if they're going to buy that. Diana would say they all chose the dueling field, but Kira chose it, too. Maybe for reasons that weren't as good as theirs. All the stuff Kira was afraid would happen to her—a job that would break her in mind and body, being used up to gratify someone else, facing death without having really lived her life? Most of it had already happened to them, one way or another. And Kira chose to defend the system keeping them all in place.

Fuck. Might as well give up and tell them to take her to hell where she belonged.

All eleven, now. All the people she faced on the field who came up short. She'd tried to talk each one of them out of it before their match. She'd used every bit of her skill to dissuade them. But it doesn't matter. They're here for her.

A sharp jab of pain runs from her ankle all the way to her neck, followed by a flash of heat. Kira groans and Diana says . . . something.

With her vision dim and her legs wobbling, Kira turns to face her final audience.

They look back in silence.

Not reaching for her. Not gloating. Not even showing smug satisfaction at her comeuppance.

Watching.

As if they're waiting for her to do something. But what?

She can barely move without falling over. She tries to speak, but her dry throat and parched mouth refuse to make any sound.

The dead stare back. Silent.

Maybe they aren't here to take her to her death. Maybe they're here to influence her life. If she wins, she'll be rich. She can make a difference. Is that what they're here for? To push her into doing something good?

Maybe she shouldn't be rich. Maybe she should just take enough to pay off her debts, buy a plane ticket back to New York, and divide the rest among her victim's families. She'll have enough to buy Lotila's father and her sister out of their lifetime services contracts. That will be good. There must be something she can do for the others.

She could give some to those people blocking the entrance the day she showed up for training, SPD or SSD or whatever they called themselves. The anti-dueling people.

Maybe that isn't enough. Maybe they expect more. But what? And if she loses, what good is she to anyone?

"If I get through this, I'll do what I can." Did she say that, or just think it? Did it matter?

Another painful spasm. Kira closes her eyes and sucks in another deep breath, willing her legs to hold and the pain to stop. When she looks again, her victims are gone. Vanished.

Maybe it meant nothing. Maybe it was an elaborate hallucination concocted by her dying brain. Maybe.

CHAPTER 33

Kira drew a cleaning pad through her pistol while resting against the judge's table in Simulator Five. Diana probably knew Kira's complaint about a sticky action was an excuse to avoid another match, but it was late enough in the day her trainer probably didn't care. A not-entirely-surprising management decree, promulgated just after the final evaluation session, confined all candidates for the professional match and their seconds to the training facility until the committee made its choice.

Faced with the restriction, Don and his trainer hit the gym. Felix and Raj established themselves in the break area, putting away sports drinks and bullshitting with the assembled staff as though they were waiting for a firing point to open up instead of anticipating the most significant gunfighter assignment made by any company in the past two years.

Diana scrounged simulator time and put Kira to work.

When they started just after noon, a small knot of trainees and staff waited on the catwalk to watch her practice, but it was now nearly five; her audience had long since dispersed, and there seemed to be little point in another run against the mech. Kira put a drop of lubricant on the hinging pin and slowly wiped off the excess.

Diana's voice came over the earpiece. "Hey, come on up here. We have company." Kira placed the pistol in its cradle and climbed the steel stairs to the control cab. She stopped with her hand on the door and got her breath under control. Should she make a big entrance or try to slide in unnoticed? A quiet entry would let her find out who the visitors were and what news they carried before she had to react. She opened the door just wide enough to slip through and closed it behind her without making any noise.

Inside the cab, Diana spoke to a man in a dark suit with his back to Kira. His jacket's cut matched his body so well it had to be hand tailored. Gold cufflinks, a white linen shirt, and shoes that probably cost more than Kira made in a month rounded out the ensemble. This was not a lackey sent to convey disappointing news.

Kira approached and got a look at the man's profile. Despite his fine clothes and high position, the executive focused on Diana and sought approval, like a subordinate delivering a report. Kira smiled to herself. By long custom, trainers were the undisputed masters of the simulator field and control cab, although it was hard to tell if the man was respecting the custom or just reacting to Diana the same way everyone else did.

Kira stood quietly, letting his words float to her. ". . . she clearly would have been the choice, regardless, but when Don's performance fell off in the final sessions this morning, the committee saw that as clutching under pressure, and it made the choice unanimous."

In the far corner of the cab, Betty Stimwald held a pair of data pads in a white-knuckle grip. Diana once told Kira that the departmental admin had held her position for as long as anyone could remember, outlasting five bosses and multiple reorganizations, apparently through a combination of efficiency and obscurity. With her plain blue dress standing out from the uniforms and coveralls worn in the training facility and no way to blend in with only four people in the cab, the admin's uneasiness was palpable.

Kira gave Betty a quick nod. Maybe that would be enough to acknowledge her presence without making her more uncomfortable. Betty responded with a stiff bob of her head.

The movement must have caught Diana's attention, because she interrupted her conversation with the executive. "Kira, this is Vice President of Contract Adjustments, Anthony Prescott."

The executive turned to Kira, and from that angle, she recognized his face from her selection committee interview. She stepped forward. "Pleased to see you again."

"Ah, Ms. Clark. Our fast, patient, and accurate blue heron, if I remember correctly."

Kira smiled, pushing aside the implications of Prescott remembering that particular detail. Executive decision-making became terrifying if she thought about it too much.

Prescott extended a hand and Kira took it, taking care to make sure her grip was as firm as his. Three gentle up-and-down pumps, three seconds, release. His smile told her she'd cleared that social hurdle.

"Ms. Clark, I'm pleased to inform you that you're the committee's unanimous choice to represent TKC in the match with United Reinsurance."

It was Kira's turn to smile. "Thank you. I hope to justify your confidence."

Again, Prescott's face told her she'd hit the right note of self-assurance without seeming arrogant and gratitude without tipping into servility. Kira relaxed and assumed an alert but comfortable stance. All she needed to do was look lethal and obedient while Prescott talked. He seemed ready to do quite a bit of that.

He began with great seriousness. "I don't need to tell you this is a matter of utmost sensitivity and importance. An amount greater than our profits for the entire third quarter is at stake."

And, of course, there's the possibility I might die. Kira kept that thought from finding its way to her face.

Prescott moved on to his next subject. "Because this is a matter of such importance, you're being asked to review and recommit to the TKC Insurance Code of Conduct."

On that call to action, Betty doled out her data pads to Kira and Diana. Prescott resumed. "Please look through these copies and let me know if you have any questions. Pay special attention to the section regarding conflicts of interest."

Kira skimmed through the document. Nothing seemed different from the one she accepted when she started work at TKC. It committed her to what the company regarded as ethical behavior: don't steal from the company, don't release company information unless authorized to do so, don't expose the company to unnecessary liability by harassing other employees or contractors, and so on. No clause seemed to explicitly rule out shooting disgruntled customers or the representatives of unhappy contract partners.

Since Prescott made a fuss about the conflict of interest section, she slowed down and read it more carefully. It stated she must "always act in the company's best interest," elaborated on that a bit, and then laid out the nasty legal and professional consequences for failing to do so. So, getting paid to throw the match to United Re was clearly frowned upon. She sped through the rest and acknowledged her understanding with a thumbprint.

Diana wrapped up at about the same time.

"Any questions?" Prescott didn't seem to expect any.

Betty gathered the data pads, and Prescott moved on to his next point. "We recognize that your preparation will require total concentration and focus, so you'll move to the annex until the match is over. There you'll be free from distractions and able to make your remaining training sessions as impactful as possible. Ms. Stimwald will show you to your quarters."

What was this "annex"? Kira's brow furrowed and she looked to Diana. Her trainer flashed a hand signal: *Later.*

Prescott was going on about the importance of this particular match and how it was falling to the team to extract the company from a difficult situation. "Team" apparently meant the entire Contract Adjustments Division, including Prescott, although no one but Kira would face an incoming round. Displaying the monumental indifference she felt toward Prescott, the division, and TKC was obviously the wrong move, so Kira adopted a pose of intense interest and . . . studied Prescott's hair. Were those lush black strands natural or genetically encoded implants? The pompadour held its shape so well, with so little evidence of hair products, he must have laid out an amount close to Kira's annual earnings to avoid baldness.

At last, Prescott went for the close. "I'll leave you in Ms. Stimwald's capable hands, and I look forward to celebrating a victory with you on Friday." He addressed the assistant. "Please take care of them. I'll see myself out."

Betty relaxed once Prescott left, her death grip on the data pads fading to a more normal pressure.

"Kira, can you give me a hand with this?" Already back at the control panel, Diana directed the mech to its charging station, the first step in simulator shutdown. Kira stepped up to the panel, reset timers, and cleared the log.

"Oh." Diana pointed to the cluster of controls on the big touch-panel just off Kira's right hand. "Don't forget to delete the video logs for the field camera and mic. They moved them under Media instead of Records."

Kira kept her face calm. The change must have come during the last software upgrade.

Diana continued, her deadpan just a bit too perfect. "If you don't erase it or move it to long-term storage, the next trainer will see you on the vid and track me down to ask if I want to keep the record." Diana paused, like a comedian about to deliver a punch line. "Professional courtesy."

Kira's mouth went dry and her throat tightened. How much trouble was she in?

Kira swallowed hard. "Sure." She caught the barest hint of

a smile on Diana's face. Did she approve of last night's escapade, or was her trainer just enjoying her embarrassment?

Kira's ears burned, but Diana didn't say any more.

With the shutdown complete, they picked up their gear bags and followed Betty out of the cab and across the floor. At a guard booth, Betty presented her ID and negotiated passage for Kira and Diana.

They entered an area building maps labeled "support equipment." Betty led them up some stairs, through an armored entrance, and finally into a hallway that could have been part of a five-star hotel, although the label on the elegant wood door at the far end declared ANNEX SIMULATOR. A sharp industrial scent underlay the stale air, and Kira's nose wrinkled. The place smelled like a clean room left unused for a long time. "What is this?"

Betty responded in a voice like a tour guide. "It's the section annex. It meets or exceeds all Guild standards for out-of-town accommodations and provides a dedicated practice area. We use it for visitors and high-stakes matches."

That accounted for the lack of use. As TKC's flagship facility, Des Moines was more likely to send gunfighters out than take them in.

"This is Ms. Reynolds's room." The admin presented the interior space as if she were selling it.

Chloe would have loved the annex. In the main living area, a kitchenette covered the right wall, separated from the rest of the room by a natural rock serving bar with matching stools made from dark wood. An oversize vid terminal bearing the logo of Blaupunkt Electronics' most expensive line dominated the left wall, and a leather couch faced the terminal. The couch exuded the scent of luxury camel skin rather than ordinary cowhide.

Betty reentered the hallway. "Ms. Clark's room is right across the hall." She opened the door to reveal the same interior arrangements in mirror image.

"Although you're free to do your own cooking, we recommend you have the staff handle meal preparation. The executive kitchen will be available around the clock until the match. They'll send your meals via the dumbwaiter." Betty pointed at a cabinet in Kira's kitchenette, then stepped back into the hallway and closed the door behind her.

"These are high-security VIP quarters. Contact the front desk for anything you need—laundry services, massage, physical trainers, anything. They'll get good people who have been properly vetted." She removed a stylus from its carrying slot and held it above her data pad. "Do you want anything from your apartments?"

Kira responded. "I'll need some clothes. All I have here is my uniforms and one set of street clothes. Can't I just go get them?"

"I'm sorry, Ms. Clark, but you're expected to be here and be focused every day between now and the match. We can deliver clothing and other necessities from your home."

Kira shot Diana a quizzical look. Diana shook her head.

Kira sent two short-term key files to Betty's handset. "Those will get you into my work locker and my apartment."

Betty made a note on her data pad. She made more notes as Kira described the contents of her closet and how to identify what she needed.

Diana's list was shorter and less complicated, partially because Howard would be available to assist with locating the items.

Betty pointed down the hall. "The Annex Simulator is reserved for your exclusive use, as is the range and exercise area downstairs. If you get an inspiration at three in the morning and want to act on it, you can. If there are any problems, use the red comm link in the control cab. That connects you directly with Executive Support, and they'll know it's a priority call." She was obviously wrapping up. "Is there anything else?"

Diana responded. "No, we're fine. Thanks for your help."

As soon as Betty departed, Diana consulted her handset. "I thought so. No outside connections, internal company only."

Kira put her hand on the wall, as if that would stop it from closing in. "It feels like we're prisoners."

Diana opened the door to Kira's room and pointed at the bottle of sparkling water and fresh flowers on the serving bar. "I'll tell you from experience, this is a lot nicer than prison. But we are sequestered."

"Sequestered?"

"Isolated. Whatever you want to call it. TKC isn't depending on those statements we just signed to keep us on their side; they're making sure we don't get a better offer." Diana returned her handset to her belt. "Also, be aware everything we say here is probably being monitored."

"They can do that?"

"Didn't you see the 'consent to any measures necessary to enforce' language at the end of the Code of Conduct?"

"I guess I didn't realize that's what it meant."

Diana laughed. "You're probably not the only one. Let's go check the simulator."

In addition to being brighter and sleeker than any equipment in the main area, the control cab smelled of new plastic and fresh paint. It looked out over a simulator field with a domed roof of its own and no connections to the rest of the facility.

Diana surveyed the equipment, fired up the console, and tapped out a few commands. She smiled. "Nice. We'll have a Mark IV mech with release 12.4 software." She pointed to the version number in the upper right corner of the screen. "They told me just this morning that update wasn't available."

The console warbled for attention, and Diana brought up the message monitor. It displayed a joint press release from TKC and United Reinsurance, announcing their respective champions for the coming duel. Kira's photo appeared under the headline on the TKC side of the statement. and next to her, on the United Re side, Niles LeBlanc's likeness stared back.

Diana stepped back from the console and faced Kira. "What do you think?"

"Chloe's ex?" Kira laughed. "And I was afraid they might pick somebody I didn't want to shoot."

"I thought it might be him." Diana folded her arms. "He's good, and it fits with being an adrenaline junkie."

Kira gave her trainer a sideways glance. "You buy that act?"

Diana shrugged. "It's not as if he needs the money. I had the underwriters take a look at potential opponents, and Niles has a sky-high credit score and an even higher estimated net worth."

Kira shook her head. "I think it's daddy issues."

Diana looked intrigued. "Really?"

"He's from an old Southern family. Chloe said his dad's people go back to a plantation someplace in South Carolina. Mom is DAR, and they live in this big old country house where the men go off to smoke together after dinner parties—actual cigarettes and cigars with real tobacco. It's wild." Kira paused, relishing the sensation of knowing something Diana didn't. "He's the youngest of three boys. The oldest followed Dad into law, the next-oldest is in the Army—"

"Wait, Dad's a *lawyer*?"

"Was. Now he's a circuit court judge."

Diana exhaled sharply and shook her head. "I can imagine how that goes over. A judge's son working in dueling—the bastard child of the bar."

"I don't think Dad's happy, but I don't think they were ever close. Chloe said Niles kept going on about how his dad's opinion didn't matter, but he did everything he could to impress him. Like, he kept saying when he made enough as a gunfighter, he was going to pay his dad back for the money he blew flunking out of Grinnell College, just to make the old man shut up about it."

"So, you think Niles has gone his own way and wants Dad to recognize him for it."

"Yup. He thinks that if he's just successful enough, Dad will have to break down and admit he was right."

"And that never happens."

"No, but I'm sure this match looks like one hell of an opportunity. With a purse this big, he'd be set."

Diana scratched her chin. "I'm sure you'll find a way to use that."

Kira conjured the cold, mocking Death's Angel smile and voice. "I'll hit him at the time and place he least expects it."

Diana chuckled. "As your trainer, I approve of that strategy."

Kira grinned with real warmth. "Can we give that executive kitchen a workout before we get started? I'm hungry."

Diana considered. "I suppose so. It's been a big day. After supper, we can get in a couple sessions to get used to the equipment and call it a night."

Diana was obviously in a conciliatory mood. Maybe conciliatory enough to answer a question that had been picking at the edge of Kira's mind all afternoon. "I heard Raj talking in the cafeteria. He said seconds always quit after a professional match."

Diana nodded. "That's true. Once you've coached a professional win, there isn't much else to do."

"He said if we lose, you probably won't have a choice."

"That's true, too." Diana's joke-that-only-she-got smile appeared. "So let's make this one a win, OK?"

Kira nodded. "As your gunfighter, I approve of that strategy."

CHAPTER 34

The transportation arrangements to the duel were ridiculous. They could have walked from the annex through the TKC facility, crossed the skywalk to the Association complex, and entered the arena—pretty much Diana's normal route to a match. However, TKC security fussed about keeping them in a "controlled environment," and the Association lobbied for the drama of having the gunfighters pass through a group of carefully vetted fans as they entered the arena. The result left Kira, Diana, and a dozen security people at the training facility's back entrance, waiting for VIP transport to complete about two blocks' worth of travel.

Two members of the security team waited in the vestibule, while the rest held positions along the sidewalk leading to the turnout where the driver would arrive. Kira and Diana waited in the hallway, Diana in her gray-and-green second's uniform, Kira in her full Death's Angel regalia of hat, cloak, and black leather.

Kira reached into her gear bag and withdrew a thin stack of paper envelopes. She held them out for Diana. "Will you take care of these for me? I don't want them stuck in the personal effects bin."

The letters, written on old-fashioned stationary with a pen Kira ordered for the occasion, contained her parting words for family and friends, the thoughts she wanted them to remember her by if she didn't leave the field alive.

It was a depressingly small stack.

Becoming a gunfighter had shrunk her circle of friends, wearing away relationships under the pressure of both distance and the uncertainties of Kira's all-consuming work schedule. How many weddings, anniversaries, and birthday parties had she sent regrets to because she couldn't fit them into her brief and unpredictable time off? How many times had changes in the dueling schedule forced her to cancel plans? And on top of all that, how many people stopped talking to her because they regarded her as little more than a well-paid murderer?

When Kira tried to justify her career to a former New York roommate, Patty had replied, "Your suffering doesn't make you innocent." Many old friends probably agreed with the rebuke, but few had the courage to say it to Kira's face. Instead, they gradually stopped talking to her.

Diana accepted the stack and placed them in a side pocket of her bag. "I'll do that. But I expect to hand them back to you after the match."

Kira gave her second a wan smile. "Thanks."

"Hey." Diana's voice was firm, but not harsh. "You're ready. It's going to be OK."

"You used to finish sentences like that with 'baby girl.'" Kira waited for her trainer's reaction. There were some things that needed to be said.

Diana looked down at her hands. "I guess it doesn't feel appropriate."

"No. That's OK." Kira swallowed past the lump in her throat. "It's . . . It's what my Mom used to call me. Right up to that last night in the hospital."

Diana looked stricken. "Kira, I am so, so sorry. I didn't know—"

"No, no. I said it's OK. I'm glad you call me that. Mom always looked out for me, just like you do. She backed me up when I got in trouble at school but then gave me the what-for when we got home. She made things right with Dad when he couldn't figure me out and I wouldn't talk to him." Kira's eyes were wet. "Diana, I let you call me 'baby girl' because you earned it, OK?"

Diana's eyes glistened. "I'm honored. I really am. But I think you're past needing that from me or anyone else."

Kira pulled a handkerchief from her pocket, dabbed her eyes dry, and offered silent thanks to the unsung genius who created waterproof mascara. Death's Angel shouldn't display that kind of vulnerability.

Diana let her finish, then spoke. "I meant what I said about you being ready."

"I'm reaching for a really big prize. What if I don't deserve it?" Kira looked down the hall and out the glass door before looking back at Diana.

Her trainer's expression became serious. "Whatever happens tonight, I'm proud of you. Not just for this, but for everything. Ever since we started working together, I've driven you hard. Harder than any of my other clients. But you did everything I asked, and you never quit. You're a good gunfighter. You deserve to win." A smile pulled at the corner of Diana's mouth. "Baby girl."

Kira responded with a smile of her own. The kind of gunfighter she was might not be her most important concern, but it was the one that would make a difference tonight. Kira latched on to Diana's words and tried to pull herself up by them.

At the far end of the hall, the door opened, and a guard spoke. "The driver's here."

WHEN TWO LIGHT *THUMPS* FROM CLOSING DOORS ANNOUNCED the security teams had taken their places in the driver's fore and aft compartments, the vehicle moved forward. From her seat opposite Kira in the cavernous, standup center section, Diana contemplated the whole needlessly complex arrangement with obvious irritation. "At least we won the coin toss."

Coming out on top during that little ritual had won the right to enter first. LeBlanc and his second would wait while Kira and Diana entered the arena, security moved Kira's fans off the premises to a theater showing a live stream from the dueling field, and Niles's followers assembled. That cut into the combatants' waiting room time, but it wasn't like either one of them might arrive late.

Kira pulled at her cloak and stared out the window. The driver rounded the corner, presenting her with her first good view of the crowd. A solid mass of humanity filled the space in front of the arena, packed like New Year's Eve partygoers in Times Square.

As the driver approached, someone angled a GO TEAM ES-
TROGEN! sign so it could be seen through the window. Kira
pointed it out for Diana, who rolled her eyes.

The driver pulled up to the spot where the broad sidewalk
leading to the arena entrance met the unloading area. Diana
stood and extended her hand. "I'll take the bags." She nodded
toward the throng outside. "Show them what they came to see."

Kira surrendered her bag, then squeezed past Diana to position herself in front of the sliding main door and prepare for
her entrance. A chime sounded to indicate full stop, followed by
soft *thumps* from the security team's doors. Outside, Kira could
make out individual faces. Men in their twenties and thirties,
the demographic backbone of gunfighter fandom, dominated
the crowd, but the group contained a fair number of young
women as well. By any measure, Kira's following had always
skewed female.

Although the sidewalk to the main entrance could easily allow four people to walk abreast, against the mass on either side
it looked like a thin line kept clear only by twin rows of Association security personnel.

Kira nudged Diana. "You know, on my first day as a trainee,
I was nervous about walking past half a dozen guys to get to
my room."

Diana chuckled, and Kira turned her attention back to the
window. Despite the celebratory air, bloodlust underlaid the
mood. While this crowd cheered for her and the one that would
replace it would cheer for Niles, they all ultimately cheered for
death. They'd shown up so they could tell envious friends they'd
been among the last to see the gunfighters alive. Kira Clark

might feel a little queasy about that, but to Death's Angel, it was all part of the show. She adjusted her hat and cloak, squared her shoulders, and set her expression, draining any hint of softness or empathy from her face. Under her breath, she recited: "I am death. I am terror. I am blood."

The leader of the security detail signaled, and the door eased open. Without filtering from the windows, harsh white camera lights made the scene resemble an overexposed photo.

The crowd responded to her appearance with a palpable roar. The noise contained no hint of support or hostility; it was simply *sound*.

She stepped down from the transport, ignoring the helping hand proffered by the guard on her right. Death's Angel was cold, perfect, and independent, beyond the need for such warm human gestures. Two guards took up positions ahead of her, and they moved down the sidewalk enough to allow Diana and the rest of the TKC security detail to assemble behind them.

At first, she couldn't make out any individual words in the random shouting, but when they got about halfway to the entrance, the sound coalesced into a call and response. Some people left of the sidewalk shouted, "Death's!" provoking the ragged response of "Angel!" from the right. After a couple repetitions, the crowd found its rhythm and the words picked up volume and punch: "Death's!" "Angel!" *"DEATH'S!"* "ANGEL!" *"DEATH'S!"* "ANGEL!" The pace accelerated as she got closer to the door, reaching a crescendo as she climbed the steps.

They might be bloodthirsty, but they were her fans, and she owed them something.

Security opened the arena doors, but she stopped at the top

stair, stepped off the direct path, and executed a slow pivot that ended with her facing the gathering.

Hand signal to Diana: *Pass me.*

Diana went on by, and whatever she said to the security guards, it kept the detail standing at the door rather than hustling the two of them through the entrance.

Death's Angel stood straight and cold, her arms extended just enough to spread her cloak, using its crimson lining to accentuate both her shape and her outfit. The chanting died away to a murmur.

After a dramatic pause, she bowed from the waist, drawing the cloak around her. She held that position until the crowd became quiet, or at least as close to quiet as a group this large could get. Then, with a gradual, deliberate motion she came upright, releasing the cloak into a fortuitous gust that made it billow freely at her back. The crowd roared. She raised her fist, provoking a fresh outburst of cheering, and then lowered her arm, turned on the ball of her foot, and entered the arena.

The security team closed the arena doors behind her and watched as she and Diana passed through the entrance check. Kira went through first, and Diana put Kira's bag through next. When the staff finished searching her bag, Kira stuffed her cloak inside it. The costume was for the crowd and cameras, not Niles. She secured the bag to her person with the shoulder strap and stood by a window to watch as the mass of fans milled around and arena guards prodded them to disperse.

"Remember, 'slinger—thou art mortal." Diana had bent down to whisper in her ear.

Kira sighed and made a sad smile. "Don't worry. I'm not

going to get too full of myself like I did with Hernandez." Kira's hand strayed toward her inner thigh. Did that wound really hurt, or was she imagining it? "I learned my lesson on that one." She pointed toward the thinning crowd outside. "Let me enjoy this a little bit. That's the best audience I've ever had."

Diana responded with a smile and a squeeze to Kira's shoulder. "There's a bigger one waiting when you win."

"Thanks." Kira lowered her eyes. "I'll get to the waiting room in a minute."

Diana let her arm fall from Kira's shoulder. "See you on the other side." Her own gear bag in hand, Diana trooped down the hallway, heading for the second's entrance to Dueling Field Six.

KIRA STOOD BEFORE THE WAITING ROOM DOOR, EYES CLOSED, centering herself. Slow breaths in, slower breaths out. Let all the obligations fall away—to Diana, to the fans, to TKC, even to herself. Relaxed body, quiet mind.

"Afraid to go in?" The loud, mocking voice behind her belonged to Niles. She turned to face him. For the occasion of the biggest duel in the past two years, he wore a plain black T-shirt and jeans, along with his porkpie hat. The strap to his gear bag crossed his chest like a bandolier.

Kira arranged her coldest possible smile. "Just wondering if you'd show or not."

Niles laughed. "As if I'd pass on the chance to see you again."

"We didn't really say goodbye, did we? You running down the hall, me with the gun and all that."

He hooked his thumbs into his belt loops. "You know, I'm

really going to have to reconsider the head shot. It'd be a shame to wreck such a pretty face."

She ignored him and pointed to the waiting room doors. "Shall we go in together?"

They drew the double doors open with slow, even pulls that matched one other. Perfectly.

Inside, Niles made an elaborate show of letting her go to the reception desk first. She made a show of accepting it as her due. The receptionist, unimpressed by either display, checked them in with indifferent efficiency.

They took up positions on their respective chairs. Kira kept her posture fluid, catlike, and focused. Niles slouched into his seat as if he were back in high school and waiting for study hall to be over.

He spent a few seconds looking around the room and finally focused on her. "So, are y'all having your period?"

Kira raised an eyebrow. "Can I ask why you want to know?"

"It just always seemed unfair to me. I mean, if you're already bleeding when you take the bullet, you're at a disadvantage, right? There should be a rule that spots you some extra time on the fall or something. Then there's the whole irritability thing. I mean, hell, when you're all hormonal like that, it's hard to tell if you'll shoot me at the judge's table or burst into tears when we get to the start point."

She made a face, as if she smelled something bad. "You've had ten days to get ready and that's the best you can do? Some pathetic line about my period?"

"Ah, so you're playing that one close to your chest." His gaze ran up and down her body like a physical intrusion. "And a rather lovely chest, even better than I remember. Did you have some work done? Or are you aging well?"

She cocked her head. "So tell me, Niles. Does this actually work? Are there women who find this attractive?"

He frowned. "I don't know, really. I think my attraction is something more, I dunno, primal. Like, pheromones or something." He leaned forward, bringing himself closer to her. "You're feeling it, too, aren't you?" He looked over his shoulder at the receptionist. "I bet she'd be willing to look the other way if we wanted to slip into one of the changing rooms, for, you know, long enough."

Kira burst out laughing.

Niles didn't budge. "I don't want you to die unfulfilled or anything."

Kira stifled her laughter long enough to get some words out. "Niles, if I'm . . ." She looked at his crotch with obvious amusement. ". . . unfulfilled, it's got nothing to do with you."

A grin spread across his face. "Oh, I get it. This is some of that acting stuff, isn't it? You're trying to, like, crush my ego and get me to fold up and quit, just like most of your other opponents. It was really expensive to learn that, wasn't it?"

Kira smiled, though it was more like baring her teeth. "How could I scare you off, Niles? You haven't missed a match in over a year. Oh, except for that one time with the Special Forces guy. Stomach flu, wasn't it? Kirk Davis subbed for you and got drilled in the head. Am I remembering that right?"

Niles shifted.

Got him.

He looked at his hands. "Well, not everybody can draw a match with a little girl."

A knot formed in Kira's stomach. Maybe it wouldn't show on her face.

He pressed the attack. "Is that what you're up to? Proving you can beat a real opponent?"

She gave him the look she normally reserved for the most naive assertions of the unbloodied. "It's about the *money*, Niles. The only thing I want to prove is that my work is worth the payout." She checked the clock. Time to play her final card. "So tell me something. Is your father watching today? Or do you have to be a multimillionaire before he cares if you live or die?"

Niles's jaw tightened and his nostrils flared, but he didn't speak. Kira kept her gaze steady, as if she expected an answer.

The receptionist preempted his response. "TKC Insurance versus United Reinsurance."

CHAPTER 35

The ward's voice comes from Kira's right. "Ms. Reynolds, Ms. Clark. The judge has reviewed the video and ruled that although Mr. LeBlanc's second did reach toward him, there was no contact and therefore no foul."

Diana's face is unchanged, but her right hand becomes a fist. "Very well. Thank you." She gives the ward a curt nod, as if dismissing him, and turns back to Kira. "Not what we wanted, but it will be OK."

Weight settles on Kira's shoulders, and pain flares in her abdomen. She steals a glance across the field at Niles. He struggles and shifts, trying to rise. Is he buoyed by the news or arching his back in agony? She leans down to get her head closer to the ground.

White mist rolls in from the edge of the combat area, and Kira's visible world shrinks until it's a circle containing nothing but her feet.

Her will collapses in the face of her body's failure, like an earthen dam giving way before a flood. Her consciousness, and maybe her life, drains away uncontrolled. She will either outlast Niles or she won't, and there's nothing she can do about it.

If she'd made any one of a thousand different choices, she wouldn't be in this position. She could have followed Diana's advice and not gone after this match. She could have taken the door instead of killing Lotila; she could have accepted the job in Minneapolis instead of becoming a gunfighter. She could have declined when TKC offered the bonus to sign up for training, or she could have refused to take on the debt in the first place, or at least stopped racking up new debt after she got her BA, or maybe not gone to college at all . . .

But could she have really made any of those other choices? Each decision seemed like the best one at the time, but they all brought her to where she was now: standing on the pseudograss with her life bleeding away and eleven deaths on her conscience, with nothing to show for her time on Earth except a trail of wreckage running through other people's lives.

Diana says something. It's so distant Kira can't make out the words, and it doesn't matter.

If these are her last moments, she's not going to spend them on the dueling field. She closes her eyes and reaches back in memory. She's just graduated from high school, and she's trying to choose between one of four colleges and an apprenticeship at the Regulus Theater, guessing at the future that lies behind each choice. The crowd attending her graduation party fills the first floor and spills out onto the deck and backyard—visiting cousins, her aunt Abigail, some neighbors, and her parent's colleagues from the university, all augmented by a steady stream of Kira's friends. Good smells from the barbecue fill the air, and in the midst of it all, there's a place for her.

Kira breathes.

ACKNOWLEDGMENTS

There is only one name on the cover of this book, but many people stand behind it.

To begin at the beginning, I've enjoyed constant support from my wife, my friend, and my partner in all things, Catherine Engstrom. She encouraged me to turn a vignette about a near-future gunfighter into a novel, edited every page of every version, and saved me from several serious errors along the way.

I also owe a huge debt to the members of the Paradise ICON Writer's Workshop and the Dire Turtles Writer's Group, who offered editorial feedback and support over several years as this manuscript took shape. A special shout-out to Catherine Schaff-Stump, who organizes Paradise ICON and always insists it's no big deal. (It absolutely is a big deal.)

I would be remiss not to mention the beta readers who helped shape the story with critiques and advice: Chris Bauer, Sue Burns, Rachael K. Jones, Ransom Noble, Catherine Schaff-Stump, Emma Smailes, and Miranda Suri.

I benefited from the generosity of Michelle Hauck and Amy Trueblood, who organized the Sun vs Snow contest, and the tremendous help with my query materials I received from Michael Mammay, my mentor for the event.

You wouldn't be reading this book without the efforts of my agent, Danielle Burby, who has been the best partner and guide to the world of publishing a new author could ask for, as well as a source of excellent editorial guidance.

And finally, special thanks to David Pomerico at Harper Voyager, whose editorial vision shaped the book, and Yeon Kim for the amazing cover, Ryan Shepherd and Kayleigh Webb for their enthusiastic support, and all the other folks at Harper Voyager who made this book a reality.

These are the people who helped create the book you are reading today, along with many others who offered advice and encouragement at difficult moments. I'm grateful to every one of them.

ABOUT THE AUTHOR

Doug Engstrom has been a farmer's son, a US Air Force officer, a technical writer, a computer support specialist, and a business analyst. He is a writer of speculative fiction and lives near Des Moines, Iowa, with his wife, Catherine Engstrom.